W9-CFB-941

Dear Theodora

Theodora looked lovely in—and out of—the water, and her fiance was ordinarily very proud of the fact. But today, he seemed anxious to curtail the bath...

Dear Theodora

Florence Irwin

EDITED BY
Heather Harpham Kopp

HARVEST HOUSE PUBLISHERS
Eugene, Oregon 97402

Cover by Koechel Peterson and Associates, Minneapolis, Minnesota.

Interior illustrations by Joneile Emery, derived from original illustrations from the Victorian period.

DEAR THEODORA

Copyright © 1998 by Harvest House Publishers
Eugene, Oregon 97402

Library of Congress Cataloging-in-Publication Data

Irwin, Florence, b. 1869.
    Dear Theodora / Florence Irwin.
       p. cm. — (Victorian reader series)
    Updated ed. of: Poor dear Theodora.
    Edited by Heather Harpham Kopp.
    ISBN 1-56507-786-5
    I. Kopp, Heather Harpham, 1964– . II. Irwin, Florence, b. 1869.
  Poor dear Theodora. III. Title. IV. Series.
  PS3517.R8617D42   1998
  813'.4—dc21   97-39736
                                           CIP

Printed in the United States of America.

98   99   00   01   02   03   / DC /   10   9   8   7   6   5   4   3   2   1

At Love's Door

"What is lovely never dies, but passes into other loveliness."

—*Thomas Bailey Aldrich*

For decades women have been rescuing beautiful old books from dusty shelves and "passing them into other loveliness." Laid invitingly on an end table or propped in a windowseat nook, these antique keepsakes bring a touch of Victorian charm to any home.

Yet, only some women have discovered the greater part of their true loveliness. For between their gorgeous covers, many of these books also contain captivating stories—romantic reads to rival the most popular present-day novels.

Dear Theodora is one such gem, and part of the new Victorian Bookshelf series. From an abundance of antique romances, we've carefully searched for those books that especially charm and entertain—books that deserve a revival among today's readers.

Written by Florence Irwin, *Dear Theodora* was originally published under the title *Poor Dear Theodora*. The story is set in 1915 on America's east coast. Women have yet to gain the vote, and social classes are rigidly defined according to wealth and ancestry.

But this is also a world on the verge of great change, as is our frank and spirited heroine, Theodora. In spite of society's objections and her family's skepticism, Theodora ventures out on her own to make a living. When she goes to work for a wealthy old lady, she must keep a sense of humor about some of her duties, such as speaking French to two spoiled poodles.

Eventually, Theodora becomes engaged—but is this the man she really loves?

Through Theodora's trials and triumphs she learns timeless lessons of the heart and spirit—what it means to forgive, to grow through suffering, and above all, to recognize when she is at love's door.

Because *Dear Theodora* was written by a woman who actually lived in the time she wrote about—versus a modern author creating a historical romance—it rewards us with the unmistakable ring of authenticity and period charm. And while *Dear Theodora* has been slightly condensed, quaint details of language, dress, and setting have been preserved whenever possible.

Readers will also appreciate the ocassional passages excerpted here from etiquette books of the day called, *Etiquette for Ladies and Gentlemen* (1877), *The Modern Hostess* (1904), and *The Book of Good Manners* (1923). We glimpse another world when we read tips such as, "Any articles of wearing apparel are distinctly improper as gifts, as are articles of intimate personal use. The gift of a pair of silk stockings is a vulgarism beyond redemption."

Yes, it was a complicated time. But it was also an era when—beneath the polished manners and ornate fashions—the simple joys of love and courtship thrived. So find your favorite cozy spot, brew a pot of your favorite tea, and let loveliness sweep you away once more.

—*Heather Harpham Kopp*

PART FIRST

A Bold,
Daring Plan

heodora stood in the center of the old drawing room and looked about her with irritation. How she detested the task before her! How often in past years had she performed it—until her accumulated bitterness had entered as iron into her soul!

The sunshine of an August morning streamed into the shabby room; when the solemn rite of dusting was in progress, blinds and shades were thrown open. Theodora knew exactly how a vase of flowers must be carefully arranged so as to hide the crack in the long mirror on the mantel. And she knew every worn spot in the rug, and just how it must be covered with a chair or a card table. (Aunt Augusta was entertaining at bridge this afternoon.)

Aunt Augusta did not possess the green felt tables so indispensable to most card hostesses—those convenient things which can be folded and put away between uses. And so instead, every table around which her guests would cluster must first be cleared of its everyday load, then dusted and carried into the drawing room; and all, with the unpleasant assurance that when the party was over the process must be repeated in reversed order.

Theodora gave a vicious little kick to an upturned corner of the rug. Why did people insist on wasting time on such festivities? Why didn't they just say, "It's no use. We're too poor. Let's stop straining," and let it go at that?

She was a perfect model of summer daintiness, slender and white-robed, picturesque from the crown of her broad hat to the toes of her snowy slippers.

Some people knew how to get the things they wanted; Theodora knew only how to do without them. A useful knowledge perhaps—or so she had always been taught. But how much better to possess gloriously, than to lack gracefully!

A voice spoke from the doorway. It was a cool, mocking voice, and it belonged to Theodora's cousin Elise, the beauty of the household. "When you've finished here, Theodora," said the voice, "Meta wants you in the kitchen. She's making the sandwiches and the cakes."

Theodora wheeled sharply. "Why don't *you* help her?" she demanded.

Elise raised arched brows of amusement; a smile parted her thin scarlet lips, revealing a row of even little teeth. She loved nothing better than to rouse irritation. "I'm attending to the flowers," she answered. "That is always my work, as you very well know. Meta said to ask you to hurry. Her icing will soon be ready."

Elise walked through the French window to the verandah and on down to the green lawn below, her ornamental garden-basket swinging from one arm, a pair of scissors suspended from a ribbon at her waist. She was a perfect model of summer daintiness, slender and white-robed, picturesque from the crown of her broad hat to the toes of her snowy slippers. She walked buoyantly, happy to have left a sting in her wake.

Theodora glanced at the clock. It was half-past ten, and Elise was just making her first appearance for the day. She never ate breakfast—that dreary eight o'clock function which Meta and Theodora dared not miss. Aunt Augusta was particularly sensitive on the subject of tardy breakfast appearances, classing them with feminine smoking and gambling and like modern evils. No one, save her young daughter and her only son, ever attempted to challenge her rules.

With the rankling picture of Elise's loveliness still fresh in her mind, Theodora walked over to the mantel mirror and stood gazing moodily into its depths. Theodora's own beauty was the sort that would outlive youth. Its chief point was an exquisitely shaped head, wonderfully set on strong boyish shoulders—shoulders that would stand small chance of being relieved of the weight of their own burdens.

Elise's shoulders were quite a different type; they were sensuous, appealing. It was a safe guess that they would slip from under every yoke, would shift every burden onto some gladly proffered masculine back. Elise had a thin-lipped little mouth, as scarlet as a pomegranate flower; Theodora's mouth was larger and more generous—but alas, no less stubborn. Elise had hair of gold, while Theodora's was as red-brown and as glossy as a horse-chestnut just out of its burr. Her hazel eyes were deep and clear and honest. On that one count she admitted her superiority over her beautiful cousin.

If Elise had a weak point it was her eyes; they were small and pointed and shallow. When she talked to a woman her eyes narrowed to agate points; but when Elise talked to a man (no matter what his age or station), her eyes grew large, momentarily revealing. Her natural attitude toward men was flirtatious, while Theodora's was that of a pal, or a chum.

The subject of beauty bothered Theodora no little. "What," she often thought angrily, "what is it that counts, about looks? I used to think that if you were pretty, you'd be attractive; I used to believe that good looks were the thing that made the difference. But they're not. In some ways, Elise is prettier than I; in others, I'm certainly prettier than she. Yet she'll go a thousand miles where I can't go an inch—and I don't even know the reason. It doesn't seem to matter that she's tricky, while I'm not; nor that I love honesty while she hates it."

Theodora said truly that she loved honesty. It was her passion. In one sense she had a right to demand it, because she most certainly gave it. She was as honest as sunlight—and as uncompromising. And like many other worthy traits, her honesty was sometimes unattractive. Theodora felt that she lacked spine, and that she constantly strived to acquire some hardness. And everyone else admired Theodora's honesty and self-reliance, but prayed that her hardness might prove to be merely the hardness of youth.

On this particular summer morning, her task completed in the drawing room, she went to the kitchen—only to be once more reminded of the subject of personal beauty. By the table in the hot kitchen stood Theodora's oldest cousin, Meta, the picture of anxiety and unattractiveness. Meta was twenty-five and looked thirty. She had a long nose and a poor complexion. Though she was the soul of goodness, in all her life no real joy had ever fallen to her. She seemed born to the role of meek drudge.

At Meta's side sat a faded, pretty woman, busily icing small cakes. At the sight of her, Theodora stood stock still. "Mother," she cried sharply, "what are you doing here? You go straight upstairs, and I'll ice those cakes. This is no place for you, with that headache." (It was one of Theodora's misfortunes that when she was most tingling with love and protectiveness, she sometimes sounded sharpest.)

"Now, my dear," answered Mrs. Winthrop, "don't get excited. This isn't hurting me in the least. I'm feeling much better anyhow."

"You're as white as a sheet," insisted the daughter. "Isn't she, Meta? And just look at those circles under her eyes! She ought to be in bed."

"I begged her not to come down," answered Meta in a tired voice. "Do go up and rest, Aunt Mollie. Theodora will help me now."

"No, it does me good to have a little something to do," replied her aunt, meekly but obstinately. Mrs. Winthrop always insisted that her daughter's stubbornness was a paternal inheritance. "Had your dear father lived to see you grow up," she would say, "I fear you might have clashed sadly!"

"What is Aunt Augusta doing?" Theodora demanded. She well knew what her aunt was doing—slave-driving, relegating to herself the easy tasks and the dominant position, while she turned her elder daughter into a cook, her sister into a scullery maid, and her niece into a cleaning woman.

"She's up in her room, tying up the prizes and writing the place cards," responded Mrs. Winthrop.

"Why don't you go and help her, then?"

"I am more useful here, my dear. Permit me to be the judge of my own tasks."

Seeing that the case was hopeless, Theodora left her mother with the cakes and took over the sandwiches. She sat in tight-lipped disapproving silence, and her mother sat in hurt meekness—so that these two who adored each other were once more at odds. Meta, for her part, was much too distracted to talk; she well knew that any culinary flaw in her mother's party would reflect on her own devoted head. It was therefore a very silent trio that worked on until lunch time.

Luncheon was a hurried meal. "Mollie," said Aunt Augusta, turning to her youngest sister, "I shall not need you at the tables this afternoon, after all. The Misses Duncan sent their chauffeur over with a note. They have had a guest arrive unexpectedly. Miss Janet wrote that, with my permission, the guest would take her place here, as they could hardly leave her at home alone. I replied that I had a vacant place at one of my tables and would certainly expect all three of them. So you needn't play, after all."

Theodora bridled. She knew that the party was virtually given for those queens, the Misses Duncan. In a community where everyone else was living on the traditions of past grandeur, they alone possessed present wealth as well—present wealth and fashion and ancestry that reached back unimpeachably into the dim dark ages.

With the exception of the Misses Duncan, Waverly had little else of which to boast—which probably made it only the more appreciative of its pair of prosperous spinsters. There may be those who are offended by an atmosphere of luxury, but certainly none of them lived in Waverly. While the rest of Waverlyites trudged afoot on roads that were muddy or dusty, Miss Duncan and Miss Janet Duncan dashed around in motors and victorias. They expected invitations to afternoon tea, and responded with invitations to elaborate dinners and luncheons. At the end of each November they went away to the gay city, leaving Waverly plunged in gloom and mud and snow—wealth being able to migrate, while poverty must hibernate.

Therefore, Theodora Winthrop realized full well that it was sheer idiocy to attempt to champion her own mother against the Misses Duncan. But Theodora was well used to butting her head against the stone wall of tradition, and she proceeded to do it once more. "I don't see why Mother has to be at the beck and call of an unknown guest of the Misses Duncan," she began aggressively.

At her tone Elise, who had been looking very bored, brightened perceptibly. Mrs. Winthrop, however, rushed to the rescue. She frowned and coughed. "I'm only too glad to be released from playing," she said. "As you know, Augusta, I care nothing for it, and I shall be delighted to lie down—that is, unless you want me to help receive your guests?"

"No, that won't be necessary. You will appear at tea time, of course?"

"Oh certainly. What shall I wear?"

"That grenadine. Meta, I have put out a lace scarf of mine for you. It will cover that blue muslin very nicely. Be careful not to get anything on it; cleaning is so expensive now. What will you wear, darling?" (This to Elise.)

"My black-and-white."

Mrs. Augusta Charrington's face clouded. "I quite hoped you would choose that pretty pink," she said. "It is so becoming and makes such a sweet contrast with Meta's blue. You seem so very young for black." (Elise was twenty-three—two years the senior of Theodora.)

"No, Mother," she answered decisively, "I can't be expected to match up my clothes with Meta's. The black-and-white is the only thing I own that is fit to put on. Heaven knows, my wardrobe is not overstocked."

"Just as you like, dear," rejoined her mother hastily. She turned to Theodora. "And you?" she asked icily, remembering her niece's recent lack of respect.

Now Theodora possessed exactly one muslin frock that was eligible for an afternoon function, but family tradition demanded that poverty be disregarded in conversation. Before the girl could reply, her mother rushed in with, "Don't you think she might wear that pretty plaid muslin, Augusta?"

Theodora possessed exactly one muslin frock that was eligible for an afternoon function . . .

"Yes. And let her wear the white ribbons. I like them better than the yellow."

Fate had been kind after all. Here was one thing Theodora could do to assert her independence—she could wear the *yellow* ribbons.

The meal ended and everyone went to dress. Elise and Theodora were expected to be on the porch, picturesquely interested in books or fancy work, before the possible arrival of any guest. Meta's place was in the kitchen; from there she would dispense the food, which was to be daintily carried in by her sister and cousin. Only at the very end would Meta appear— just in time to give the impression that she was entirely a person of leisure.

The party proved hardly more of a success than the luncheon. Of course, everyone said it was quite lovely, but there remained a sense of failure.

In the first place, the Misses Duncan and their guest won none of the prizes—those beautiful centerpieces so daintily embroidered by Meta. These had been carried away by the least

16

attractive of the guests. Aunt Augusta was nettled. Her idea was to give to those who already had the most.

Then Miss Duncan's guest, Mrs. Neilson, had been almost rude. She had quite frankly expressed her surprise to find people still absorbed in bridge in August 1915; she had been shocked that Waverly boasted no Red Cross chapter, and that it had not taken madly to knitting; in fact, she talked almost exclusively about the European War, a subject in which Waverly was but faintly interested.

And on top of that, Mrs. Neilson had added insult to injury by taking a marked interest in the stubborn niece of her hostess.

Theodora, on her part, had been disgusted by the very evident efforts of Elise to ingratiate herself with Miss Duncan and Miss Janet. She understood her cousin's motive well. The two spinsters made a long motor tour each September, and Elise regarded herself as a desirable guest for the approaching one.

With all Meta's care, her ices had been a little soft. Fewer than usual had been eaten, and in a spirit of deep depression she had put the remainder back into the freezer to harden.

And last but not least, Ned Charrington had not come home to supper, for the third time in less than ten days. There were two deep lines of worry between his mother's eyes.

"Did any of you hear Ned say anything about staying late tonight?" she asked. When no one had, she hastened to excuse him. "I know they're keeping him very hard at work," she said. "Miss Janet Duncan said she thought it was perfectly splendid for the boy to work during his vacation this way."

As a matter of fact, Ned Charrington's college course was a financial burden his widowed mother could ill afford to bear. And Ned insisted that it would be better to forego college entirely than to forfeit the fraternity life that nearly tripled his legitimate expenses.

Finally, on his own initiative, Ned had procured a position in a banking house in the nearby city, thus rendering his present vacation a source of income. There was nothing to make a summer in Waverly attractive to him anyhow, and he said that he got more fun working, going and coming by train each day, than by sitting around in the "dead hole" of his hometown.

As the family rose from the supper table, Meta seemed to pluck her courage in both hands. "Mother," she said, "Dr. Sewall thought he might drop in for a moment this evening. Would it be all right for me to serve the rest of the ice cream? I don't believe it will keep till tomorrow."

There was so odd a note in her voice that Theodora glanced up quickly. She was surprised to see a vivid blush spreading over Meta's sallow face.

"Good gracious," she thought in amazement, "is that the way the wind blows?"

The idea of Meta being interested in any man was shocking. Everyone knew that she had been faithfully helping this new physician with his poor patients, but that was entirely natural. Meta lived for others; she had a great gift at charity, and had always done as much as her limited means allowed. Such a thing as a love motive, however, was a totally new development.

Mrs. Charrington gave permission, and then said she thought she would go to her room—an example which her sister speedily followed. It had been a trying day.

The three younger women moved to the wide verandah where they were presently joined by Dr. Sewall. It was his first social call at the house, and Theodora looked at him with new eyes. In spite of Waverly's lack of eligible young men, she could not see him as a desirable, or even a possible, suitor. He was tall and angular and serious and quiet, and even a little awkward. It was difficult to imagine either him or Meta in a love affair.

Elise was unusually silent. She sat in profile to the rest of the group and scarcely even replied to direct questions. When her sister left briefly to get more ice cream, Elise turned a little more directly to the guest and murmured a sentence or two. At one point, her scarf slipped from her shoulders and she stooped to regain it at the same moment that the doctor sprang to restore it. There was a confused moment of intermingled heads and hands, of laughter and apologies, and then the lacy scarf was once more draped over Elise's pretty shoulders.

Soon she rose, saying that she felt the dampness. Just as she passed Dr. Sewall's chair her ankle turned, and she escaped a fall only by grasping his shoulder. However, she was very brave about it and refused all help, though she limped perceptibly as she disappeared into the dim-lit drawing room. Then the sounds of soft music floated out upon the night. Elise was playing some plaintive old Scotch ballads—those simple and compelling ones that seem never to lose their appeal.

Theodora detested ballads, having had an overdose of them all her life; but she could not help admiring the tactful way in which Elise had removed herself. It had been done, of course, in order to give Meta her chance of a *tête-à-tête*. Theodora must not linger and spoil everything. Murmuring something about "letters to write," she said good night—but not without a feeling of awkwardness. Any man must see through such a ruse.

As she passed a turn in the dark old stairway, Theodora was astonished to see Meta and her guest enter the drawing room and to hear the doctor say something about his fondness for music. He took a seat near the piano. Elise went on playing; she never even turned her head. Yet for some unknown reason

Theodora was assailed with a sudden desire to murder her. But after all, what had Elise done? Nothing but get out of the way.

After the doctor went home and the house grew silent, Meta stopped at Theodora's door to say that Ned must have decided to spend the night in town again. There was but one more train and that was not due till nearly two. He surely would not come at that hour. So she had locked the house and put out the lights.

Tired, as she was, Theodora could not sleep. She lay staring into the darkness, going over in memory the events of the day just passed, wondering how many more such days her life must hold. A desperate plan had been forming of late in the back of Theodora's brain, but it was too wild and impossible to give rise to much real hope.

Suddenly she raised herself on her elbow, alert, listening intently. Surely that was a whistle under her window!

Theodora's room was a small one at the back of the house—the four main second-story bedrooms being used by Mrs. Charrington, Mrs. Winthrop, Elise, and Ned. Meta was upstairs and front. So, too, was the servant—on the other side of the front. Theodora alone occupied the back wing. Beneath her were the kitchen and pantry, above her the huge storeroom.

As she listened, the sound which had aroused her was repeated. It was certainly a whistle. She hurried to her window and looked out.

"Brownie," said a hoarse whisper ("Brownie" was Ned Charrington's pet name for the cousin of whom he was so fond), "Brownie, tha' you? You 'wake?"

"Is it you, Ned?"

"Yes. Come down 'n' open door."

How oddly he spoke! "Are you sick?" she demanded in fright.

"No. Not sick. Come down 'n' open door, I say."

Trembling violently, Theodora donned a dressing gown and crept down the back stairs. How they creaked and groaned! Surely the whole household must soon be roused.

As she opened the door, Ned lurched through and almost fell on her. Regaining his balance with an effort, he propped himself against the wall and stood grinning inanely at her. He looked ghastly and unnatural. "Kep' askin' you come down 'n' open door," he repeated foolishly.

At that moment, Theodora became conscious of a horrid odor and realized in a flash what was the trouble. To her mind, murder could have been no worse. Never before in the entire course of her narrow and sheltered life had she spoken with a drunken man.

"Ned," she said wildly in a voice that was low and tense, "Ned, look at me. Look straight in my eyes. You must come upstairs quietly. Do you understand? They're all asleep—"

"All 'sleep? That's good. That's fine."

"Yes, and I'll help you to your room. Here, sit down on this chair and let me slip your shoes off. Now wait a moment—I'm going to wet a towel and wipe your face with cold water. . . . There, doesn't that feel better? Hush! Now lean on me. Give me the shoes, I'll carry them. Oh, Ned, can't you step more quietly? There, don't try to talk. I know everything you want to tell me. Just be quiet. . . . Hush! Don't you understand me, Ned? I say *hush*!"

Painfully, they made the perilous ascent together. Just as they reached the threshold of Ned's room, Mrs. Charrington's door opened and she came out. Wearing a long white wrap and with her pale hair braided down her back, she looked like a ghost. By the light of the dim taper candle, Theodora caught a glimpse of her ravaged face. Never had the girl pitied anyone so much! Never again would she feel quite the same dislike of her aunt. Poor, *poor* Aunt Augusta! *She* had evidently spoken to a drunken man before.

"I'll attend to Ned, Theodora," she said, with lips that seemed too stiff to move. "He has had several of these attacks lately. His father had them. It is his heart. I shall consult a doctor if they continue. You may go to bed now. Thank you for what you have done."

"Oh, Aunt Augusta, can't I help you?" whispered the girl in an agony of compassion. She scarcely recognized her aunt in this wild-eyed shaking woman.

"No. I understand the case. Thank you, just the same. Go to bed now. . . . Theodora?"

"Yes, Aunt Augusta?"

"I'm sure I need not ask you to speak of this to no one."

"Oh, Aunt Augusta! Of course not! How could I?"

"Very well. That is all. Thank you. Good night."

Mrs. Charrington turned to the prostrate form of her son, who had tumbled across the bed the moment he got inside the room and who was now breathing heavily. Noiselessly she closed the door, leaving Theodora in the corridor outside.

The girl felt weak and frightened. She crept back to her own room and into bed. There she lay, trembling like a leaf. After a time, she began to sob quietly. How awful this thing was! How terribly it added to the dilemma in which she had so long felt herself entangled!

Ever since she was seventeen, Theodora had been certain that there was nothing either in her present life nor in her future outlook to warrant either happiness or hope. The inferior position to which Aunt Augusta always relegated her younger sister and her niece was galling. The poverty of the combined household was another sore point. *Someone* must get out and earn money. Naturally, it could not be either of the two older women; it would never be Elise; Meta could not be spared—most of the burdens fell on her shoulders as it was.

Theodora had long yearned to break away from her confines, to try her luck in the world. But she well knew that her conservative family would be horrified. She'd never be able to persuade them—she, the youngest of them all, and the one whose ideas they deplored! She would only succeed in butting her head once more against the stone wall of tradition.

Whenever this truth had weighed heavily upon her, she had always comforted herself with the thought that Ned's college course would soon be over, and he would be able to help. He was such a dear sweet-natured boy. He and Theodora had always been special chums—they both detested Elise, they both pitied Meta, and they both kicked against Waverly's high society.

But now! How the outlook was changed by tonight's unhappy experience! And it evidently wasn't a first offense. Aunt Augusta's whole attitude proved that. Ned would become another financial burden instead of a provider. In that case, who was left to assume the role, save Theodora herself?

"I'm the only one to go out into the world," thought the girl. "Every day shows that more plainly. And I want to. I'm not afraid—not the least bit. The only thing that frightens me is the thought of staying on here forever, doing nothing, seeing nothing, hearing nothing, getting nothing. But how can I make them see it? How can I get away?"

Round and round in a circle her thoughts ran till finally, spent by shock and worry, she fell into blessed slumber.

CHAPTER

⚜II⚜

heodora awoke the next morning to a feeling of depression—one of those mysterious mental hangovers with which everyone is familiar. It was but a moment before she remembered the cause. The night had failed to soften its shock. She wondered what had happened after she fell asleep, and how long Aunt Augusta had kept watch over that terrible bedside.

But apart from Ned's tragedy, there was another vague trouble in the air. What was it? Ah, yes, now she remembered. She was booked to spend the day in the hot city with Elise, who had shopping to do and who was considered too beautiful and precious to travel unattended into the haunts of men. Theodora detested these shopping bouts. The selfishness of her cousin was always at top pitch. After a difficult night, the coming day was bound to be trying.

Elise could get up to breakfast when she had a reason. She appeared, cool and lovely in a fresh holland frock with white gloves, hat, and shoes. Theodora herself had a similar gown and would have liked to wear it, but her cousin always objected to "dressing like twins." Ordinarily this would not have deterred Theodora, particularly as her frock had been bought first and Elise—taking a fancy to it—had copied it. But today the

24

prospect of unnecessary bickering didn't appeal to her. With a sigh, Theodora donned her only other possible choice—a darker and thicker gown.

Aunt Augusta was already seated at the table when she went down. Theodora threw her a quick glance. She looked almost ill, yet she met her niece's gaze calmly. For the first time in their lives, there was a bond of sympathy between them. Nothing could alter the fact that Augusta's niece shared her secret and stood ready to help her fight the world.

Mrs. Charrington turned to Elise with an ill-concealed effort. "How much money will you need, dear?" she asked.

Her daughter hesitated. As usual, she wanted all she could get. "How much can you spare me?"

"Could you do with ten dollars?"

Elise's face clouded. "Our tickets, alone, will be nearly two dollars," she said. "And we can't go all day without a little something to eat. I couldn't do much shopping on seven dollars." There was a stubborn look on her face.

"I'm afraid I can't spare you any more today," said her mother. "If you could wait till next month, I shall have a little money coming in then."

"If you'd only spoken about this before I got all ready and made all my plans, I could have arranged to stay at home." Elise's voice was disagreeable and peevish. "Summer will be over next month. I suppose, if there's no money to spend, we might as well not go. There's no use wasting the time for nothing."

But everyone at the table knew that Elise didn't mean that. She had no intention of changing her plans. She was merely testing the strength of her mother's purse.

"I have given Theodora the money for her own ticket," Mrs. Winthrop hastened to remark. Just then, Meta entered from the kitchen and took her place at the table.

"Ned stayed in town last night, didn't he?" she asked. Poor Meta! She was born to the misfortune of inappropriateness.

Not for a moment did the eyes of Theodora meet those of her aunt, yet again that strange unspoken sympathy ran between the two women. Incongruous as they might be as a pair of conspirators, that was certainly what they were becoming.

"No," replied Mrs. Charrington, "he was kept late at the office, dined with a friend, and came home on the last train. He was tired out and I have let him sleep." Here she turned to Theodora. "I thought," she continued, "that after you reach town, you might telephone the office and explain his absence." It was noticeable that she asked this service of her niece rather than of her daughter. A telephone was a luxury that the Charrington-Winthrop household did not afford.

As the two girls walked to the train Theodora had a taste of what the day held in store for her. Elise's disappointment on the subject of money could not go unexpressed. However, there was a lull in Elise's protests when they reached the station platform. There, an audience waited to be impressed. Elise must look charming.

Long ago, Waverly had been one of the most aristocratic summer suburbs of the nearby city. In those times, wealthy people possessed a winter home in one city, and a summer home within easy reach of it. Except for a journey to Europe every four or five years, this was the height of their adventure.

But with declining fortunes, many of these old families had been forced to accept Waverly as an all-year residence—a summer home and a winter asylum. They dropped gradually out of all urban gaiety, as its pace quickened and its cost became prohibitive. In consequence, they were soon virtually forgotten except by those few old friends who were still faithful to Waverly summer life.

So matters had stood when, some two or three years ago, the natural beauty of the place had appealed to a newly rich multi-millionaire who happened to be driving through. With his tobacco fortune, he proceeded to buy eighty acres outside of town and to put up a palace. In his wake came other fortunes—beer, chewing-gum, patent drugs, more tobacco.

Horrible tales went around concerning the palace—gambling, drinking, betting, scandalous dancing, feminine smoking, and the like.

Waverly shivered and drew its respectable mantles close about its thin shoulders. Horrible tales went around concerning the palace—gambling, drinking, betting, scandalous dancing, feminine smoking, and the like. The thing that made the matter worse was that Waverlyites stood no chance of selling property to the newcomers who, according to the taste of a modern era, preferred to live outside a village rather than in it.

Thus every summer morning two distinct groups stood on the platform of Waverly station, between whom no bow of greeting was ever exchanged. Arriving daintily afoot came those ordinary folk who found themselves obliged to spend a day in town. They stood at a certain spot, and remained there in sweet converse with lifelong friends. Presently, with honking of horns and rattling of chains and cracking of whips, the wealthy newcomers arrived—in motors, or carriages, according to individual taste. They formed a group apart—unabashed, luxuriously apparelled, a little too highly ornamental, a trifle too loud, but by all worldly standards a group to be envied.

Elise Charrington, as always, played up to the group of new-comers. She insisted on standing a little higher up the platform. "You know perfectly well, Theodora," she said fretfully, "that it is impossible to get a good seat from this end." She placed herself in profile to a nearby knot of the strangers and drew up her figure, flexing her rounded throat and throwing her pretty outline into highest relief.

She soon had her reward. "Gad, what a little beauty," said a masculine voice. "Look, Travis, did you ever see anything sweeter?" The remark was accompanied by two very bold stares.

Theodora was the only person who resented them. It mattered not to Elise that the speaker was sixty or more, nor that he had a portly figure, a ruddy face, and dissipated-looking eyes. He was a *man*, and there never seemed to be any younger ones in these wealthy groups. Had there been, life in Waverly might have possessed some zest.

At any rate, judged by the standards of Elise Charrington, the day began well; but it speedily degenerated when they reached town and realized the inadequacy of the purchasing power of eight dollars. Patiently Theodora trotted around from shop to shop in her cousin's wake as each fresh disappointment was visited on her innocent head. "I *hate* to be poor!" said Elise viciously. "What good are looks, if you never have a chance to do anything with them?"

The cousins lunched cheaply and inadequately on ice cream and buns. By three o'clock, Elise's funds were exhausted and she declared that she was ready to go home. But that morning, Theodora's mother had pressed a five-dollar note into her hand. "I wish I could give you more, dear," Mrs. Winthrop had whispered. "My greatest cross is that you can not have the things you deserve. But this will buy you a pair of shoes at least, and those you must have."

The girl had protested. She always suffered a feeling of shame in accepting money from her unselfish mother—though where else she might have hoped to get it, short of the fruition of her cherished plan, it would have been hard to say. However, she had been forced to take the money, and now she wanted to spend it.

There was immediate trouble. Elise's head ached, and her feet were tired, and she feared she'd be ill if she didn't get home in time to rest before dinner. She finally consented to go to just one more shop, and there Theodora picked up the first possible pair of shoes—thankful to get any.

At nine o'clock that night Theodora sat in her little room, robed in a dressing-gown, absently brushing out her magnificent hair, and nerving herself to a terrible task. Whenever she was out of her narrow home circle—even for a day, even under circumstances as adverse as those of the day just past—she felt particularly brave and capable. She was determined to strike while her courage was up; tomorrow she might be again in shackles.

She rose, went to her mother's room, and knocked.

"Come in, dear," said the pretty voice. With the feeling of a murderess about to stick a knife into a trusting heart, the girl entered.

"Well, dear, did you have a pleasant day?"

"No, Mother. Quite horrid, thank you. But that wasn't your fault. It was Elise's, as usual. Mother, why do I have to chaperone her? She's twenty-three and I'm twenty-one. It's ridiculous!"

"I shouldn't call it *chaperoning*, my dear."

"Well, it amounts to the same thing."

Silence fell for a few moments. Then all at once, her pretty prepared preambles forgotten, Theodora took her plunge. "Mother," she said, "I want to work. Someone has to make money for this family, and I seem to be the one."

Mrs. Winthrop was frankly dazed, and looked it.

"Work how? What do you mean, Theodora?"

"I don't know just what I mean, but I want you to help me find out. Lots of girls work and support themselves. Why can't I?"

"What are you thinking, Theodora? What could you do?"

"That's the trouble. I don't know. But there must be something. I'm not a fool. Perhaps I could be a nursery governess."

"You mean that you want to go away and leave me?" The mother's voice was plaintive and accusatory. A son is supposed to have his own life, whether married or single; a daughter is not.

"Leaving you," answered the girl, "is the only part of it that bothers me. But I couldn't make any money here. Would you come away with me if I could find some work? I could advertise. Would you come, Mother?"

"Theodora! How could I? Do you know what my income is?"

"No, Mother. Of course, I know it's small."

"The interest on ten thousand dollars—your father's life insurance. That is every cent I have in the world."

"Then, that's all the more reason why I should go to work. Half of this house is yours, isn't it?"

"Yes. But what good would it ever do me, except to live in? It couldn't be turned into a source of revenue."

"No, I suppose not. Was it left to you and Aunt Augusta equally?"

"Yes, by our father. But you must remember that your Aunt Augusta's mother was his first wife, while my mother was only his second wife."

"What difference does that make? The house was his, not his wife's; and he was your father just as much as Aunt Augusta's."

"True. But I was the child of a second marriage. Your aunt was ten years old when I was born, and she has always had a very dominant nature—"

"I know all about Aunt Augusta's nature," began Theodora. Then she remembered the past night and stopped, to her mother's relief.

"I'm made differently, I suppose . . . Meta's Meta, and Elise is Elise, and I'm Theodora."

"Your aunt's mother was a woman of some little property," continued Mrs. Winthrop, "which she naturally left to her daughter. My mother left nothing."

"That makes no difference. Miss Duncan told me that she had often heard her father say that my grandmother was one of the loveliest women he ever knew."

"But she was a second wife," repeated the parent with dogged persistence. The lesson had evidently been well drilled into her head. "Then, in addition to what your aunt inherited from her mother, her husband left her a little something. Not much, it is true, but sufficient to give her an income considerably larger than mine."

"Oh, well," said Theodora indifferently, "it doesn't matter. Let's get back to business." There followed a long discussion, the main issue being constantly dodged by the mother, insistently dragged again to the fore by the daughter.

"Why can't you be content to live on here, just as you've always done?" demanded the perplexed parent at length. "Why must you be so much more restless than your cousins?"

"I don't know. Because I'm made differently, I suppose. Why are my hair and eyes a different color from theirs? There isn't any *reason* for such things. Meta's Meta, and Elise is Elise, and I'm Theodora. That's the only reason that I know. But I haven't been 'content' for a long while, Mother. This isn't life."

"And do you imagine that working for your living would be 'life,' as you call it?"

"It would be better than this, I'm sure of that. Day after day, year after year, we sit here with no change, no chance, no experience; doing nothing interesting, learning nothing—"

"What do you want to learn?"

"What the real world is like."

"And when you have discovered, you may well wish yourself back in your sheltered home."

"Perhaps, but at least I shall have tried it. Here, I know everything and everyone by heart; I know just what each and every person will say and do and think. I could write it all out beforehand. My wildest excitement is a day's shopping in town. We all sit here, afraid to move because it would cost money, afraid to work because our dead ancestors wouldn't like it. If they were so fine—if we're so fine—I should think we could afford to take a chance at independence."

Mrs. Winthrop sighed wearily and leaned her head on her hand. Her daughter was filled with immediate compunction. "I'm tiring you to death," she cried. "Go to bed and get a good rest. But may I speak to Aunt Augusta about this, tomorrow?"

"If you insist. But I may as well warn you that it will do no good."

"I think it will," answered the girl with an odd smile. "Anyhow, I'll try it. And if she consents, will you?"

"I suppose I must, since your mind seems to be made up. But she will never consent."

Stooping, the girl kissed her mother. In spite of occasional surface prickles, these two were in very close accord. "Poor mother," said Theodora, "it's awfully hard on you to have a queer daughter like me."

Just as she reached the door, her mother spoke. "Suppose your aunt refuses her consent, Theodora?"

"Mother, I shall go just the same. I must. Aunt Augusta is not my guardian. She has no right to dictate to me. I must live my own life. Now good night."

She closed the door gently behind her, leaving her poor flustered parent to imitate the time-honored hen who has hatched a duckling and sees it headed straight for the dreadful pond. Powerless to understand, to dissuade, to aid, she could do nothing but cluck anxiously and vainly on the bank.

⚛III⚛

t eleven o'clock the next morning, Mrs. Charrington entered her sister's room to talk over poor dear Theodora's latest whim. The girl had been closeted with her aunt for the last half-hour. To Mrs. Winthrop's very great surprise, her sister did not entirely veto the venture.

"I'm devoutly thankful," said Aunt Augusta, "that neither of my daughters is afflicted with this terrible modern restlessness." (And to this, Mrs. Winthrop might well have answered that she was "devoutly thankful" that her daughter was not as homely and meek as Meta, nor as selfish and peevish as Elise. But, of course, she didn't, and her sister proceeded.) "Poor dear Theodora has always been odd. I believe, Mollie, the best way to convince her of her mistake is to let her try the thing on which she seems so set—provided, of course, that a sufficiently protected position can be found."

"Ned went to work in preference to sitting around here," ventured Mrs. Winthrop.

"That is entirely different. A man may do what a girl may not.... Who is that coming? Oh, Mollie, there is Miss Duncan's motor. I'll hurry down. Will you run and ask Meta to make some iced drinks? Then come and join me in the library."

It wasn't long before Theodora and Elise were also summoned. Mrs. Neilson, who accompanied the Misses Duncan, had conceived a novel plan, and had asked particularly for the young people, whose help she wished to enlist. "Whenever I find myself in a new locality," she said, "I am possessed to turn it into a workfield. These wartime days are so urgent; there is so much to be done, and every little helps. I am surprised to find Waverly so detached."

There was an awkward pause. As a matter of fact, Waverly was always detached, of necessity, where matters of charity were concerned. With the exception of the Misses Duncan, all of the inhabitants of Waverly were exclusively occupied with keeping their chins above water. They couldn't afford such luxuries as giving. Wars might come and wars might go, but Waverly could do little to help.

As Mrs. Neilson spoke, she was conscious of a lack of response. All her hearers were immediately embarrassed by the thought of money. The subject of giving was taboo in Waverly.

"You know," continued Mrs. Neilson cheerfully, "everyone gives now. Everyone has to—even if it is only a mite. Mites mount, you see."

Theodora dropped her eyes. Too well did she know that everyone did not give. Elise, on the other hand, continued to gaze at the speaker—hating her, the while.

"There is a girl in the city who is a great friend of mine," Mrs. Neilson went on. "She has just returned from France where she has been doing wonderful work. She's here to raise money for a greatly needed hospital. A hundred and twenty-five dollars will support a cot for a year. Just think of the brave men that one cot may hold in a year's time! I thought if we could get this Miss Bend to come out here to speak, we might raise the price of a cot for her."

"We'd never do it," cried Theodora. Her cheeks were scarlet and her eyes looked worried.

"My *dear*," remarked the guest in a tone of disappointment.

"I mean, Mrs. Neilson, because we're all so poor."

This was a bomb. Poverty decently disregarded was one thing; poverty blazoned, quite another. Mrs. Neilson, however, saved the situation by the naturalness with which she took the comment. "That wouldn't matter, dear," she said. "No one need give much. But if everyone came and gave what they could spare, quite a nice little sum might be raised. Even if it weren't enough for a cot, it would help. The point is, that after hearing Miss Bond speak no one can ever again sit down with folded hands. I'm convinced of that. She, herself, has no money, and just wait till you hear what she has done."

"You see," explained Miss Duncan, "my sister and I would ask some of our friends to motor over from a distance, and we should offer our house for the talk. Mrs. Neilson will be with us and she will write and ask several of her friends. If everyone in Waverly comes, we'll have quite an audience."

"And I don't think I'd have tickets," said the astute Mrs. Neilson. "I saw it very nicely arranged once before. Three or four girls handed around boxes decorated with big bows of ribbon and with slits cut in their lids. People put in just what they could afford—checks, pledges, bills, small change—anything that they felt they could spare."

This was a relief.

Conversation began to flow more easily then. The date for the function was settled—provided Miss Bend was available that day. "We can put notices in the windows of the public garage and the drug store," suggested Mrs. Neilson. "All the motorists stop at those places."

"My dear Ellen," cried Miss Janet Duncan in shocked tones, "that is rather too public for Waverly."

"But, Janet, these are public times. The war is a public calamity. There's no class distinction about suffering and need and danger. The great thing is to get as big an audience as possible for Miss Bend. You don't care who sits in your chairs for one afternoon, do you?"

"These are the days when women are striking out for themselves in every direction."

"No, I suppose not. But, we've always been so very guarded against theatrical publicity, here in Waverly. We like to keep the old standards."

"My dear, you're about to see very great changes in standards. Mark my words, the day is not far distant when you'll marvel at your present ones, as at something entirely antiquated."

Here Meta entered with a tray, and discussion stopped for a moment. Theodora saw her opportunity and seized it. "Mrs. Neilson," she said, a little breathlessly, "I have been begging my mother and my aunt to let me change my standards—and theirs." And she told of her plan to go to work.

To Meta and Elise the idea sounded incredible. Meta was frightened and Elise was furious. No one could ever tell what hope of social advancement might be ruined by the appearance of a freak in the family. One did not boast of poverty. Theodora was totally lacking in decent pride.

But Mrs. Neilson immediately applauded Theodora's courage and good sense. "In your place," she cried, "I should do the very same thing. You are a sensible girl. These are the days when women are striking out for themselves in every direction."

Aunt Augusta proceeded to settle her debt of the night before with her niece. "I think we will permit her to try it," she said, not without an effort. "The world is not what it once was, and the young seem restless. I hope poor dear Theodora will not find her experiment disappointing—"

"She won't," predicted Mrs. Neilson, with a brilliant smile at the girl. Theodora gave her hand a grateful squeeze.

On the appointed afternoon, the drawing rooms of the Misses Duncan were being rapidly filled. The occasion was raised to an even greater level of importance by the announcement that the bishop of the diocese would be present to introduce the speaker. Waverly was much more interested in bishops than in modern and mistaken young women who went flying around Europe unchaperoned.

Every chair was filled and eyes were beginning to consult watches, when a tremendous clatter arose outside. Four beautiful motors drew noisily up under the *porte-cochére*, and deposited a group of twelve or fourteen elderly, high-voiced, overdressed women, who came clicking over the marble entrance hall on French heels so exaggerated as to be veritable stilts. The heavy breath of artificial perfumes preceded the party.

Miss Duncan looked at Miss Janet, and Miss Janet looked at Miss Duncan. They recognized this group, from previous stolen glances on the station platform, as the wealthy newcomers from the palaces. Blissfully unconscious of the outrage which had been perpetrated against the Duncan hospitality, Mrs. Neilson was happily thinking that these strangers suggested wealth and would probably give generously.

The bishop's introduction was beautiful—at least, so Waverly said afterward. He bewailed the war, and commended Miss Bend, and thanked the Misses Duncan, and

From the moment that Miss Bend began to speak, nothing else existed for Theodora.

all in very eloquent words. But Theodora was used to bishops. She thirsted for the greater novelty. And from the moment that Miss Bend began to speak, nothing else existed for her.

Never had she imagined such situations, such heroism, such sacrifice. *This* had been happening in the world while smug little Waverly sat safe and idle, its sole tribute to the war's existence a perfunctory shudder now and again.

> The knot of newly-rich, a little loud, posed haughtily, questioning each other absorbedly as to the hour of arriving chauffeurs.

Why was anyone in the whole world sitting still? How dared anyone do it? Oh, for freedom, for opportunity, for money! *Money*! That was what one needed! Its lack hampered the whole of life! Hitherto, Theodora had wanted money for herself and her mother. Now, she saw farther. Money was indeed as necessary as she had come to think it, but for far better reasons. . . . If one couldn't give, if one couldn't help, then one might as well be dead. In fact, one was dead.

As in a dream, Theodora rose with the other girls to the task of passing the boxes. She noted not a single face as she moved mechanically from chair to chair. At the close of the lecture everyone pressed forward to meet the speaker who stood on a slightly raised platform at one end of the room. The knot of newly-rich, a little loud, posed haughtily, questioning each other absorbedly as to the hour of arriving chauffeurs. They flattered themselves that they gave a perfect imitation of indifferent superiority. But they were at a disadvantage. Although expensively clad, although salved by the happy consciousness of just having given generously, when they arrived in front of the plat-form, they were received with frigid politeness by the ladies of the house.

Miss Duncan and her sister judged that they had been tricked. They felt that opportunity had been seized to invade their sanctuary. Had these women been strangers with whom their present hostesses would probably never again have come face-to-face—the matter would have been different. But living in Waverly, using the same station and the same trains, standing in wait on the same platform, the two elements would now be faced with a hitherto unknown problem. Standing erect, with hands hanging limply by sides, they merely bowed their heads gravely to each unwelcome guest. Then they pronounced the names of Miss Bend and of the bishop—with no attempt to learn those of the strangers nor to make the introduction mutual.

The bishop and Miss Bend were happily removed from such vexing problems. They were equally charming to everyone. But it took more than that to cover the Duncan snub, and that "more" Mrs. Neilson immediately proceeded to supply. She greeted each newly-rich effusively, thanked them all for coming, asked all their names, and introduced them all over again to Miss Bend. Her kindness had its reward.

"If you'd give us your address, Miss Bend," said one of them in a voice that was conspicuously raised, "we'd be pleased to send you some pledges for cots. I gave all the money I had with me, but I'm willing to give a cot beside, and I guess some of these ladies with me feel the same way. We're not in the habit of hanging on to our money when there's good to be done with it."

"How perfectly lovely," cried Mrs. Neilson as four other women testified to like sentiments. "Miss Bend, do you hear that?" And Miss Bend, beaming with pleasure, added her warm thanks.

Later, the money was counted. Nearly seven hundred dollars had been taken. It didn't seem possible, but it was quite true. Seven hundred dollars plus five cots, was the marvelous reward for an afternoon of work and worry.

"I shan't sleep tonight," cried Miss Bend. "I shall certainly lie awake singing the Doxology. Rest assured, I shall never forget Waverly and its kindness."

Theodora, with her mother and aunt, lingered after the other guests had gone. Mrs. Neilson had suggested that they consult Bishop Wysong about finding a position for the girl, and the idea proved to be a good one. He was very encouraging, and promised both to make inquiries and to keep a watch over the advertisements in the church papers.

His approval and sympathy were balm to Aunt Augusta's spirit. If Bishop Wysong (who had christened Theodora and confirmed her) saw no objection to her making her living, it couldn't be such an awful thing to do, after all!

Theodora was very silent on the way home, and her silence continued for the balance of the day. Dinner was a trial to her soul. Though her mother, her aunt, and Meta, all paid full tribute to Miss Bend and her wonderful work, the subject made them uncomfortable because of their inability to help. They therefore took refuge from it.

But the conversation presently took a turn very much for the worse and concerned itself with the strangers and their exhibition of bad taste.

Elise had been sitting silent and discontented. The sight of money and luxury invariably depressed her, and today she had had more than she could bear. Her feelings gathered and broke. "I can't see anything so very terrible in those women coming to a charity lecture," she said fretfully. "Where would we have been without them?"

"No one denies their very great generosity, Elise," said her mother stiffly. "I trust we all appreciate that. It is their *taste* that we question. Forcing an entrance where they could never otherwise hope to penetrate—"

"I don't believe they cared a pin about that. What are two prim old maids to them—"

"*Elise!*"

"Well, Mother, don't get hurt. I only mean that those women have everything in the world that they want—"

"Except good taste and birth."

"Just look at their clothes."

"I saw their clothes, Elise, and I thought them quite terrible. Would you want to see your mother dressed so?"

"Certainly. Why not?"

"Will you excuse me, Aunt Augusta?" demanded Theodora suddenly. "I'm not very hungry, and my head aches a little." She rose to leave the room, but before she reached the door her mental vow of silence was broken. "I think such agonizing sounds simply ridiculous in the face of what Miss Bend told us today," she said excitedly. "What possible difference could it make for those women to sit an hour in Miss Duncan's room? They're perfectly decent, I imagine. Suppose this were Belgium or France! Do you think we'd have time to split such hairs?"

"Fortunately for us, it is neither Belgium nor France," replied Aunt Augusta tranquilly. "When this war is over and forgotten, Theodora, matters of good taste and good breeding will still be considered important. They are the foundations on which society is built."

"Look at Mrs. Neilson," Theodora flung at her aunt. "She is certainly as good as anyone there today, and yet how differently she acted!"

"Mrs. Neilson," answered Mrs. Charrington, with uplifted brows, "faced no permanent problem. She could well afford her position. Do you know, Mollie, that Miss Bend is very well-born. She is the daughter of Lydia Tremaine, whom we used to know."

"Lydia Tremaine! That quiet gentle girl! And she actually permitted her daughter to go off to Europe unchaperoned, at such times as these!"

Theodora, escaping, heard no more. Such, however, was the tradition in which she had been bred, the mold into which she had been forced, ever since she could remember. Nothing but very great natural sturdiness could have succeeded in resisting it!

It wasn't long before Mrs. Winthrop received a letter from Bishop Wysong, who had not forgotten his promise. The church paper had solved Theodora's riddle. A certain Mrs. Robert Delafield Stuyvesant, resident in New York and at Grosvenor-on-Hudson, wished a highly recommended companion possessed of every virtue of character, disposition, birth, breeding, and education. Letters were exchanged, and Theodora was engaged to make her appearance at Mrs. Stuyvesant's country home on the first of October.

Ned insisted that Theodora was a brick. Elise thought she was a fool. She was secretly envious about New York, but devoutly thankful that soiled linen was to be laundered so far away from home. Meta was too dazed to think. Aunt Augusta said nothing whatever.

The real wrench was the parting between mother and daughter. But Theodora insisted that the separation would be short, and that all her leisure should be devoted to finding a position so well-paying that her mother might join her. "Just think of a little home together, Mumsie," she kept repeating, "with no one else to bother us, nor to rub me the wrong way!" And Mrs. Winthrop did what all good mothers have done from time immemorial—put her own feelings aside in the interests of her child, and covered an aching heart with a smile.

There was a flurry of dressmaking and trunkpacking, and at last the great day arrived. Theodora set out on her journey, smothered in directions and cautions and advice—and full of so many conflicting emotions that she hardly knew whether she was happy or unhappy. She couldn't believe yet that the whole thing was not a dream.

〜IV〜

s the little station-motor rolled between the entrance gates of Fair Acres, a dazed but eager Theodora leaned forward to catch the first glimpse of her new home. She saw a lovely old park, whose velvety lawns were showing the first touches of autumn dryness. Magnificent forest trees flung banners of deep red and dull gold to catch the slanting rays of the late afternoon sun. Then a sudden turn in the drive gave Theodora her first glimpse of the house.

It was exactly what she would have wished—an immense grey stone pile, irregular in outline, flanked by wide verandahs. Off in the distance gleamed hothouses, their multitude of panes transformed into flaming mirrors by the shafts of sunlight. All in all, a stately and beautiful home!

The front door was opened by a butler, and Theodora had just time to catch a general impression of wide halls, heavy tapestries, soft rugs, crackling fires, and the delicious odor of hothouse flowers, when another figure appeared. This was an ultra-correct maid in black uniform, around whose feet and ankles frolicked two of the darlingest, snowiest, curliest little dogs Theodora had ever seen. She longed to kneel down and pet them. One of them wore a huge pink bow, and the other a blue.

The maid was plainly bored by them. She shoved them aside with her foot. "Miss Winthrop?" she asked (she was French, and Theodora's name was difficult for her tongue); "I am to show you to your room, please," she continued.

Theodora followed her through long corridors and up a stairway that seemed far removed from the principal one. They made so many turns, she wondered if she would ever be able to retrace her steps. But her room, once reached, was wholly charming to her unsophisticated eyes. Of fair size, hung with flowered chintz, boasting both writing table and fireplace (Theodora's two pet luxuries), possessed of bookshelves and an easy chair, it left nothing to be desired.

"They'll send up your trunk, Miss Winthrop, as soon as it comes," said the maid. "Would you like a tea-tray, or will you wait for dinner?"

"What time is dinner?"

"Yours will be at seven tonight. Madame is entertaining at dinner at eight, and she told me to order your tray an hour earlier."

"Then I'm not to see her tonight?"

"No, Miss; not until tomorrow. She is resting now. When the maid brings your tray you can ask her for anything you need. There is a bathroom directly across the hall. Will that be all?"

"Yes, thank you," replied Theodora, and was immediately left to her own devices. Somehow, she felt lonely and neglected. This arrival was such a tremendous thing to her, yet it seemed to mean nothing to anyone else. She had assumed that she would see her employer soon, and had been full of apprehensive anticipations. The delay made her nervous and she had no means of reassuring herself.

It was quite a comfort when a nice-looking Irish girl brought up a dinner tray. Theodora had a little talk with her, and thereby learned something of the routine of the establishment. The maid who had received Theodora was Louise, Mrs. Stuyvesant's personal maid. Louise had been with her mistress for years—in fact, nearly all the servants were old employees. The companions seemed to be the only ones who failed to stay. "They change pretty frequently, Miss," the parlour-maid had admitted, and had then held her peace, frightened by her own talkativeness.

She would soon be making familiar acquaintance with that magic street, gazing into its windows which today had been so tantalizingly glimpsed.

Following the example of her mistress, Theodora was to have a breakfast tray in her room each morning. She was then to await Mrs. Stuyvesant's orders. Luncheon and dinner she would probably eat in her mistress' company, unless there were guests; at such times, solitary trays would be her lot. It was a side of the question that had not occurred to her. Eating alone would be a new experience. Theodora couldn't help smiling when she considered how her cousin Elise would have chafed under the implied inferiority; then honesty forced her to admit that she didn't greatly care for it herself.

The parlour-maid withdrew, and Theodora applied herself to her dinner. On the tray was a half-pint bottle of claret, which she didn't touch; it set her thinking of her cousin, Ned Charrington. From him, her thoughts passed to Waverly in general, comparing it with what little she had already seen of her new home. Even the Misses Duncan had never dreamed of engaging a companion. Even they would not be apt to send up wine on a dinner tray. Even to an employee, who was likewise a gentlewoman, they would have accorded a personal greeting on the day of her arrival. Yes, there were certainly differences.

Theodora had plenty of material to keep her thoughts busy. The day had been a whirl of new impressions. For the first time in her life she had travelled—and on her own initiative, at that. She would never forget that marvelous first drive up Fifth Avenue—a drive which had ended all too soon. To think that she would soon be making familiar acquaintance with that magic street, gazing into its windows which today had been so tantalizingly glimpsed, mingling with its fascinating throngs!

But travelling is unfortunately no preventive of homesickness. Never before had Theodora been so far away from her mother. She would sorely miss that good-night kiss without which she had rarely slept—and the knowledge that her mother would be missing it equally, only served to increase the sadness. Sitting down at her desk, the daughter wrote a three-sheet letter with which to follow up the postcard that had already carried the news of her safe arrival at the Grand Central station.

This done, she prepared for bed. As she floated off to sleep, she heard laughter and gay discussion. She wondered what it was like downstairs. Would she, herself, ever be permitted to get to the real core of life? How strange and unfair it seemed that a miserable accident such as lack of wealth should forever bar one from joy and experience and usefulness! How wretched that a thing like money should be the controlling power of the world!

With this thought, Theodora fell asleep and forgot all her woes.

❦ ❦ ❦

It was eleven o'clock the next morning before her summons came. Mrs. Stuyvesant, it appeared, rested late after entertaining.

Therefore Theodora had the long half of a morning on her hands before the meeting took place. And when the moment actually arrived, she faced it with a nervous dread. Louise, who had come to fetch her, knocked lightly on a closed door and disappeared.

"Come," cried a voice, and Theodora entered.

"Ah, Miss Winthrop! Pray sit down." No hand was extended in greeting and Theodora, who had been on the point of crossing the room to offer her own, sat down abruptly, blushing hotly and feeling snubbed. Of course, she was now a paid companion; but wasn't she Theodora Winthrop, just as much as ever? Had she become a social outcast by the mere fact of working for her living?

One thing, however, she was forced to admit: Her employer was wonderful—to the eye, at least. Simply wonderful! She was the very picture of a brilliant old worldling, perfect to every slightest detail!

Mrs. Stuyvesant's hair was snow-white and it lay in beautiful coils and masses atop of the most proudly held head Theodora had ever seen. Beneath this frame of hair, big dark eyes under coal black brows, and a pair of faded but still delicately tinted cheeks, made an arresting ensemble.

"You are rested from your journey, I hope?" said the older woman with perfunctory politeness.

"Yes, thank you. I enjoyed the trip. Travelling is a novelty to me."

"Travelling?" There was a mocking smile on the rather scornful old lips.

Theodora felt hot, but she looked levelly back into the amused eyes.

"From my standpoint, Mrs. Stuyvesant," she answered quietly, "it was travelling. You see, I am unfortunately quite inexperienced."

It was a pity she couldn't know how cleverly she had done. Like all autocrats, Mrs. Stuyvesant admired spirit more than anything else in the world—admired it, and spent her life trying to kill it in those around her. Naturally, she didn't expect to permit it in a companion; the possibility had never arisen with any member of that timid army that had preceded Theodora, and had been summarily dismissed one by one.

"You have never worked before I believe, Miss Winthrop?"

"Never."

"Why did you decide to begin?"

"Poverty."

"You have lost money recently?"

"No, Mrs. Stuyvesant. I never had any to lose. But until recently, I should never have been able to persuade my family to let me work."

"And you are not doing it for amusement, nor because you want to be of use in the world?"

"I'm doing it for money entirely."

The keen black eyes gazed straight into the honest hazel ones. Unknown to herself, Mrs. Stuyvesant's lips softened a trifle.

"How old are you, Miss Winthrop?"

"Twenty-one."

"I take it you are not greatly given to untruths?"

"I should hope not." Theodora's voice was very scornful.

"You will have ample opportunity to test your truthfulness. I have never yet had a companion who dared to tell me the invariable truth. You believe, I'm sure, that a compromise with truth is never excusable? Well, you have much to learn."

This was unexpected. Theodora was left to wonder whether her truthfulness were being commended or belittled. Not that it mattered, however.

"Is your room comfortable?" continued her employer.

"Indeed, yes. It is simply lovely, thank you."

"Do you read French well?"

"Aloud, do you mean?"

"Yes."

"I read it very easily, but I don't know what you will think of my accent. I've never been abroad."

"In that case, it is probably atrocious. However, one can't have everything. Are you fond of dogs?"

"Oh, I love them. I saw two such sweet ones in the hall last night."

"Yes. Those are my children. They are wonderfully clever. I like them to be exercised intelligently, and my stupid servants merely walk around with them. You can take them out in the mornings before I am ready for you. Around the park and into the village. Their walks must not be too monotonous. And if your French is not too bad, I should like you to speak to them in that tongue. They prefer it, though of course they understand English."

"What are their names?" asked Theodora.

"Blanchette and Poilu. Do you play bridge, Miss Winthrop?"

"Fairly well."

"I may need you occasionally to fill in. . . . You knit, of course? I shall have a great deal of Red Cross work for you to do."

"I'm sorry, but I never learned to knit."

"Never learned to knit! How shocking! Where have you been living? Louise shall teach you at once. She knits beautifully—"

At this moment, there was a knock and Mrs. Stuyvesant's physician was announced. A cloud passed over the proud old face. "Stay a moment," she said, as Theodora rose. "I want you to meet Dr. Powers. Then you may wait for him down in the library. When he has finished his visit to me, he will have a word to say to you."

As Theodora sat awaiting Dr. Powers, she looked around on the most beautiful room she had ever seen. Mrs. Stuyvesant's morning room had been charming—it was luxurious and dainty and sophisticated and intimate. But this library gave assurance of the intellect of a long line of owners. There was a smell of Russia leather; books stamped with gilt coats-of-arms lay on the tables; rare editions lined the walls; beautiful porcelains and etchings, together with a collection of Japanese armour, surmounted the cases; on one table lay the current issue of every periodical of which Theodora had ever heard, as well as innumerable others which were strangers to her—they seemed to be in every tongue but German. Selecting one of them, she was just settling herself to enjoy it when Dr. Powers appeared.

"Miss Winthrop," he began, "there is a subject on which I must warn you. Mrs. Stuyvesant has been my friend and patient for many years. Some eight years ago she underwent a terrible experience—her only son died under particularly painful circumstances, and she has never recovered from the shock. In addition, she now has angina pectoris." He stopped and regarded Theodora. "Have you had any experience with that disease?" he demanded.

"Never. I know almost nothing about sickness."

"Ah! That is rather a pity, under the circumstances. It is my firm conviction that Mrs. Stuyvesant's companion should be a trained nurse. However, she won't hear of it. She knows the nature of her trouble, but she never wants it mentioned. Remember that. She has already had several serious seizures, and she should never be alone. Now I must instruct you as to remedies."

He proceeded to teach Theodora about the various drugs which she must always have on hand—those for quick seizures, those for more ordinary use, the methods of administering them, and the signs by which she must recognize symptoms. It all sounded rather frightening. "Have you noticed Mrs. Stuyvesant's hands?" was Dr. Power's next question.

"No," answered the girl. "I've seen her only once. I got an impression of lace ruffles and flashing rings, but I didn't notice her hands. Why?"

"They used to be very beautiful—one of her chief sources of pride. Noted sculptors begged permission to model them in marble, and so on. Now they are knotted and twisted with gout, and she avoids showing them. I have actually seen her play cards in gloves. You will undoubtedly find that one of your duties is pouring tea in the afternoon—at least, that has been the case with all those who have held your present position. This house is a notable gathering place in the afternoons—particularly on Sundays. At tea time, my patient is apt to get excited and overtired. I want you to watch her closely and whenever such signs appear, you must drop three drops—no more, no less—from this brown bottle into her second cup of tea, which she is sure to take. Give the bottle to the butler, and tell him to see that it is always on the tray."

"It seems a terrible responsibility," said Theodora.

"You'll be equal to it, I'm sure," answered the doctor kindly.

Soon after his departure luncheon was announced, and Theodora made her first acquaintance with the dining room. She couldn't fail to appreciate the delicious food. Wine appeared again, and noticing that the girl never lifted her glass, Mrs. Stuyvesant turned on her sharply.

"You don't take wine?" she demanded.

"Not often."

"May I ask why? I trust it is no question of principle. If there's anything I detest, it is puritanism."

Theodora thought of Ned and of that awful night at home. But had she, indeed, any general principles against wine, or was Ned merely weak, falling where another might safely stand? She hardly knew her own views of the matter.

"My mother considers me too young to take wine habitually," she answered truthfully.

"Hm! Provincial standards. Still, that seems a sufficiently legitimate reason. I don't mind that."

"Don't you indeed?" thought Theodora the independent. But as Mrs. Stuyvesant wasn't Aunt Augusta, she could say nothing.

After luncheon, there were some notes to be written before Mrs. Stuyvesant rested. These, Theodora found simply astounding. Two-thirds of them were answers to appeals for money or help. Very few were refused. The girl filled in checks amounting to hundreds of dollars, and handed them over for signature. She wondered if this were an ordinary occurrence.

There was one letter concerning an unpopular matron at a certain hospital; a movement was afoot to replace her. At Mrs. Stuyvesant's dictation, Theodora wrote the answer to this and then proceeded to read it aloud. She came to a certain sentence: "Although I am aware that Miss Ross is no saint, she still has many traits that make her valuable to us; I think you would better think twice before sending her off."

"What is that?" demanded Mrs. Stuyvesant suddenly and sharply. "Read that last part again."

Theodora complied.

"Did you say, 'I think you *would* better think twice'?"

"Yes, Mrs. Stuyvesant."

"Why did you write such a sentence as that?"

"Because it was correct."

"Correct? It most certainly is *not* correct. Change it at once."

Now as it happened, Theodora had had an English teacher who had given particular attention to that phrase—and the girl had ever since prided herself on her correct use of it. She longed to point out to her employer that "would think" was correct grammatically, but her lips were sealed.

> *She would have been content to sit and listen greedily to the bright talk purling so smoothly around her.*

"Do you want me to write 'had better think twice'?" she asked constrainedly.

"I certainly do. And you may copy the entire letter. I think you'll find your duties here sufficiently varied, Miss Winthrop, without attempting to add English lessons to them. Provincial standards may do very well in small places, but they do not hold in the real world. Ring for Louise please; I must rest."

❧❧❧   ❧❧❧   ❧❧❧

At afternoon tea, Theodora forgot her irritation. She very rarely harbored grudges. The sun always came promptly out from behind her clouds—only it helped such a lot if she could first give vent to her feelings. As she put it, she hated to be "bottled up." However, it was a lesson that she had to learn now.

Few persons could have failed to yield to the spell cast by that charming tea-hour. Fourteen or fifteen guests dropped in, all attractive, all interesting, all primed with the latest tidbits of news and gossip. From nearly every guest, Theodora received first a smiling bow, and then a much more careful scrutiny. Before the afternoon ended almost every one had made occasion for a little chat with her.

But even failing that, she would have been content to sit and listen greedily to the bright talk purling so smoothly around her. Here was life, indeed!

At home, if two or three were gathered together they were probably discussing a new stitch in embroidery, or how the chewing-gum millionaires had attempted to bow to Miss Duncan on the platform. Ah, she had been lucky—more than lucky—to get a chance to widen her horizon!

"Miss Winthrop," said Mrs. Stuyvesant suddenly, "my last cup of tea is simply wretched. It is perfectly cold."

"Oh, I'm so sorry," cried the girl contritely, the quick color rising to her cheeks. This was a scolding which was probably well deserved, and it was only injustice that Theodora resented. She had been so absorbed that she had forgotten her duties.

Her penitence was so genuine and so graceful that it made everyone her would-be champion. Even her imperious employer was mollified.

"Never mind," she said. "Probably the spirit-lamp wasn't working properly. Towner has been shockingly careless of late."

"No," answered Theodora, "it is quite all right. I'm afraid the fault is mine, Mrs. Stuyvesant."

"Well, let it go," answered the older woman with unexpected mildness. "What were you saying, Edith?"

❧❧❧ ❧❧❧ ❧❧❧

That night before she slept, Theodora wrote to her mother.

Dearest Mother,

Everything is lovely. I wish you could see my room. A perfect dear, with a fireplace all my own! Tell Elise I'm to have a breakfast tray every morning. The house looks like a palace to my untutored eyes, and Mrs. Stuyvesant is simply wonderful—very beautiful and aristocratic. Like Aunt Augusta, she is never wrong. I think they would hit it off marvelously, except that Mrs. S. would never meet Aunt A. as an equal. Did you know, lovely Parent, that we in Waverly are simply provincial nobodies? How do you suppose that fact escaped our notice all these years—for it seems to be established without question, and I am evidently to be kept constantly in mind of it.

I poured tea this afternoon, and the talk was so wonderful that I forgot my duties and let everything get stone cold. I heard important names being bandied about with a familiarity that made my head swim. Mrs. Stuyvesant and her friends evidently know *everyone*, except such poor worms as are not eligible to their circle. To be honest, life here seems to me so big it's amazing. The people are interested in everything important and useful, and they appear to give away fortunes. That, I confess, makes me green with envy. However, it's just the accident of money. If we had it, we'd do the same.

The burning question at present is, whether my French is good enough to be inoffensive to the ears of two highly intelligent poodles who prefer to be addressed in that tongue. I'm to be tried out tomorrow. If I pass the test, I'm to exercise the pair of canines daily, in French.

I gather that Mrs. S. is contemplating giving a big house party in the near future. Of course, it won't touch me, but it will be exciting to live under the same roof with it. That is nearer than I've ever yet come to excitement. Good night dearest Mother. Crowds of love and bushels of kisses. Miss me, but be happy. And above all, keep well.

Your own,

Theodora

PART SECOND

An Intriguing Young Man

CHAPTER
V

heodora had just finished writing the invitations to the house party. There they lay, a goodly pile—blazoned, sealed, stamped. The girl wondered about their recipients. It went without saying that they were all rich and fashionable; almost certainly they were interesting—to the extent, at least, of having seen the latest play, heard the latest music, read the latest book, and met the latest celebrity.

For her own part, she was conscious of an ever-increasing admiration for the old woman with whom she lived—even while admitting her numerous obvious imperfections. Many times, their two dominant personalities clashed; but Theodora had always to yield almost before she resisted. Often she was silent, knowing herself to be right (as in that grammatical discussion on her very first day). At first difficult, this was becoming less of a cross. Where it had formerly been bitterness, it was now merely a nettle sting.

Could Theodora sometimes have read her employer's mind, she might have been quite a bit astonished. The girl must be broken, of course, Mrs. Stuyvesant concluded. Imagine permitting herself such a degree of personality! But what a relief—oh, what an ineffable relief—to be free from the irritating exhibition of stupidity, and petty falsehoods, and cringing, afforded by all those other companions. What a grim sort of satisfaction never to be able to pick a real flaw in the innate breeding of a paid attendant, to be sure of looking constantly on daintiness and wholesomeness—and even beauty, to have one's ears caressed by a really lovely voice, to watch the quick flash of intelligent response in honest young eyes, the avid grasp of ideas by a fresh receptive young mind!

> She knew that her cousin Elise got many secret books from a library in town, that she kept them hidden and read them on the sly.

"You've finished the letters, Miss Winthrop?" asked Theodora's employer.

"Yes, Mrs. Stuyvesant."

"Then I think we'll have time to go on with the French book before luncheon."

Theodora's accent passed muster, so she had been introduced to a realm of literature whose art and subtlety held her spell bound. In the protection of her own fireside she would never even have heard of such books. This morning's reading gripped the heart, intrigued the mind, but brought a puritan modesty up gasping. "Read that again," said Mrs. Stuyvesant of a certain sentence.

The girl obeyed. "'The terrible experimental inquisitiveness of youth is responsible for most of the tragedies of life.'"

"Do you agree with that, Miss Winthrop?"

Theodora considered. "No, Mrs. Stuyvesant," she presently answered.

"Why not? It is quite true."

"Well," said the girl, "take this war! It certainly is one of the tragedies of life, yet it has nothing to do with the inquisitiveness of youth."

The older woman threw her a quick glance of appreciation. She liked people who thought for themselves. "That is true," she admitted. "But this book was written before the war. I'm rereading it, you see. I imagine it means individual tragedies, perennial tragedies, general recurrent tragedies. Do you get my idea?"

"Yes," answered Theodora, and again she considered. She knew few young people, and none like herself. The thought occurred to her that she might have little or none of this natural experimental inquisitiveness, and that by its very lack she was rendered sub-normal! She knew that her cousin Elise got many secret books from a library in town, that she kept them hidden and read them on the sly. Theodora had always felt a strong repugnance for a certain class of topics and thoughts. This repugnance, though innate, had been greatly fostered by an old-fashioned training, coupled with a natural obedience. Perhaps Elise had a surplus of this trait of inquisitiveness, while Theodora had none! That might explain many things.

"I'll think that over, Mrs. Stuyvesant," she finally said. "It's rather interesting." And she went on reading.

Before luncheon, Theodora went to her room where she found two letters awaiting her. The one in her mother's writing she naturally opened first. Her eyes flew over its pages. Suddenly she gave a sharp exclamation.

What was this? *Elise* engaged to Dr. Sewall? It couldn't be! Mother must mean Meta. But no—the name appeared again and again. Elise was to be married very soon, with the quietest of ceremonies. She seemed to be happy. She would have a pretty home, two servants, and the doctor's professional car.

In a fit of disgust, Theodora threw the letter on the floor. "The cheat," she exclaimed. "The wretched little cheat! She's no more in love with that man than I am. To rob her own sister— and such a sister as Meta! It's a disgusting shame! I hope she'll never know what happiness means—the miserable little thief!"

The other letter was one of Ned's rare notes. He now wrote:

Dear Brownie,

I've been meaning to write and ask how you are getting along. It's a confounded shame that you had to get out and hustle for the needful. Isn't money the very devil? I'm in the deuce of a mess over it this minute. Don't quite see yet how I'm coming out, but I may strike luck. If not, they'll probably expel me. I bet I can count on you to stick by me in that case. But I'd sure hate to disappoint Mother.

Hope they're treating you decently where you are. If not, just get up and leave. Don't let them try to put anything over. You're a brick anyhow. It'd be fine if there were more like you. Here's wishing you luck.

Yours,

Ned

Theodora's salary was fifteen dollars a week and she had just received her second payment. She sat down instantly and wrote:

Ned Dear,

I was overjoyed to hear from you. Sorry about the money trouble. Of course, I'd stand by you; but I trust nothing need happen. I've just been paid and I haven't an expense in the world. Thirty dollars isn't much, I know, but would it help any? You're more than welcome to it.

I'll write soon again—nearly luncheon time now. Ned dear, I don't want to preach, but do be careful about one dreadful thing. You know what I mean. Oh, Ned, be my own dear, and never do anything of that sort again.

Your loving,

Brownie

The sum of Theodora's worldly wealth was just thirty-five dollars, so her offer was no small act of generosity. She had planned the luxury of pledging herself to the Red Cross for ten dollars a month, but that must wait now. She'd have to content herself with knitting harder than ever at the grey and khaki garments Louise had taught her to make from the apparently inexhaustible supply of wool furnished by Mrs. Stuyvesant.

On the morning of the day when the house-party guests were due to arrive, Theodora had Ned's answer. It was grateful and loving, but it absolutely refused the offer of the loan. "Not on your tintype," wrote the boy. "When the day comes that I have to take money from a girl—and a girl who is supporting herself, at that—that'll be the day when I buy a revolver and shoot myself. Don't you worry, Brownie old girl, I'll come out all right."

That was all. Not a word about her small warning; but the girl felt happy, nevertheless. Ned wasn't the sort to lay his burdens on the shoulders of a girl, anyhow. Dear old Ned!

Theodora realized that while the house-party lasted, she would be consigned to almost total solitude; she would even be robbed of that daily treat that she had come so to anticipate. One of Mrs. Stuyvesant's guests would always be there to pour tea, thereby saving the crippled old hands and dispensing with the exclusive services of the butler. "When my tea must be poured by a servant," Mrs. Stuyvesant was fond of saying, "I shall cease to ask my friends to share it with me."

> The men seemed such attractive worldlings; the women were like fashion-plates. . . . To the watching girl, it was like a scene in a book or on a stage.

She had been showing quite a bit of concern over the lonely evenings in store for her companion. Could Theodora have realized how little anxiety her predecessors had evoked, she would have been touched.

"I shall be all right," she kept insisting. "I love to read, and I'm used to depending on myself."

"You must spend your evenings here in my boudoir. You can't stay all day and all night in the same room. Come in here with your book or your writing, and stay till bedtime."

"Thank you," smiled Theodora. "That will be lovely."

It was from that boudoir that she watched the arrival of the guests—Mrs. Stuyvesant having gone to her bedroom to rest, in order to be equal to the strain of dinner and the evening.

How gay they all looked and sounded! The men seemed such attractive worldlings; the women were like fashion-plates. Their merry voices and trilling laughter formed a pretty accompaniment to the deep bass of the men. To the watching girl, it was like a scene in a book or on the stage. How wonderful to be born to a life that flowed always among such settings.

And yet, after all, what an odd sort of reception it was, when one came to think of it—almost like a hotel or a roadhouse. A room-clerk assigning quarters, a porter sent to fetch trunks

Amusing Guests at a House Party

Strictly speaking the house party consists of from four to twenty guests gathered in a country home, from three days to a fortnight.

When the party is assembled, the time is devoted to the enjoyment of the best-planned and most varied entertainments that the hostess can provide. Horses, golfing, tennis, sailing, boating, dancing, are obvious diversions to suggest during the day.

At night, a dinner, followed by a dance, a card party, private theatricals, a fancy-dress ball, a casino dance, a picnic, or a moonlight drive are some of the expedients for filling the evenings, which even in a modest house party, must not be left entirely empty for yawning and boredom to creep in.

To invite a dozen persons to one's home and leave them entirely to their own devices is indeed brutal; but the contrary error of over-entertaining is to be likewise avoided.

—The Modern Hostess, 1904

and bags, no sign of a hostess nor of a personal welcome! Theodora giggled a little at the thought. In Waverly, the rare guests were always met at the train by some member of the expectant household. It was never neglectful of the formal relationship between visitee and visitor. The new way was much more fun, of course; but wasn't it also much more selfish?

Soon halls were aflutter. The guests must all have elected to go to the library for their tea and drinks. The tap of high heels, the frou-frou of lacy tea-gowns, and the wafting of faint perfumes testified to their passing. The sounds of laughter and voices, the faint rattle of china, the tinkling of ice against glass ascended again from downstairs.

If a house-party could so set veins a-tingle at this distance, what must it be like at close range? Theodora had a premonition that she should presently grow sad and homesick unless she pulled herself together. "Don't be a goose, Theodora Winthrop," she admonished herself. "You can't have everything. Suppose you were still in Waverly, with no money and no chance to earn any! Be thankful for your good luck!"

She hadn't much appetite for dinner, however, and she couldn't fix her mind on a book afterwards. It was rare when that solace failed her. About nine o'clock she decided she might as well go to bed. The thought had barely crossed her mind, when the door of the boudoir was pushed open and a man entered. Seeing Theodora he paused.

"I beg your pardon," he said. "This is still Mrs. Stuyvesant's room, isn't it?"

"Yes," answered Theodora. "I'm her companion, Miss Winthrop."

"And I'm her nephew. It's awfully nice to meet you, Miss Winthrop. I've been hearing quite a bit about you, of late."

Looking at this man, Theodora couldn't help wondering if he were a fair sample of those downstairs. If so, she certainly had a right to be depressed over her isolation. It would not be too much to say that he was the most attractive-looking man she had ever seen. Tall, blond, bonny, with a look of friendliness in his laughing grey eyes and with that interested manner all women love, he was evidently one of those fortunates to whom all the world holds out quick hands of welcome.

Feeling that she was staring rather stupidly, Theodora blushed a bit. "Can I do anything for you?" she asked primly.

"Can you? Well, I wonder. My aunt sent me to ask her maid for a certain scarf. You might find that, if it wouldn't be troubling you too much. But after all, that would be more of a service to her and her maid than to me, wouldn't it?"

"Which scarf did she want?"

"The white Spanish lace. And do you know, I'm beginning to think I'll accept that offer of yours, and let you do something for me, as you so kindly suggest."

Theodora could control her lips better than her eyes. She dropped the latter hastily, but not before her companion had seen in them that which made his own smile.

"I'm going to let you in on a secret," he said, with the most engaging air of camaraderie. "I'm bored to tears tonight. I don't happen to feel like bridge, and I've been talking all through a stupid dinner. I'm going to take this scarf down and then, if you'll let me, I'm coming back up here to hide. May I? And will you wait for me?"

Theodora shook her head. "I'll still be here, if that's what you mean," she said.

"That is exactly what I mean. I'm glad you're quick at catching meanings—it helps such a lot." He had the most beguiling smile; so gay and friendly. "Well," he continued, "in just a moment then—" and he started for the door.

"But what will they think of your absence?" cried Theodora.

"Nothing—for they won't know of it. In the first place, my partner dropped out of the party at the last minute—some important war work kept her, to my aunt's very great disgust. You may have noticed that she hates to have her plans upset. That leaves me, you see, an unattached blessing, and at the same time makes the party uneven. The card-sharks will think I'm in the drawing room engaged in sweet converse. The others will take it for granted that I'm playing bridge in the library."

He spoke very fast, as though to forestall any objection on her part. "You'll wait?" he urged.

"I don't think I should."

"But why not?"

"Well, because—"

"The usual delightful feminine reason. Somehow, it always fails to convince me. You are expected to be in this room, I take it?"

"Yes. Mrs. Stuyvesant particularly told me to spend my evening here."

"Exactly. And I have had the run of the house all my life. So you see, it's all right. Where is my aunt's maid?"

"Downstairs. She'll be there till bedtime."

"And by that time, you'll be in your own quarters, and I shall have rejoined the boring crowd. Wait for me please." And he was out of the room before she could say either yes or no.

❧ VI ❧

f course, she waited. In the first place, because his logic—though not entirely flawless—was plausible; in the second place, because she so much wanted to; and in the third place, because this course meant merely *in*action, while any other would have meant action. "I know he isn't coming back," she told herself; "I'm not so silly as to believe that he is"—and she fell to wishing that she had changed her frock, as on other evenings. And then, in an incredibly short time, he was there.

The lack in her costume was not apparent to him. (Women habitually overrate the importance of such trifles.) In her severe blue serge, with its snowy collar and ruffles, he thought she looked wholly charming.

"Isn't this cozy?" he asked. An open fire was crackling and sputtering, and the lamplight was soft and shaded. Drawing a deep chair near the fire for Theodora, the man took another, which he carefully placed so as to get the best view of her. "So you're my aunt's new companion," he began, as he settled himself comfortably in its depths, "and your name is Miss Winthrop. What goes in front of that?"

"Theodora."

Drawing a deep chair near the fire for Theodora, the man took another, which he carefully placed so as to get the best view of her.

"Theodora Winthrop! How awfully pretty! And you look just like it, too."

"And you're Mrs. Stuyvesant's nephew?" Theodora rejoined a little hastily.

"Yes. Beeckman by name. Alan, to my friends. Are you of a friendly disposition, Miss Winthrop? If not, I'm disappointed, for your looks belie you."

They both laughed.

"What do you do with yourself, shut up here alone?" continued the man; "a young thing like you!"

"Have Mrs. Stuyvesant's other companions been older than I?"

"Well, rather! At least a quarter of a century, I should think."

Theodora gave a little unconscious sigh which did not escape her companion.

"Tell me about the party," begged the girl suddenly. "Is it very gay?"

"By no means. Just so-so. Not up to my aunt's usual standard. But this time she struck hard luck. As I told you, the nicest girl—in fact, from my standpoint, the only really interesting girl—didn't come." (Theodora edged mentally away from the thought of this girl. To be able to turn down a wonderful house party at the last minute and to leave everyone mourning for you, is really too much luck.)

"I wish you were downstairs," said the man suddenly. "Not at this moment, naturally, but as a member of the crowd. I assure you it would help a lot." He smiled, and nodded at her in such a friendly way that she felt happier, at once.

"I watched you all come," she confessed, "and it looked fascinating—"

"No, I'm inclined to think your term is too strong. I should certainly save that word for a more appropriate use. It's the usual crowd. . . ."

Silence fell. Theodora hastened to break it; this man mustn't find it stupid both upstairs and down. "I suppose," she said, "the girl who didn't come was Miss Gary? You see I wrote the invitations and I remember there were very few unmarried girls. I think I wrote 'Miss' on only two envelopes."

She had paid for her nervous haste by bringing the talk back to the unwelcome subject of that wonderful girl.

"No," said Beeckman, "the girl who didn't come is Miss Helen Burrill, and she's simply a peach; I hope you'll meet her some day. She's the cleverest girl I know—does everything wonderfully. She dances beautifully—really beautifully—and her game of bridge is so remarkable that there isn't a man in town who wouldn't run a mile to play with her. And yet with it all, her one idea is doing good—charity work, and that sort of thing. I doubt if she would have even dreamed of accepting this invitation, except as a kindness to my aunt who is perfectly devoted to her."

"Little Marjorie Gary, now," went on the man, "is quite a different sort of proposition. In the first place, she is a mere child. This is her first season. She and her youthful gentleman make an exceedingly incongruous element in this particular crowd that my aunt has gathered. But there's a strong reason for their presence. It's quite a juvenile romance!"

Urged by the eagerness of Theodora's eyes, he began to tell her about it, then suddenly pulled himself up. "But this must bore you terribly," he cried. "Let's talk of something more interesting—you, for instance."

But she wouldn't let him. "No, no," she insisted. "I'm longing to hear about this romance—that is, if you don't mind telling me?"

"I'd love to. Well, to begin at the beginning, Mrs. Stuyvesant—who, by the way, is my great-aunt—is childless.

She lost an only son some years ago—"

"Yes, I know. Dr. Powers told me."

"All about it?"

"No. Just that."

"Ever since his death my aunt has seemed to cling particularly to her one niece and her two great-nephews—my cousin, Van Rensselaer Beeckman, and me. We three are nearer to her than anyone else. Her niece is Mrs. Gary—the mother of this little witch downstairs."

"If they'd let Marjorie alone, the whole thing would probably have died out. Then again, . . . There does appear to be such a thing as true love."

"Is she lovely, this little Miss Gary?" asked Theodora.

"Simply lovely. The most entrancing piece of spoiled prettiness I ever saw. She's an only child, and in her whole life she's never once been crossed. Well, about a year ago, while she was still in school, what did she do but proceed to fall desperately in love with an ineligible—some young cub that she'd met at a college prom. It came to the point where the family took alarm, but it was too late. They merely succeeded in fanning the flame. If they'd let Marjorie alone, the whole thing would probably have died out. Then again, it might not have. There does appear to be such a thing as true love."

"But they're so young!"

"Too young for love, do you think?"

"Oh, I don't know. Tell me more about it. I'm quite thrilled."

"You see, in addition to their extreme youth—which is urged as the main objection, because everyone thinks the child will change her mind when she's older—there's another crime

75

laid at the boy's door. He isn't a member of the particular little set in which Marjorie was born and must marry."

"I know all about the traditions of blood, and the way they can hamper one," nodded Theodora.

"The Garys admit that this boy is a nice fellow, good-looking and well-bred, but they had set their hearts on something different for their small princess. He hasn't a red cent, I'm told, but that needn't matter. Marjorie has more than enough for both of them."

"But why is she here? Is the boy here, too?"

"Heavens, no! She's here to be weaned away from him."

"With her mother? I remember writing to a Miss Marjorie Gary, but I didn't write to any Mrs. Gary, I'm sure."

"No, she wasn't asked. Marjorie has conceived the notion that all her family are spying on her and trying to separate her from her true love—and at that, she isn't far wrong. However, things have come to the point where she is cold to her mother, and suspects every servant in the house of being a detective. Mrs. Gary is breaking her heart over the affair, and my aunt has asked the child up here, together with a youthful gentleman on whom the family would smile."

"But he must be young, too."

"He is; but by this time they're so worried they'd waive that point in favor of his eligibility. The families have been friends for generations, and all that sort of thing. And they've concluded that you can't have everything. Just the same, it's the most absurdly managed piece of work I ever saw; absolutely *bungled*! They'll merely succeed in making her hate a nice chap she might otherwise come to like. What girl ever found any fellow attractive when she was desperately in love with another? And what spoiled child wouldn't fight like the very devil to get the first thing that had ever been denied her?"

"I wish I could see her," cried Theodora. "Is she so very pretty?"

"Perfectly lovely. The prettiest child I ever saw. Now, Miss Winthrop, I've done nothing but talk. Do tell me something about yourself and your life here? Is it fairly pleasant?"

"Oh, yes, indeed! I'm awfully happy."

"Not very gay for a young person of your years, I should think. How do you spend your days?"

Theodora sketched him a brief outline. He looked at her rather wonderingly.

"Don't you ever get blue?" he asked.

"Not often. I was just a little bit homesick tonight; you see, this is the very first time I've ever been away from home. While I was eating my dinner I could catch an occasional murmur of the voices downstairs there, and it made me feel lonely. But that was silly, of course."

"It's a perfect shame," exclaimed the man impulsively. "I'll tell you something, though. In a fortnight or so, Helen—that is, Miss Burrill—and I are coming out here for a little visit before my aunt returns to town. Just a quiet little visit—that's the kind Miss Burrill likes best. When that happens, you'll spend all the evenings downstairs with us, I'm sure. You see, we'll be just four for bridge. You play, I suppose?"

"Oh, I play. But not in the class with you and Miss Burrill. My game would bore you to death."

"I assure you it wouldn't bore me to death, Miss Winthrop." Suddenly he began to laugh, as at some memory. "We had the warmest discussion at dinner tonight," he said. "I never saw my aunt more excited. And on such an odd subject, too; by no means the sort of thing that ordinarily interests her. It was a question of good English."

"Good English?"

"Yes. Aunt Honora asked us if we had ever heard anyone use the 'absurd' term 'would better' in place of 'had better'—"

Theodora sat up quickly, eyes shining. "And what did you say?" she demanded.

The man looked at her admiringly. "By Jove," he cried, "I believe she's been throttling you on that subject—"

The girl nodded. "It was on my very first day here," she answered. "What did you say about it, Mr. Beeckman?"

"I told her it was grammatically correct, of course."

"Which? Would, or had?"

"Would."

Theodora clapped her hands in delight. "Did you convince her?" she asked.

"Certainly not. So you stood up to her too, did you?"

"Yes."

"Good! Keep it up, Miss Winthrop. It's the only way. She'll like you all the better for it—though, of course, she'd never admit it. I believe my one hold over her is that I never in my life knuckled to her. She's a perfect old dear, of course, and a wonder. But she's just a trifle, well, domineering. I'll bet quite a bit that it takes more than that to frighten you!"

"I'm afraid I lost my temper."

The man smiled. "I like spirit," he observed. "I inherit that from my aunt."

A clock chimed ten. Beeckman looked up incredulously. "By Jove," he exclaimed, "what a short hour! And also, what a charming one!" Rising, he walked to the fireplace, and stood looking down on Theodora. "What's your morning schedule?" he asked.

"The poodles first," she replied. "I exercise them immediately after my breakfast."

"And that is?"

"About eight o'clock."

"Lucky little beasts," he exclaimed. "I'm glad they're sufficiently intelligent to appreciate their advantages. Well, good night, Miss Winthrop. You've given me a charming time." He held out his hand.

After his departure, Theodora retreated to her room feeling both excited and depressed. What fun it had been, and how soon it was over! Probably she'd never see him again—unless indeed, the second visit came to pass as he had predicted. What would Mrs. Stuyvesant think of this evening's performance, if she ever came to hear of it? Would she object? Almost certainly she would. Yet on what grounds?

When she finally saw who it was, an extra wave of color leaped to her cheeks, making them worthy of the admiration accorded them.

Theodora met her guests in her library, and chatted with them there. She was certainly well within her rights in spending her evening in the room assigned to her use. Mrs. Stuyvesant had herself sent her nephew for that scarf. If a man came into the room where one happened to be sitting, one couldn't imitate a deaf mute, could one?

All very pretty reasoning. Nevertheless, Theodora knew quite well that the damning point lay in the fact that she had waited for Beeckman's return at his suggestion. There was no comfortable skewing of truth in her moral vision. "I shouldn't have done it," she acknowledged.

It was astonishing how long she thought of her new acquaintance before she slept, how she went over her conversation with him word by word. She was still harking back to it in memory the next morning when she started out in the dewy autumn freshness with her two intelligent canine companions—thinking so hard, that for a moment she failed to recognize the figure that advanced to meet her. When she finally saw who it was, an extra wave of color leaped to her cheeks, making them worthy of the admiration accorded them by the man who, cap in hand, stood blocking her path.

"Mr. Beeckman," she gasped.

"The reward of virtue," smiled the man; "from my standpoint, that is to say. While all those lazy people up there are wasting the best part of the day in bed, I'm out for exercise—and finding pleasure. How are my clever friends, Blanchette and Poilu? Do they still prefer French to English?"

"They're said to."

"Then suppose you and I talk English," he suggested, "and leave them out of the conversation. It will be two duets instead of a quartet. I've always had an uncomfortable feeling, anyhow, that those dogs sneered secretly at my stupidity. Don't you think they're very subtle?"

For a delightful hour he walked with Theodora along the country roads, through the little village, even on beyond it (the mentality of the poodles demanding variety of scene). When they reached the park gates on their return, Beeckman paused. "I'm going to leave you here and walk on a bit," he said. "*Au revoir*, Miss Winthrop. There's nothing like early morning exercise, is there?"

Theodora entered the park alone. As she neared the house she became aware of gay groups dotted over the lawns. The beautiful day had evidently tempted Mrs. Stuyvesant's guests out early. Some were climbing into motors, some were amusing themselves on the charming little golf course, some were mounting horses held by waiting grooms.

Theodora altered her course, meaning to avoid them all by approaching the house from the side. As she walked along a shaded path, she found herself facing a youthful pair—a girl and a boy—who were seemingly in the midst of a quarrel. The girl's head was up and her face was aflame; the boy followed a little in her wake, evidently seeking a hearing. Suddenly spying Theodora and the two poodles, the girl made a beeline for them.

"Oh, the darling dogs," she cried. "Go away, Billy, they don't know you and they're very nervous and high-strung. They hate strangers, don't they?" she asked Theodora, in a beseeching tone. "I'm an old friend, and I want to talk French to them. That's all they understand. Don't you hear me, Billy? Go on around to the front and wait for me. I'll join you in a minute."

The young fellow could do no less than withdraw slightly, though he did it with a bad grace. He managed still to keep well in sight. Theodora knew instantly that the girl must be that Marjorie of whom she had been hearing—and certainly she was lovely, as Mr. Beeckman had said. She had the features of a cameo, and the eyes of a dove. She knelt over the dogs, as though to caress them, and suddenly began to speak very low and very fast.

"You're Mrs. Stuyvesant's companion, aren't you? Do you speak French?"

"Yes."

"Kneel down then, as if we were both stroking Poilu. There, so! I want to implore you to do me a favor. It's quite all right— a mere nothing. I simply have to send a telegram, and I'm watched like a convict. All the servants are spying on me I'm sure, and if I attempt to telephone a telegram, I'll be overheard. My mail is watched and my maid is a traitor. Won't you be an angel, and walk to the village with this message? I give you my word that it's all right. It's all written out, on the chance of finding a way. The money's inside. Don't bother about change; of course, I don't mean it as a gift. But for heaven's sake, get the message off for me. I'll bless you for ever. I swear to you that it's all right. Don't trust the errand to any one else, will you? *Please* do it yourself, if you want to help a poor girl out of a barrel of trouble."

During the whole of this speech she kept patting the dogs—laying her soft cheek against their silky backs quite as if that were her only thought, and smiling up into Theodora's face in perfect imitation of a friendly conversation. The youth who watched from a distance could certainly have seen nothing suspicious. Drawing a folded handkerchief from her pocket, the girl made a show of using it, saying from behind its thicknesses: "Here, take this handkerchief. Don't unfold it. Everything's inside it. Thank you for ever. Good bye." And, with a sudden brilliant smile, she rose and ran to rejoin the waiting boy. Theodora could hear her coaxing him back into a good humor as they walked off.

For her own part, she was dumbfounded. She couldn't accomplish any further communication with the pretty creature who had blown across her path like a perfumed whirlwind; she couldn't betray her trust without a word of explanation; she couldn't turn the errand over to a servant; and she couldn't consult anyone. Yet she was decidedly uncomfortable about assuming the responsibility.

All through luncheon she argued the matter out with herself. Her final decision was that she must do as she had been requested. Had any other of Mrs. Stuyvesant's guests asked a service of her, she would certainly have been expected to comply. While Mrs. Stuyvesant was resting she would simply walk down to the village and send the message from the telegraph office there. What it contained was not her affair; if she had been asked to post a letter, she would never have demanded to know its contents.

She carried out her plan, merely handing the folded paper to the woman in charge of the office. "The money is inside," said Theodora. "The message is not mine and does not concern me. Just send it, please, and give me the change."

The employee took her pencil and ran it over the words. "What is the name?" she asked in a matter-of-fact tone. "It's blurred by the fold. It's Charrington, isn't it? Edward F. Charrington, D. K. E. Fraternity House, Yale University. Is that right?"

᭜VII᭜

s the clerk read off the address, Theodora stared at her in absolute bewilderment. Then, a look of terror crept into her eyes.

"What!" she cried sharply. "On, no, that *can't* be right. It certainly can't be right." The clerk shoved the message over for her inspection, "No, no, I don't want to see it. It—it isn't mine. Just send it, please, and give me the change. Don't read it to me. It doesn't concern me in the very least."

The clerk thought she was a lunatic. "The signature is 'Marjorie,' I think?" she said freezingly, as she pushed a little pile of notes and silver back across the sill. There must have been a bill of some size enclosed in the message.

For the remainder of the day Theodora could settle to no task. She wandered restlessly, turning her puzzle over and over. One thing was sure; she couldn't betray the girl who had trusted her, and that meant that she couldn't consult anyone. She tried to comfort herself with little Miss Marjorie's repeated assurances that it was "all right." She thought of telegraphing Ned on her own account, but what could she say? She knew nothing of the contents of that other message.

She was convinced of one thing; this could have nothing to do with that love affair of which Mr. Beeckman had spoken. It was some side issue. Marjorie Gary had met Ned somewhere and was telegraphing to him for help. Ned was a go-between. Perhaps he knew her lover. Yes, that must be it. They were probably college chums—perhaps even class-mates. Nothing more than that. The idea of Ned as the hero of a mad love affair was too absurd. He was a dear, of course—but he was just Ned.

> *Theodora had changed her frock in order to eat her solitary dinner in a pretty, light one; and for this fact she had reason to be glad.*

On that evening, Theodora had changed her frock in order to eat her solitary dinner in a pretty, light one; and for this fact she had reason to be glad, for shortly after nine o'clock there entered to her Mr. Alan Beeckman.

All through the early part of their conversation, he kept watching her oddly. Finally, as though obeying an impulse, he spoke. "You look to me like a young person who could keep your own counsels," he remarked.

Theodora, remembering how she was doing so, smiled a little palely.

"I'm going to make a confidante of you," said the man. "I'm in a bit of a quandary. You see, I pride myself on being something of a psychologist and something of an amateur Sherlock Holmes. These last two days I've been taking note of signs, and unless I'm grossly mistaken, there's something brewing beneath this roof. You remember the pretty child I mentioned last evening—Marjorie Gary?"

Theodora's heart gave a great lurch. She nodded her head.

"Well, do you know, I'm almost sure she's planning an elope-ment?"

"Oh, no!" cried Theodora sharply.

"Yes. She's very young to be carrying the burden of so weighty a secret, and I've been watching her closely. She couldn't manage a thing of that sort in the daytime, because she's never alone. But at night she'd have a far better chance here than in her own home. I'd be willing to wager quite a bit that she came with that express idea in her head."

"But how can she plan a runaway marriage," cried poor Theodora, "if the boy has no money?" (She was suddenly oppressed by the consciousness of how little money Ned had.)

"Oh, they'd merely marry to avoid permanent separation, and to make her ineligible to any other match her parents might plan. She's getting desperate. They'd go to a clergyman or a justice of the peace—probably the latter—and get the knot tied; then she'd go home and he'd return to college. Her idea would be that she'd bring her parents round when the thing was settled—but she never made a bigger mistake in her life."

"You think so, if they adore her and spoil her and give her everything she wants?"

"I'm sure of it. You see, I know Kirkland Gary, her father, as well as I know myself. If he thinks he's been duped, he's adamant. Marjorie will simply ruin her chances. If she'd stay at home, refuse to go out, be languid and sad—even a little ill— pet her father and get him thoroughly worried about her, he'd be wax in her hands by spring. But with the devil-may-care course she's planning, she's inviting a lifelong estrangement that would be tragic for all of them. The trouble is she is just as stubborn as her father."

"What can you do?" Theodora's voice was worried and tense. The thought of that telegram was burning into her brain.

"I shall keep watch. You see, it would just about kill Aunt Honora if Marjorie should succeed in eloping from here. If the thing is to happen at all—and mind you, I'm convinced that it is—it must happen tonight or tomorrow night—"

"So soon?"

"Yes, because Marjorie's booked for home the next day—she's not staying as long as the rest of us—and her maid is a strict chaperone. Once back under the home roof, little Miss Marjorie's chance is gone. So I'm going to keep watch for two nights. The child's room is immediately opposite that little alcove writing-room in the north corridor. At bedtime I'm going to change to morning clothes and sit there all night. There's a curtain, as you know, that can be drawn across the opening of the alcove, and every sound in the hall can still be heard."

"And suppose nothing happens?"

"So much the better. But something will, I'm perfectly certain. Tonight, or tomorrow night."

"Why don't you telegraph her parents?"

"I don't want them to know. It would ruin in advance the clever course I'm going to help her plan out, when once I've caught her."

"Couldn't you tell her first?"

"Miss Winthrop, your sympathies are too much on the feminine side of this thing. Marjorie would never listen to me unless I caught her red-handed. She'd probably deny the whole thing—and what proof have I? No, I must trap her in the act. Her parents mustn't know, the servants mustn't know, and my aunt mustn't know."

"And if it doesn't happen tonight?"

"Then I must try again tomorrow night—and there lies the one flaw in my almost perfect scheme. I'm horribly afraid I shall doze off the second night. She might slip me! The trouble is that I can never sleep in the daytime—"

"Mr. Beeckman," said the girl suddenly, "if nothing happens tonight, let me go on watch tomorrow night."

"You! Never in the world!"

"Please! I beg of you to let me! I can stay awake beautifully and I—I have a very special reason for wanting to help. Please, please let me."

With every passing moment, Theodora was getting more worried over the sending of that telegram. She realized that she had acted very unwisely—to put it at its mildest. If her own cousin, Ned Charrington, the boy who was almost like her brother, had indeed been asked to help in any such miserable business as an elopement, what a terrible complication it would make. Oh, it would never do—never in the world!

But the chance to repair things had come in the nick of time. Theodora glimpsed it with breathless relief. It took a long time to persuade Beeckman, but he finally yielded. Theodora harped skillfully on her most persuasive string—the danger of the man's falling asleep and of thus having his plans frustrated. It was arranged that he should watch the first night, and she the next; she had to promise to get a very long sleep tonight, in order to be fortified for the vigil.

On the morrow, Beeckman again shared her morning ramble. He showed the loss of sleep, and nothing had happened. When he came up to the boudoir that evening, they arranged the night's plans. Theodora was to sit in her own room until the house was quiet. She was then to go to the writing room and keep watch there. At the slightest sound, she was to peep through the crack between the curtains. And finally, if little Miss Marjorie were indeed in flight, Theodora was to allow her time to get past the turn in the hall, then she was to hurry to Beeckman's door and give three taps; he would be fully dressed, even though asleep.

"The moment you're sure I'm roused," he warned, "hurry to your own room and go to bed. We don't want any scandal over this thing."

It seemed to Theodora that the house would never get quiet, and the lights would never go out. As a matter of fact, it was only about half-past one when she took her eerie walk through the quiet halls of the sleeping house. Her own room was far from the north corridor, and as she crept along she wondered if she could indeed be that same girl who, up to a few weeks ago, had scarcely ever spent a night outside a simple Waverly bedroom, had never even met a fascinating young man, had never assisted at any sort of intrigue whatsoever, and had regarded an elopement as sensational claptrap!

Until half-past three, Theodora watched fruitlessly. She was beginning to hope that Beeckman had been mistaken about the whole thing, when her ear caught a sound in the hall. It was scarcely a breath—just a tiny rustling, a carefully turned knob, the brush of a garment against the door—all momentary, all slight. Only the most keenly strained ear would have noted anything. It was a dread act, in that tomblike silence, even to part the curtains for a peep. But the peep, once ventured, revealed the quarry. Little Miss Marjorie was actually in flight. Theodora's eyes, accustomed to the darkness, discerned that the fugitive carried nothing but a small wrist-bag. Evidently she did not want her progress hampered.

Beeckman's voice answered to the second of Theodora's timid taps. "All right," he whispered, "I'm coming." And the girl sped to her own quarters.

For her, that ended the affair. It was not till Beeckman joined her, later in the morning, that she heard how well the thing had gone. He had overtaken the fleeing girl before she left the park. They had sat down in the little summer house, and had there discussed the situation. By humoring the sobbing child and by sympathizing with her, her cousin had won her confidence. The whole world was in league against her, and for no reason. She would never give up the man she loved. Fearing her family would finally succeed in driving him away, she, herself, had planned this elopement, and had begged him to accede to it.

"From his standpoint, you see," said Beeckman to Theodora, "there was nothing to do but agree. He couldn't very well hang back when his girl proposed to him."

"Where was she going?"

"She was about to walk to the village, where she would hire a motor to take her to a station some miles farther south. There she could catch a very early train for New York. Then she planned to hurry to Stamford, meet her waiting beau, marry him, and go home to announce the fact to her parents. You see, the trouble lies in the fact that they're both legally of age. Marjorie was eighteen some months ago, and the boy has passed his twenty-first birthday."

"Mr. Beeckman," said Theodora suddenly, "would you mind telling me his name?" And the next moment she could have bitten out her tongue because of the question.

"Certainly not. It's Charrington. He's a junior at Yale."

"Oh, no!"

"Yes. Why, Miss Winthrop? Do you know him?"

"Know him? He's my own first cousin—almost my twin brother."

It was the man's turn to be astounded. "What?" he cried. "And you knew nothing of the affair?"

"Not a word. Not a suspicion. Except for this absolute proof, I would have vowed that it couldn't be so. You don't think that there could be two boys with the same name in that class, do you?"

The Perils of Elopement

The paternal consent refused, the devoted suitor has only two alternatives: to refuse in turn to accept the refusal as definitive, and use every social and other influence to change the father's mind—or to elope.

Only extreme circumstances justify an elopement, which at best always carries with it a suggestion of the underhand. The crux of such a situation invariably lies with the attitude of the girl concerned, and on this her suitor should place his main reliance. If she is of age and is convinced that her future happiness is at stake, she is entitled to feel that she has a moral as well as legal right to marry, though her father object.

However, if she lacks the strength of character to be firm—once she feels she is right—and fears to tell her parents definitely she must disregard their disapproval, she shows that her affection is not equal to its first great trial, and this fact should lessen her suitor's regret at losing her.

—The Book of Good Manners, 1923

Beeckman shook his head.

"But Ned couldn't plan marriage," cried the girl. "He hasn't a penny."

"But you forget; he didn't plan it. Marjorie did. The ethics of twenty-one would make it impossible for him to refuse her. To think of his being your cousin!"

"It's awful," cried poor Theodora. "I mean, considering my position in this house. But, Mr. Beeckman, Ned is a dear, just the same."

"I'm sure of it. You see I also have Marjorie's testimony to the fact."

"And," went on Theodora, "he *is* well-born—"

"Why, of course he is!"

"No; you'd say that. But while we're on the subject I want to tell you about it. I haven't been in this house three weeks without learning Mrs. Stuyvesant's ideas about social position. She thinks that nobody is anybody, unless they happen to be born in her particular little set. Now to me, that is perfectly ridiculous. All my life I've been taught that, whatever else I might lack, I had ancestors, at least. We've been told that it was just as vulgar to brag of birth as to brag of money, but that anyone who knew anything at all, could recognize its marks. And I think our teaching was right."

The man was regarding her in admiration. "Certainly it was right," he agreed heartily.

"Well, then, you can see that it is a little irritating to sit with sealed lips, and hear myself and all my family relegated to outer darkness—not by actual word, of course, but by manner."

"And take my word for it, Miss Winthrop, my aunt—well, she likes to keep people decently modest—her own friends, I mean, and her relatives. I believe she regards it as a duty. You should hear her try to make me eat humble pie." He paused a moment, as though to censor his own words, and then continued: "I admit that there is a great deal of arrogance in New York society, and a great deal of snobbery. But those traits are not confined to New York. Surely, Miss Winthrop, you must have met them elsewhere?"

"Ned's a perfect dear—but he's just a boy. He's just Ned. I can't possibly picture him as the hero of a romance."

Theodora thought of the Duncan sisters and their crowd. In Waverly, she herself had happened to be well known and inside the pale; but suppose she had been outside—and a stranger! Suppose she had come there to make a living!

"Yes," she admitted, "I have."

"Exactly. It's merely human nature, you see. Those who are constantly fawned upon become either irritated or vain. They are made to think too highly of themselves. If no one cared a fig about them, they couldn't possibly care so much about themselves. Miss Burrill and I have discussed this subject with my aunt till she vows we are both disgusting socialists. But as to your case, I'm sure she appreciates you tremendously. She couldn't help it. I wish you could see your predecessors—then you'd understand."

Theodora was beginning to feel very happy and light-hearted. She reverted to the subject of the attempted elopement. "Do you think they'll try it again?" she asked.

"No. I have Marjorie's promise for six months, on condition that I will help her all I can, and that her parents shall never know of last night's escapade. I showed her how unfair to Charrington this thing was—how it would make him look like a sneak to her family. She'd never thought of that, and it turned the trick. She consented to let me telegraph to him at Stamford, and to go back home as though nothing had happened. She's to manage her adoring parents according to the scheme I outlined. But you should hear her rave over this cousin of yours."

"That," said Theodora in a puzzled voice, "is the oddest part of the whole thing. Ned's a perfect dear—but he's just a boy. He's just Ned. I can't possibly picture him as the hero of a romance."

Beeckman laughed. "The cousinly point of view," he cried. "According to Marjorie, he's the loveliest lover that a girl ever had. His two sole faults, as she admits them, are youth and poverty. As she sagely observes, 'he'll get over the one, and the other doesn't matter. I have money enough for both of us, and it will keep us comfortable while he's making good. What else is money for?' And by Jove, I think she's right, at that. Miss Winthrop, a wonderful thought has just struck me!"

"What is that?"

"That when those two infants marry, you and I will be cousins."

"Oh," cried Theodora, "for goodness sake never suggest such a thing to Mrs. Stuyvesant. She'd send me off at a moment's notice."

Then they both laughed, and felt very friendly and intimate.

It came to pass that Theodora saw Beeckman every morning and evening of his stay. He always ran up to the boudoir after dinner, if only for a few minutes, and he invariably shared her morning walks. And then, on the very last morning, a terrible thing happened. Beeckman had just been telling Theodora that his plans for returning presently for a more quiet visit had all been upset by Miss Burrill, who was leaving at once for Chicago to help organize some Red Cross work.

"You must miss her when she's gone." Theodora's voice was rather low.

"Oh, no end. But I have to get used to it these days. The rest of the girls seem tame and boring in comparison with Helen. She's always full of interesting ideas, and I've never known such enthusiasm. You certainly must meet her. I'm dining with her tonight, and I'm going to tell her all about you. I'm only sorry that her changed plans will keep me from seeing you again, before you come to New York. It seemed to me we'd have such a cozy little time, with Bridge each evening. However, it won't be long till you're in town."

Theodora walked along, looking down at the ground and feeling more disappointed than she would have cared to confess. She had been unconsciously counting on this return of Beeckman's. And then, all of a sudden, tragedy overtook them. Poilu, who had never done such a thing in his life, spied a mangy-looking bull pup down a side street, disliked him at sight, and made a dart at him. The pup responded as might have been expected, and soon a terrific fight was in progress. Turning, snarling, leaping, rolling, it was a battle of the wildest sort.

Theodora was almost weeping, "Hold Blanchette!" she shrieked, and darted into the thick of the fray. But she felt herself thrust aside. Her companion was a sportsman, and he knew a thing or two about fights. He had picked up the panting Blanchette and now turned her over to Theodora. "Stay out of this," he commanded. "I'll separate them."

He did, but it was the work of some strenuous minutes. Upon examination, Poilu was found to have escaped with some flesh wounds which appeared not to go very deep. But he was a mass of mud and blood and filth. Theodora felt as if the end of the world had come.

"I'm going to get a cab and send you home with this wretched cur," said Beeckman. "I'd like to come with you, but I'd better not. As soon as you get back, turn the beast over to one of the men; then call my aunt's maid and tell her about it. Go to your room and stay here. Shall I tell Mrs. Stuyvesant the news, or would you rather do it?"

"Oh, wouldn't you mind?" she cried in a burst of relief.

"Mind? Certainly not. Why should I mind? I only want to do what will be best for you."

"I'd rather die than tell her," confessed Theodora.

"Very well, then. That settles it. The only thing is, I shall have to say that I was with you—and that might be visited on your head. However, I'll just tell her that I was walking in the village."

"Mr. Beeckman?"

"What, you poor child?"

"You honestly don't mind—I mean you don't care on your own account what Mrs. Stuyvesant thinks?"

"Care? I should rather think not. I was thinking only of protecting you."

"Then please don't tell any fibs on my account. Just say we were walking together. I'll take the consequences. I'd rather, honestly. I couldn't be comfortable otherwise. She can't do worse than dismiss me. And no matter what she did I'd like it better than fibbing. Anyhow, I haven't done anything wicked."

"You poor little thing! Of course you haven't. But it seems such a sneak on my part. I'm the one who's responsible for the whole thing. I'll tell you what I'll do; I'll stay over and see the thing through. I'll just wire New York—"

"No, no. Tell her the mere facts and go, please. I'd a thousand times rather. Thank you just the same. You're awfully kind."

And she gave him her hand, biting her lips to keep back the tear. To be dismissed in disgrace! It was too awful!

"The poor little thing," thought the man, as he watched the cab drive away. "She's simply a brick! Why, in the name of common sense, didn't I let her alone? I wish I could take this thing off her shoulders. Anyhow, I'll do my best to muzzle Aunt Honora."

Theodora did as he had directed. She was only too glad to have a sane plan of action laid down for her. Turning Poilu over to Louise and one of the footmen, she went to her room and began to pace the floor in a tempest of vain regret.

What a fool she had been! Here she, Theodora Winthrop, the girl who had always felt rather sure of herself—who had believed if one were truthful and honest everything would come out all right—had done little but make a series of wretched mistakes ever since entering this new home. To have sent that awful telegram! To have been the compliant recipient of a regular set of stolen visits! Why, a servant wouldn't have acted otherwise! Her employer would naturally think her an ordinary intriguing schemer.

She sent away her luncheon untasted. Some two hours later there was a knock at her door, and her summons came. With a long tremulous sigh, she moved to obey it.

☙VIII☙

ome," cried a voice in answer to Theodora's knock, and the girl walked in to face her doom.

"Ah, Miss Winthrop! Sit there, please." Mrs. Stuyvesant's tones were icy, her eyes were hard, and the chair she indicated placed Theodora's tear-ravaged face in the most uncompromising light. It was a new position for the chair, which had evidently been especially set for the trial.

"Will you kindly tell me about this unfortunate affair?" said Mrs. Stuyvesant.

In a toneless voice, Theodora related the circumstances. "You know, Mrs. Stuyvesant," she concluded, "you told me to take the dogs down to the village. You wanted them to have change of scene."

"Very true. But there never before seemed to be any vicious mongrels around. This one must be shot, of course."

"Oh," cried Theodora, "it wasn't his fault! He was merely defending himself. Poilu began it. He attacked the strange dog in cold blood."

"That may be, but it fails to alter the case. Poilu is a valuable and a high-strung dog; the other is a mere mongrel. He must be shot. Of course, I shall pay his owner."

There was a pause.

"Are you quite sure you were giving your attention to your duties when this thing happened?" pursued the older woman.

"I think so, Mrs. Stuyvesant. I was walking with your nephew and talking to him but I was watching the dogs. Poilu ran so quickly I couldn't possibly have stopped him. No one could. It all happened in a moment."

"How long have you known my nephew, Miss Winthrop?"

"Since the first evening of your party."

"How did you meet him?"

"He came into this room for your scarf. He said you sent him. I was sitting here, in accordance with your permission."

"Did he stop to talk?"

"A little while. Then after he had taken the scarf down, he came back and stayed for an hour." The girl paused, and then added: "He said he'd come back, and I waited for him."

"I suppose you thought that my nephew was asked here entirely on your account?"

"No, Mrs. Stuyvesant." (This almost with contempt. The older woman had been guilty of the first false move.)

"Didn't it seem strange to you that he should be making engagements with you, my hired companion, to whom he had never even been introduced?"

"Yes, it did. But I was where I had been told to be, and Mr. Beeckman said he had the run of the house."

"You could have gone to your room, Miss Winthrop."

"Yes, Mrs. Stuyvesant."

"May I ask you why you didn't?"

"I wanted to stay."

"Humph! And was that the only time you met?"

"No. I saw him every morning and every evening."

"By appointment?"

"Never." Another pause, and then: "But after the first time, I thought he'd come, and I hoped he would."

"How did he know your habits?"

"I told him about them the first evening. He merely came into the room where I sat, and walked on the roads where I walked. It seemed as though he had a perfect right in both places, and I certainly had."

There followed the longest pause of all. Theodora drew a deep breath of relief. It was over, and she was still alive! In fact, after the beginning, it had been easier than she had expected. And above all, there was the blessed certitude that nothing was hidden, nothing hanging over her head to fall upon her later. Whatever might be in store for her, it would happen soon and be over.

"I have had the veterinary in," said Mrs. Stuyvesant at length. "I trust you will be glad to hear that Poilu has not suffered too severely, and that he will probably soon be well again."

"Oh, I'm so glad!" cried Theodora.

"As to my nephew," continued the older woman, picking up a jeweled fan and holding it to her face (Theodora knew that fan; it was a Spanish one, and it had eye-slits), "as to my nephew, he is the most amusing person I have ever known; a trifle selfish, perhaps, when it comes to a question of his own entertainment. Most men are. As it happened, the girl who was asked here especially on Mr. Beeckman's account was unable at the last moment to come. He therefore took his temporary amusement where he found it waiting for him, as would any man of the world. It was very kind of you, Miss Winthrop, to be willing to furnish it."

It stung. There wasn't any question about that. Theodora's face flamed scarlet. Nevertheless, she was game. Many mistakes might she make, but never one of cowardliness nor yet of too great meekness. She looked her employer straight in the eye. "I'm glad, Mrs. Stuyvesant," she said levelly, "if I was able to add to the success of your party—even by amusing a bored guest."

The older woman stared incredulously for a moment, then she picked up the Spanish fan again. When she spoke, her voice was cool and non-committal. "That is all, I think, Miss Winthrop," she said. "You may go. Your dinner will be served in your room, as Louise is going to put me to bed at once. I have had a wearing day."

Was the man laughing in his sleeve? It didn't seem like him, yet she knew almost nothing of men and their ways.

Theodora went to her room, quite unsure of her position. She couldn't decide whether she was to be dismissed or not. Nevertheless, there was a feeling of lightness in her heart, its only bar being that rankling thought about Alan Beeckman and his Helen. Theodora couldn't help wondering if she had indeed made herself cheap. Was the man laughing in his sleeve? It didn't seem like him, yet she knew almost nothing of men and their ways. Anyhow, she wasn't going to worry over it any more than she could help. She went early to bed, and was fortunately soon asleep.

In the middle of the night there came a quick knock, followed by a frightened voice. "Miss Winthrop, please," said Louise's tense tones, "can you come at once? Madame is very ill."

Theodora hurried into a dressing-gown and flew. She sent servants to telephone for the doctor and a nurse. Then she applied the crisis remedies and fell to rubbing the patient's hands and feet. Minutes seemed hours. The doctor arrived in a short time, but it was none too soon. It was pale dawn before the danger was finally past. A nurse in uniform had arrived on the scene, and Theodora was sent off to bed. The doctor assured her that she had been wonderful, and that it was thanks to her quick and efficient work that tragedy had been averted.

As she walked through the halls with throbbing conscience, she wondered how greatly the affair of the dogfight might have contributed to this seizure. "Oh," she thought, "after this, I'm going to stick to my duties without bothering about anything else. If I stay here, I hope I shall never forget this night. I hope I shall never again be as foolish as I've just been!"

As Mrs. Stuyvesant grew better, it became apparent that Theodora was still regarded as a fixture in the household. For some three weeks her life at Fair Acres was as quiet and uneventful as ever it had been in Waverly. Then at the end of that time, Mrs. Stuyvesant was well enough, and the season was late enough, to warrant the move to New York. Theodora looked forward to this with the greatest interest. New York seemed to Theodora Winthrop the pinnacle desire, the place where Opportunity made her dwelling. She soon found herself installed in another beautiful home; it was modeled on the same general plan as Fair Acres, though it was not so huge. The library, however, was even more impressive, and it was the room that the girl came to love best.

But the streets and their wayfarers were a never-failing joy and delight. Even when Theodora exercised the poodles in the early morning along Fifth Avenue at those unholy hours when delicate worldlings were still in bed, when lights were crude and winds were raw, Theodora thrilled to the lure of the spell. How much more, then, when she drove with her employer in the sparkling afternoons, or enjoyed her weekly half-holidays alone. She contented herself at first, on these free afternoons, with mere walks on the great thoroughfares and through the biggest of the shops. Before long, Theodora learned to extend her pleasures. She found the museums and libraries and theaters. Sitting along in the highest gallery, watching the matinee performance of a clever piece, she was probably the happiest person in the audience.

The first Sunday afternoon in town was a grand occasion. Looking regally handsome, Mrs. Stuyvesant held court while Theodora sat happily in her shadow, pouring tea for her guests and receiving gratefully the crumbs of conversation that fell to her. Everyone had come back to town early on account of war activities, and Mrs. Stuyvesant's return was always accorded a celebration.

Alan Beeckman was not among the visitors. Half-eagerly, half-nervously, Theodora watched for him; but he did not come. Neither did Miss Burrill. There did come, however, a certain Mrs. Beeckman from whom the girl could hardly take her eyes—so fascinating was she, so clever and animated, so sure of herself and her audience. They called her Blanche and, next to her hostess, she held the center of the stage.

"How's suffrage, Blanche?" asked someone.

"Suffrage is all right!" responded the vivacious Blanche, with a quick little nod of emphasis. "It's coming, and it's coming soon. Then all you fossils will be making appointments with me, in order to learn how to vote properly."

This unloosed an avalanche. Theodora listened to some red-hot arguments, for suffrage and against it. Mrs. Stuyvesant was as arrogantly against it as was Blanche for it. But it surprised her to find fashionable women on the side of equal suffrage.

"Aunt Honora, I'm going to convert you. I shall take you to our next meeting," said Blanche.

"Indeed you will not, my dear. I haven't come to that yet."

Mrs. Beeckman, looking around, caught Theodora's tense gaze. Then I'll take Miss Winthrop," she cried, "if she'll come. Will you, Miss Winthrop?"

Theodora glanced at her employer. "Thank you, Mrs. Beeckman," she answered a little doubtfully.

"Would you like to?"

"Yes, indeed. But unless it were Wednesday—"

"It's Tuesday afternoon. You can spare Miss Winthrop then, can't you, Aunt Honora?"

"I can spare her, certainly. But I warn you not to make a convert of her. That would be more than I could bear."

"Is she an anti?"

"Certainly she is."

"Are you, Miss Winthrop?" persisted Blanche.

"Yes, Mrs. Beeckman, I think so."

"Then there'll be all the more glory in converting you," cried Blanche cheerfully. "I'll do my best, Aunt Honora. Tuesday afternoon, then, Miss Winthrop, at a quarter of three, sharp. I'll stop for you here."

When Tuesday afternoon arrived, Theodora entered Mrs. Beeckman's limousine with a distinct assurance of her pleasure in being with her brilliant hostess, but with considerable doubt as to the balance of the program.

"Are you a screaming anti?" demanded Mrs. Beeckman.

"I fear I am," admitted the girl.

"And have you ever heard any really good arguments or debates on the subject?"

"Never."

"All your friends are antis, I suppose, and all your reading has been on that side?"

"Yes, that is true."

"I thought so. That is the general idea of 'reading up' on any subject—reading only what concurs with one's preconceived opinions. Now, I approached this thing with an absolutely unbiased mind, and I studied it thoroughly before coming to a decision. I'm convinced that it is right, fair, and necessary that women shall vote. All that I ask of you this afternoon is to listen to our arguments without prejudice."

When they arrived at the meeting place, Mrs. Beeckman was nearly devoured by her admirers in the waiting crowd. Even as early as this, the temperamental differences in the sexes were made apparent. What crowd of men, thought Theodora, would so fall over themselves to make an impression on a social lion?

Not all the women here were Beeckman followers, however. The bulk of them were, but there were others who stood aloof and looked disdainful. It was a motley crowd that had gathered. The top notch of fashion hobnobbed with skimpy skirted, short-haired, bespectacled, dowdy women.

Leaving her guest in the front-row seat, Mrs. Beeckman took her place on the platform and called the meeting to order. Theodora was immediately impressed with the knowledge of law—parliamentary, municipal, federal, national—that these women appeared to possess. To that, she gave full and admiring credit. But she heard not a single argument which she considered conclusive, nor one which she herself could not have refuted.

A certain speaker was introduced as Mrs. Felton. "Mrs. Felton," said Mrs. Beeckman graciously, "is with us today for the first time. This is her maiden speech for us, but her efforts for the cause have been untiring. She has formed in her own home village a Suffrage Club of which she is president, and the membership has increased from ten to thirty-four in less than a year."

"Eight months," amended Mrs. Felton modestly and made her bow.

She was a thin pale woman who looked as if she needed a tonic and good food. Her face was clever and her manner direct. She gave the impression of having been a whining, fretful, delicate, clever child. She spoke well, as far as enunciation and vocabulary were concerned; but to Theodora, at least, her superlative statements were simply astounding. Give women the vote, and there would never again be a war. Let women vote, and there would be no more drunkenness, no saloons, no unhappy homes. Gambling halls would disappear—did anyone think they were run for the benefit of women? Sexual vice would cease to exist, since women were now but its powerless and unwilling prey. Child labor would no longer be permitted. Fraud would die—it being an established fact that women have a higher sense of honor than men.

After the meeting, there was a great deal of informal talking, as well as introducing. Theodora could see that she, herself, acquired approval merely through being the guest of Mrs. Beeckman.

"We'll go and have some tea," said Mrs. Beeckman as she and Theodora got into the car. "It's all right. I told Aunt Honora." And thus it was that the girl had her first peep at a fashionable hotel during tea hour. Mrs. Beeckman had a cocktail before her tea, rum in it, and innumerable cigarettes after it. Theodora couldn't help thinking that suffrage would hit her rather hard, if Mrs. Felton's prophecies proved true.

They discussed the speeches and the Cause. Mrs. Beeckman, though delighted with Theodora's keen pleasure in discussion, was disappointed to find her so little converted. "Still," she admitted, "it often takes quite a while. I'm sure you will be one of us eventually. You have too good a mind to continue as an anti."

"There's Mrs. Stuyvesant—" began Theodora.

"Oh yes. But she belongs to a past generation," said that lady's niece easily.

A number of attractive-looking people—men and women—stopped at their table for a word or a chat. Theodora reflected with honesty that she was enjoying the tea much more than she had enjoyed the meeting which had preceded it. "I'm about on a mental level with Elise," she thought.

Upon her return home, she was told that her dinner would be served upstairs, as Mrs. Stuyvesant had unexpected guests. Getting into a dressing gown, Theodora settled herself for a long cozy reverie. A tap at the door, and a maid entered with a letter and a dinner tray. Theodora quickly seized the former. She wrote to her mother two and three times every week, and even amid the whirl of her new life, she eagerly awaited the replies to her letters. It was one of her great crosses that Mrs. Winthrop was still at Waverly, tyrannized over by Aunt Augusta, irritated by Elise, deserted by her own daughter. Oh, for money—for piles and piles of money!

But the letter she opened drove even the thought of money from Theodora's head. Elise was to be married quietly and immediately. Meta was wretched, and seemed on the verge of a nervous breakdown. The doctor had ordered a change, and the Misses Duncan had been kind enough to invite her to spend a fortnight with them in the city—though how the Waverly household would survive her absence remained to be seen.

Theodora crushed the letter into a tight little ball. Poor, poor Meta! Selfish, miserable, feline Elise! With the impatience of her years, Theodora always wanted justice to be both immediate and adequate, whereas, as a matter of fact, it is rarely the one and inevitably the other.

The dinner on the tray was particularly dainty, but it was quite ruined by the irritating news. Theodora was still turning this over in her mind, when there came another rap at the door. Would Miss Winthrop please hurry downstairs? Mrs. Stuyvesant wanted her in the library for Bridge.

The summons was as unwelcome as it was unexpected. Theodora had never touched a card since leaving Waverly. Even there, she didn't play often. Probably Mrs. Stuyvesant and her guests were "sharks." Beside which, here was Theodora caught in a dressing-gown with her hair braided down her back.

"Say that I will be down immediately," she cried, and began to dash around, making a hurried toilet. It goes without saying that her hair was stubborn, that her buttons wouldn't button, and her hooks wouldn't hook, and that she finally entered the library feeling disgruntled. Then, all at once, her heart flew to her mouth and she wished she'd been given time to dress properly, for the man who rose to his feet at the entrance was none other than Alan Beeckman. On no other night in the past weeks could Theodora have been caught so unready. Her annoyance took the form of stiffness, especially when she became aware of how Mrs. Stuyvesant was watching her.

She remembered uneasily how this man before her had "amused" himself at Fair Acres at her expense, and how sarcastic his aunt had waxed on the subject. She reflected how untidy she must be looking, and how inadequate her game of bridge must soon prove—in fact, how entirely at a disadvantage they all had her! She knew intuitively that the slender creature in the deep chair must be "Helen," and she reminded herself that she had always disliked paragons. So she got even by making her manner as unattractive as she imagined everything else to be.

Little could she guess how skill-fully Beeckman had engineered this meeting, how he had played upon his aunt's weakness for Bridge—leading the conversa-tion to the game, and lamenting that there was not a possible fourth for tonight. Helen, who was always an angel, was to meet this new companion and to be especially nice to her. If the man expected any per-sonal pleasure out of the arrangement, he was doomed to disappointment. Theodora was cold and detached, and never once met his eyes directly. Helen, on the other hand, was sweet and winning to the last degree.

Her skin was tinted like a sea-shell, and her manner was charming and gracious. Yet there lay about her a suggestion of sadness.

Helen was tall and fair and delicate-looking, with soft ash-blond hair and big dark eyes. Her skin was tinted like a sea-shell, and her manner was charming and gracious. Yet there lay about her a suggestion of sadness, a soft appeal that had the effect of far-away music. She was like moonlight—sweet and lovely, but vaguely sad. She called Mrs. Stuyvesant "Tante," and her relationship with Alan was conspicuously intimate. He turned to her and waited on her and appealed to her, and she received it all in a way that plainly showed how used to it she was. Once, Theodora distinctly heard her call him "dear," and the sound of the word was a lash to her own pride.

Mrs. Stuyvesant was right; men were selfish creatures and the girl who held herself lightly was a fool.

Helen was not as young as Theodora had expected. She looked twenty-six or twenty-eight—as old as Alan himself. But that might be because of her seriousness.

As to the game, it went much better than Theodora had dared hope. Although she had played far less than any of the others, she had played under the sternest of teachers. Aunt Augusta was a severe task-mistress, and for that fact her niece was now unexpectedly thankful.

At the end of the game, Beeckman tried hard to get a word with Theodora; he was really anxious to know how she had come out in that affair of the dog-fight. Helen, noting his efforts, encouraged them. But he was foiled by his aunt, and by Theodora herself. She said good night, and went upstairs.

She saw him again the following Sunday afternoon, but under circumstances still more adverse. The room was full when he came. Mr. and Mrs. Gary (the parents of Ned's lovely Marjorie), had been the first arrivals. They were consumed with concern over their darling's health: Theodora was forced to sit with lowered eyes and listen to much uncomplimentary talk about "that unfortunate affair."

"Keep firm," was Mrs. Stuyvesant's grim advice to her niece and nephew. "It won't last. Bring her down to Palm Beach this winter, and I'll warrant the cure."

The worried parents sighed; they didn't feel so sure. In fact, so well had they been managed by their astute child, they were on the point of yielding in despair. However, they would never have admitted this to their hostess. The arrival of other guests put an end to the family council.

Finally the butler announced "Mr. Beeckman" and Theodora looked hastily down at her cups.

She might have saved herself the trouble. The man who soon sought her side to beg for some tea was not Alan Beeckman. The newcomer proved to be Mr. Van Rensselaer Beeckman,

The Courteous Card Player

1. He does not criticize his partner for real or supposed error, but gives him credit for his good plays.
2. He does not blame his "bad luck" when losing.
3. He does not audibly congratulate himself on his "good luck" when winning.
4. He does not play erratically, so that his partner is at a loss to know what he really holds, and then reprove the latter for not winning.
5. Affectations of manner; exultant exclamations, cardtable drumming, noises, using cards as facial massage accessories, etc., are all tabooed by the well-bred player.
6. Never should a player afflicted with a poor partner make him plainly aware that he is so regarded.

—The Book of Good Manners, 1923

and he, too, addressed Mrs. Stuyvesant as "Aunt Honora." This afternoon, however, he didn't spend much time addressing her—preferring to devote his efforts to Theodora, with whom he conversed in tones which were carefully lowered. Lowered tones were his habit with women.

"I wonder if it was your wife who took me to my first suffrage meeting," said Theodora after some time. "I met her here last Sunday."

"Then you're luckier than I am," smiled the man. "I haven't met her for three years—in fact, not since she divorced me."

At Theodora's heightened color and look of distress, he laughed appreciatively. "Don't worry, Miss Winthrop," he begged. "No one else does, I assure you. Mrs. Beeckman and I often find ourselves in the same drawing room, but we always manage not to 'meet.' It's rather good fun. This, however, is one house where our skill is never called into play. My aunt is far too clever to permit such mishaps.

The man took frank pleasure in Theodora's bewilderment. "You should always look astonished," he observed, lowering his voice an extra shade.

"Why?"

"Because your eyes are so lovely."

"Van?" said his aunt rather sharply, at this particular juncture.

"Yes, Aunt Honora?"

"Come here and talk to me. I haven't seen you for an age."

He went immediately, but he returned to Theodora's side the moment that another arrival set him free. His aunt, however, had him on her mind. She kept casting side-glances in his direction. These worried him not at all, but they made Theodora very uncomfortable.

"Don't you think you'd better go and talk to someone else?" she suggested. That, of course, riveted him to her side for the balance of the afternoon.

"By no means," he answered, settling himself deeper in his chair. And at that precise moment, his cousin Alan entered. Naturally, Alan's conversation with Theodora was limited to commonplaces.

Mrs. Stuyvesant vented her displeasure on Theodora when the guests were gone; very unfairly, the girl thought. But the quasi-scolding leaped to the forefront of her mind some three days later, when she met Mr. Van Rensselaer Beeckman on the street. It was in the morning and she was exercising the poodles near the park when the man overtook her.

"Did you catch it?" he demanded, holding out his hand.

Theodora feigned denseness.

"Well, I did, anyhow," Beeckman informed her. "I have received strict orders to let you alone. That being so, I want to make a date with you for your first free afternoon. We can have some tea. Will you?"

Theodora's pride was instantly in arms.

"Thank you very much," she said stiffly; "but certainly not."

"No one will ever know it," he said, misunderstanding her motive.

"It isn't that. That isn't the sort of thing I do."

"I see." But this professional woman-eater had no intention of letting a little country Miss think she had piqued him. He turned and joined her, talking easily the while. In fact, he gave her quite the uncomfortable feeling of having treated a molehill like a mountain.

Presently, he raised his hat to someone across the street. Theodora, following the direction of his eyes with her own, recognized Alan Beeckman.

"You know my cousin, don't you?" asked her companion.

"Yes."

"Have you met Miss Burrill?"

"Yes." Then almost in spite of herself, Theodora asked. "Are they engaged?"

Something in her voice made her companion glance at her sharply. Then he smiled—glad of so easy a chance to pay off his recent snub. He had but to tell the truth. "Yes," he answered smilingly. "They are engaged, and everyone says it will be a match made by the gods!"

PART THIRD

Startling
Revelations

CHAPTER
☙IX☙

y the time she had been in New York eight weeks, Theodora discovered one of the odd traits of modern American society—its restlessness. Having spent the summer at Newport, the autumn at Fair Acres, and the early part of the winter in town, Mrs. Stuyvesant began to talk of Palm Beach. She would take Louise, Theodora, and the poodles.

Wonderful hours came to be passed in the studios of New York's great modistes. Theodora had never hitherto suspected the importance of clothes, nor the cult which their worship had given rise to. Surrounded by a multitude of hushed, absorbed women, she sat in a darkened room by her employer's side, and watched a procession of models parade and pose, contort and simper. What must their homes be like? What must the inside of their minds be like? What must be the effect of their mode of life? Scampering around in front of men, clad in the closest of tights under the thinnest of negligees, posed almost nude on blocks while masculine hands draped thin chiffons over their bare shoulders—to what sort of careers must such an atmosphere tend?

Very much to Theodora's distress, Mrs. Stuyvesant insisted on ordering two simple dresses for her evening use. The girl's objections were all overruled.

"Consider them uniform, Miss Winthrop, if that will ease your pride," said the old lady. "Remember that you will be in my party, and that I am the best judge as to how it should appear." But she stole a side glance when the girl was not looking, and saw an odd little satisfied smile on her lips. The young creature of the so-called weaker sex who can resist pretty clothes, can resist most things.

The luxury of modern travel was a revelation to the girl. Mrs. Stuyvesant had a drawing room, Theodora had a compartment, and Louise had a section. Meals were carried into the drawing room. From certain hampers, Louise produced wine, bonbons, fruit, and thermos-bottles of special tea and coffee. New magazines and books were skimmed and given away to porters. And all on a journey of thirty-six hours!

They arrived at night and went straight to their rooms, through a hushed and deserted hotel. Even so, soft southern breezes crept through Theodora's curtains and fanned her cheeks; the rustling of palms was in the air; perfumes were strange and lovely; in spite of the darkness, the girl's searching eyes discerned the oddness of the exotic picture outside her window. She was so excited she could hardly wait for the morning. It would be her own, as Mrs. Stuyvesant was to rest till noon.

Theodora was awake early. By nine o'clock, she had had her breakfast and was out to meet the day. How sparkling it was, how beautiful! Languorous air and musical sounds, golden sunlight and purple shadows, azure sky and green-blue sea, scarlet hibiscus making gorgeous splashes against dark green palms, tawny sands—and everywhere the kaleidoscope of animated human life!

At noon she sat on the verandah, at a little table by Mrs. Stuyvesant's side, sipping orangeade, listening to wonderful

Before they were in sight of the hotel, the tinkling sound of dance
music came floating out to meet them; and then, a turn in the
driveway brought them face to face with a marvelous sight.

dance music from a double band, and watching the dancers. So happy was she that she forgot even to envy them.

After luncheon, she found herself booked for a long chair-ride with the pampered poodles. A double wheeled-chair, a negro driver, and an intelligent and excited girl were all pressed into the service of two sleepy (and soon snoring), beasts. Theodora had one of the most beautiful and memorable experiences of her life. Rolling smoothly along the shore of the lake, watching the ascents, flights, and descents of hydroplanes, peeping eagerly at the beautiful homes on her other side, listening to the soft "plomp" of an occasional coconut into the water, smelling the delicious breath of orange blossoms. Theodora pinched herself to see if she were dreaming.

A double wheeled-chair, a negro driver, and an intelligent and excited girl were all pressed into the service of two sleepy (and soon snoring) beasts.

It was nearly twilight when they made the homeward trip. Before they were in sight of the hotel, the tinkling sound of dance music came floating to meet them; and then, a turn in the driveway brought them face to face with a marvelous sight.

"Oh," cried Theodora to her driver, "what is that?"

"Coconut Grove, ma'am," answered the man, showing all his teeth in a sympathetic smile. "Like to stop?"

"Oh, no," Theodora assured him, "I'll go on to the hotel." So that was the famous Coconut Grove, that paradise of palms with a dancing-floor laid round their base. Festoons of pink lights were looped from tree to tree and a red sun was just slipping away behind the waters of Lake Worth. Mrs. Stuyvesant was taking tea with friends, inside that sacred railing. Probably

Theodora herself would never get a nearer view than now, but she was content. The longing that filled her heart was not for greater pleasures and blessings for herself. If only her mother could have been by her side, she would not have had a wish in the world ungranted.

The new life soon became an accustomed joy. Day followed day, languorous and dreamy, scintillating and sparkling. Mrs. Stuyvesant's circle was constantly added to. The Garys appeared—father, mother, and lovely daughter, the latter in the role of invalid.

"You don't look very ill to me," said Mrs. Stuyvesant, scanning her sharply.

"Ah, but I am, Aunt Honora. I don't sleep well, and I have the tiniest little appetite. Ah, Miss Winthrop, how do you do?"

"You know Miss Winthrop?" demanded her aunt sharply.

The child threw Theodora an imploring look. "Yes," she answered, with perfect aplomb, "I met her at Fair Acres one morning, when I went to greet Blanchette and Poilu."

"Miss Winthrop seems to have made acquaintance with all my Fair Acres guests," remarked Mrs. Stuyvesant caustically.

"If they all thrust themselves upon her as I did," replied the pretty child with a spirit that would have amounted to pertness had it been less soft, "she is much to be pitied."

Here a boy came up and begged Miss Marjorie for a dance, whereupon she moved off with a lethargy and slowness that left her poor parents pouring their fears into the unsympathetic ears of Mrs. Stuyvesant. "Dr. Homans fears tubercular trouble," sighed the mother.

"Dr. Homans is a fool," snapped the aunt.

"Oh, Aunt Honora, how can you say so?"

Just then, Theodora felt a hand laid on her shoulder. "My *dear*," said someone, "what are you doing here?" And the girl turned to meet the eyes of Mrs. Neilson—that friend of the Misses Duncan who had so sympathized with her desire to go to work.

They greeted each other with delight, and then Theodora paused. She was at a loss as to her course. Mrs. Stuyvesant herself solved the difficulty.

"Introduce your friend to me, child," she said, and her voice was very kind. Nothing ever escaped her. She had seen Theodora's difficulty and appreciated her delicacy. As it happened, she and Mrs. Neilson had many friends in common, and the older woman was particularly gracious. After inquiring about Theodora's plans and ascertaining the fact that she took the dogs out each afternoon, Mrs. Neilson turned to Mrs. Stuyvesant.

"May I join Miss Winthrop on her ride this afternoon?" she asked.

"Certainly," smiled the old lady. "My chair will be at your service." Then to Theodora, "Louise may take the dogs to the beach today, and you and Mrs. Neilson may chat undisturbed." Cutting short the girl's thanks, she turned again to Mrs. Neilson. "I hope you will have tea with me some day soon," she said.

"That is a very charming woman," she observed later to Theodora, when they were alone. "I shall hope to see her often."

Helen Burrill soon appeared upon the scene, though she insisted that she could not stay more than ten days. As she was under the chaperonage of Mrs. Stuyvesant, it followed that Theodora saw a great deal of her. No one was surprised when Alan Beeckman arrived a couple of days later.

Both he and Miss Burrill were delightfully friendly with Theodora, and she soon forgot her slight grudge of the New York days. After all, what was there to preclude her pleasant relationship with a girl and a man who were engaged to each other?

What possible difference could their engagement make to her? The more good friends one had, the luckier one was; and down here in this happy easy-flowing life, quarrels seemed silly.

She saw a great deal of Miss Burrill and Mr. Beeckman together, and she saw still more of Mr. Beeckman alone. The explanation of that was simple. Men and working women are on the scene many times when luxurious women are not; in the early morning, for instance, when the beach is as beautiful as it is deserted; before dinner, when men are dressed and women still dressing.

It was about this time that the girl began to experience an odd feeling. It was a vague sense of happiness, of complete satisfaction with life—as if just around the next corner one might suddenly catch up with unexpected bliss. When she came to examine this sensation, she found that there was really nothing to warrant it. It was all a lotus-dream—the effect of the tropical climate. That lovely thing that seemed to have bloomed in her heart, was nothing but an exotic plant of the senses.

One morning as Theodora sat on the verandah reading to Mrs. Stuyvesant, she glanced up at the turning of a page and saw Bishop Wysong coming toward her. He was her own bishop, the man who had known her since her childhood, who had confirmed her, and who had recommended her for her present position. He had never met Mrs. Stuyvesant, but he evidently intended to, for he was approaching them with all the haste that was compatible with dignity. In his bishop's garb and with his beautiful face, he was easily the most conspicuous figure in that gay throng.

Mrs. Stuyvesant received him with marked pleasure; after some little conversation, she sent Theodora upstairs on an errand. This was exactly the opportunity that the bishop wanted; he was anxious to find out how the girl's experiment was working.

"That child has always been a great pet of mine," he observed. "She is very fine."

Now, Mrs. Stuyvesant had always hated to have her opinions dictated. It irritated her and made her stubborn. From a Bishop she might possibly have tolerated it, but this morning happened to be bad timing. Not two hours earlier, Alan Beeckman had sought his aunt's permission to take Theodora to the Cocoanut Grove some afternoon; he and Helen had decided that it was a shame she shouldn't see it, and they wanted to give her a little party.

Mrs. Stuyvesant—who would have hated to have anyone guess how attached to Theodora she was secretly growing—had vetoed the request vehemently, insisting that such a festivity would be "out of keeping." Alan had argued, but his aunt had not yielded. In consequence, she had ever since been oppressed with a feeling of remorse which was in no wise mitigated by Bishop Wysong's praise of Theodora. She stiffened visibly.

"She's a headstrong piece," she observed dryly.

"My dear Mrs. Stuyvesant, you surprise me! Is she really? *Strong*, I know her to be—but I should never have said *headstrong*! Is she not obedient to your wishes?"

"If she were not, I should certainly have dismissed her."

"I see. Then she has perhaps an ungracious manner of obeying?"

Mrs. Stuyvesant was fair and she was truthful. "I think possibly," she said coolly, "we have a different conception of the word headstrong."

The bishop beamed. "Ah," he cried, "that is undoubtedly it. You use the word in the sense of *spirited*? That, she most certainly is.

It required great spirit, dear Mrs. Stuyvesant, for that child to start out in the world. She comes of a long line of proud and conservative ancestors. Her own family happens to be at the end of the line where the money has all disappeared, but the pride and conservatism have not gone with it. In the face of her entire circle, this plucky child carried her point. As you say, it took spirit to do it."

Mrs. Stuyvesant, aware that she had said nothing of the sort, let the matter pass.

"I am simply delighted," continued the Bishop, "to see in what pleasant places her lines have fallen. Theodora has evidently reaped the reward of her courage."

"If you are not engaged for this afternoon," said Mrs. Stuyvesant, suddenly, "come and have a cup of tea with me in the Grove. It is quite an informal party."

Theodora, passing at the moment, heard the invitation and noted the Bishop's rapt attitude. At three o'clock on that same afternoon, she was getting into her chair with the dogs when she heard herself called. "My dear," said Bishop Wysong, "can you make room for me in there?"

"Indeed I can," cried the girl. "You won't mind the dogs?"

"Not the least in the world. Will you have me back at the Grove at a quarter before five?"

Theodora promised, and they started off. "Have you seen Mrs. Neilson?" was the girl's first question.

The bishop had.

"She rides with me three and four times a week," said Theodora happily. "She's simply a dear, isn't she? How recently have you been in Waverly, Bishop Wysong?"

He gave her all the Waverly news, then he said: "Your experiment is turning out beautifully, my dear, isn't it?"

"Oh yes, Bishop Wysong. More than beautifully."

125

"You have a very kind friend in Mrs. Stuyvesant."

The girl's reply was noticeably slower. "Kind, certainly," she finally answered. "I'm not so sure about the friend. Sometimes I think she likes me, and sometimes I'm sure she doesn't."

"I can set your mind at rest on that point. She assuredly does."

"Well, I'm glad if she does. She's—well, you know, she's a decidedly strong character, to put it mildly."

The Bishop threw back his head and laughed aloud. "She made nearly the same charge against you," he cried. "And it is quite true in both instances. I suppose, between two such strong characters there are occasional rubs?"

"I shouldn't call them *rubs*, exactly—"

"I know. But we'll let that go, for want of a better term. What I wanted to say to you, my dear child, was this: Sympathy is the greatest softener in the world; not necessarily *expressed* sympathy, but sympathy of feeling—the effort to put oneself in exact mental accord with the other person. Even when it doesn't seem to work, the chances are that it does. Understand me, I fully appreciate pride. Did you lack it, I should urge it upon you as a priceless possession. But there is no necessity for that; no one will ever accuse you of lack of pride. Therefore, being so happily assured on that head, let me recommend softness to your favor."

"But Bishop Wysong, I'm as soft as mush! I am, truly! You needn't laugh. I don't want to boast, but I must tell you that I never dream of answering back—"

"I should hope not, my dear."

"Well, it isn't always so easy. . . . And I never balk at orders, and I keep my temper—really, I do everything I'm told, without a word or a look."

"Dear child, I never doubted it. I wasn't even thinking of your actions; I was thinking of your heart. Never let it feel hard and cold and resentful. Never harbor small grudges. Don't be too insistent of your pride. Guard against all inward bitterness, my dear, and keep the heart of a little child—the sweet, honest, trusting child that I have known and loved for so many years."

Turning toward the girl, he was surprised to find her eyes full of tears. Impulsively she put out her hand and grasped his. "I'll try," she whispered shyly. And so for quite a space they rode in silence, hand in hand. And when they parted, Theodora went home feeling strangely light-hearted and tender. Bishop Wysong had used his own remedy of sympathy, and it had worked.

The next day the divorced Mrs. Beeckman appeared on the scene. Theodora found that she was known as "Mrs. Delafield Beeckman." She couldn't help wondering how Bishop Wysong would look upon her if he knew her history and standards—for his own opinion on the subject of divorce was uncompromising. But in the midst of these thoughts, Theodora remembered the bishop's small sermon of the previous day—and hastened to put the matter out of her mind.

The season was growing positively hectic as it approached its end. Theodora saw it wane with sorrow. She didn't want this wonderful winter to be over.

One morning she sat facing the doorway through which a crowd was pouring out onto the verandah for the morning dance. In spite of wars in Europe, life at Palm Beach seemed to be all dancing; one danced in the morning on the wide verandahs, in the afternoon under the palms and the sky, and in the evening amid the more conventional setting of ballroom or Palm Room.

Among the moving throng, Theodora noticed Marjorie Gary—but what a transformed Marjorie! No longer listless, she was sparkling with animation; no longer pale, she was flushed into a divine rose. She walked as though on air, and her head was turned over her shoulder as she spoke to the boy who followed in her wake. Theodora, following idly the direction of her eyes, nearly gasped in amazement. She couldn't believe the evidence of her senses. There, not ten feet from her, stood her own cousin, Ned Charrington.

He didn't see her for a moment, then he came bounding in her direction. "Brownie," he cried, "what in the world are you doing here?"

"Didn't they tell you I had come? But that is not the question at all. What in the world are *you* doing here?"

"Greatest piece of luck in the world! One of the fellows had a governor who was just starting down here in his private car, and he brought three of us along. A perfect cinch! We have only four days, but you can bet your bottom dollar we'll know how to make the most of them. The exams were late this term on account of an epidemic that broke out at the usual time. Your old lady brought you down, I take it?"

"Yes. And Ned, what do you suppose? My Mrs. Stuyvesant is Marjorie Gary's godmother and great-aunt."

It was the boy's turn to be astounded. "What!" he cried. "Then she must hate my very name. And do you know my girl, then?"

"I certainly do."

"Isn't she some love?"

"Yes, Ned, she is. But what are you ever going to do about it?"

"The Lord only knows. The one thing I'm sure about is that I'm perfectly crazy over her. I can't think of another thing. Sometimes I feel as happy as a king, and as if I owned the world" (Theodora nodded with a strange sensation of comprehension), "and then again, I want to kill myself in despair. . . Here she comes now. That donkey with her won't get another dance, if I know myself. See you again, Brownie, old girl!"

And he was off, in answer to his sweetheart's seeking eyes.

After the dance, Marjorie herself came running to Theodora's side. "Ned's just told me," she whispered. "To think of our being cousins some day! I've always had such a warm feeling toward you—a sort of special drawing, if you know what I mean. From the very first moment. Of course it was this! Isn't it too wonderful?" And with a quick little hand-squeeze, she too was gone.

Van liked her beauty, and tried to flirt with her. Alan and Helen became her warm friends and planned to relieve the monotony of her position.

Theodora smiled tenderly. Of course, the child thought she was telling the truth, but it was plain to see that any relative of her Ned's would have seemed an angel to her enamored eyes.

Mrs. Stuyvesant was extremely irritated. As no one could read the real reason for her fit of temper, she got less credit than she deserved. As a matter of fact, this girl whom she had discovered for a companion suited her wonderfully in that capacity. She had even brains; she had even breeding; her friends were delightful; left to herself, Mrs. Stuyvesant would soon have become warmly devoted to Theodora, and eventually would even have insisted on forcing her down the throats of her world.

But instead of this pleasing and proper process, her world seemed to be in league to force the girl down the employer's throat. From the very first moment, the Stuyvesant circle had been Theodora's champions. The guests at afternoon tea spoke of her charm. Blanche Beeckman admired her intelligence. Van liked her beauty, and tried to flirt with her. Alan and Helen became her warm friends and planned to relieve the monotony of her position. (*That*, if you please, was a trifle too much). Mrs. Neilson and Bishop Wysong never lost a chance to praise her. And now, that headstrong chit, Marjorie Gary, had fallen madly in love with the girl's ineligible cousin. It was too tiresome! So fumed Mrs. Stuyvesant.

Alan Beeckman made early occasion to chant Ned's praises in Theodora's ear. "He's a fine chap," he said warmly. "I don't wonder Marjorie fell in love with him. Don't worry over the affair, Miss Winthrop; it's sure to come out all right. I'm sorry, you know, that this must be our last talk here" (he and Helen and Blanche were leaving that night), "but you'll soon be coming north yourself, and then I shall hope to see a lot of you."

Theodora felt unaccountably depressed as she bade him goodbye; she had always had a strong gift for friendship and great loyalty toward her friends. Bishop Wysong had gone too, and Mrs. Neilson. The beautiful season was fast drifting into the past.

Ned came hurrying to her. "Brownie," he cried, "do you think you could get the afternoon off and come down onto the beach with me? It will be our one chance for a good talk. Marjorie's sent me off. She has to have her hair shampooed and dressed for the dance tonight. See if you can't get off."

When Theodora returned with the permission, she found her cousin fuming. "It's a confounded shame," he cried, "that you should have to go and get leave for an afternoon off just like some servant. You, the equal of anyone here! I don't suppose you've had one ocean dip, have you? Not since I came, I know—

or at any rate, not when the crowd went in. And not one dance, nor one afternoon in the Grove! It makes me hot."

"But Ned, that's only because I'm a worker. Everyone has been lovely to me and I've had a wonderful time. Fancy being at Palm Beach at all! A year ago that would have seemed like a mad dream."

"That may be, but all the same it's unfair that money should make the difference. Come on down to the beach, and let's sit on the sands and talk about it. There won't be a soul there at this hour, yet it's as beautiful as a dream of love. The afternoon lights on the sands and the water make me wish I were one of those painter chaps."

Once esconced on the sun-kissed sands, Ned broke out again with his grievance. The money question was breaking his heart.

"Isn't it the very devil," he demanded hotly, "that a thing like money should make all the difference in life? If I had a dozen millions, you'd see Marjorie's parents running to meet me with outstretched hands—not that I'm much, at that. But I'd be plenty good enough if I could flash such a roll. I'd bring mother and poor old Meta down here, and I'd dress them like the Queen of Sheba. You could bring Aunt Mollie. I'd never bring Elise, no matter how much I had. The little cat!"

"Ned," said Theodora suddenly, "how are you going to get back?"

"The old boy who brought us down is going to send the car north again with us. We leave tomorrow night at one o'clock."

"Do you know," said the boy moodily, "if I were left alone in a room where a million dollars were lying loose, and if I knew that my taking them would harm no one and cast suspicion on no one and that I'd never be caught, I'd do it as quick as a wink."

"Ned! You wouldn't."

"I certainly would. Mind you, I said if no one would be hurt or suspected, and if no one would be made poor by it. Say it was some embezzled money, or something of that sort."

"But it would be stealing, just the same."

"Then I'd steal."

Theodora was frightened. The remembrance of that night in Waverly, when she had helped this boy to bed, came flying back into her mind with all its old horror. Perhaps Ned was weak through and through—charming, but weak. The remembrance of how she herself had been coveting money for these last months or years, gave her a curious feeling of guilt.

"You're joking, of course," she said.

"I'm not," persisted Ned doggedly. "I wouldn't do it to anyone's hurt—"

"But your own!"

"But my own. And I wouldn't do it for any paltry sum. Simply, a million dollars is my price. If the world insists on making money the sole aim of existence, the price of all happiness, then I claim a right to take it if I can get it as readily as that."

"And you think money so gotten would bring happiness?"

"I'd risk it," nodded the boy. And then, to his cousin's relief, he began to laugh.

"Poor old Brownie," he said. "I got you all worked up, didn't I? Don't worry. I imagine I'm as honest as the next chap, only I'm honest in making startling statements, too."

Theodora wanted to change the subject. "Ned," she said, "do you know, it was I who sent you that telegram last October—about that trip to Stamford, you know?"

"*What!*"

Then the story came out. "And you're the only living soul to whom I've ever told it," said Theodora.

"You're a brick, Brownie. An absolutely joyful brick!"

"But Ned, you must never plan such a thing again. It would make you look like a sneak and a coward."

The boy hesitated. "People do elope," he said. "Nevertheless, I agree with you that it's a pretty poor way."

She noticed with pleasure that he laid no blame at the door of his lady-love. "It will come out all right in time," she comforted.

"I'm not so sure. If it doesn't, I might just as well commit suicide. I don't want to live without her; I can tell you that much."

"Ned dear, there's just one other thing—"

The boy looked up quickly. "That night in Waverly?" he forestalled her.

Pulling his hatbrim well down over his eyes, he lay looking at the silver sand which he was sifting through his hand. "I've been wanting to tell you about that," he said. "I've cut it out."

"You mean you've given it up entirely?"

He nodded. "Never touch it," he answered briefly.

"*Ned!*"

"Well—Marjorie and Mother, you know. I got to taking the stuff in the first place because I was so unhappy. Then I found it was mighty hard to stop. You see, some chaps can drink and others can't. I happen to be one of those who can't, and that's all there is to it."

"Oh, Ned, I can't tell you how happy I am!" Theodora's voice was very low. "Was it hard?"

"You bet your life it was hard. I hope I'll never have to go through anything like it again."

As they rose to leave, Theodora said:

"You *were* just joking about that money, Ned?"

But again the boy laughed. "My million?" he cried. "Indeed *not*! I'd take it as quick as a wink!" And she couldn't make him say anything else.

Theodora was perturbed about that million of Ned's. Even as a joke it was disconcerting. She had been growing disgustingly impressed of late with the importance of money. Suppose Ned, in his unhappiness, had overreached her!

He and his friends left that night, and the following morning Theodora's chambermaid—a conspicuously friendly individual—was full of important mystery. "Last night a gentleman was robbed of six thousand dollars he'd just made down at the Club," she said. "They think it was stole off of him by some of the folks that went north—they was an awful pile of them. Ain't that terrible? A high-toned place like this!"

With sickenly churning heart, Theodora asked the details. It appeared that the gentleman in question had made a sensational winning and had cashed in. He had put the notes in a wallet, and the wallet in the breast-pocket of his dinner jacket. But he must inadvertently have transferred it to the pocket of his topcoat. Arriving at the hotel, he was told by the night clerk that he was wanted on the long-distance wire. He threw his topcoat on a chair, believing that his money was still safe in his other pocket. His message had taken an unusually long time; when he returned his coat was gone, and with it his money. So, too, were the passengers north.

Theodora felt sick. She knew that Ned couldn't have taken the money, but she kept thinking "suppose he had!" The thing was grotesquely impossible, but what if it were true? She conjured up for herself a sort of vision—a long dark car, a pile of luggage, a light topcoat. Then, behind the closed door of a state-room, a guilty boy going through the pockets of his loot. So persistently did her mind return to this picture, it came to seem like a sort of revelation. It wasn't true—she knew it couldn't be true—but why had Ned said that awful thing, down on the beach?

Two days later the chambermaid returned to Theodora with the solution of the mystery. In the hotel there was a gentleman who had a private car. This, he had sent north with his son and two friends. After half of the trip had been made, a light top-coat which didn't belong to any of the young gentlemen had been discovered among their luggage. It had evidently been flung down beside their waiting pile, and the night-porter who had taken them to their car had gathered it up by mistake. They had telegraphed back about it, and they would express the coat as soon as they reached New York.

So the coat had been in the car, but Ned had been blameless and Theodora had made a simpleton of herself. She realized how ridiculous her fears had been; nothing but that absurd speech of Ned's would ever have put such an idea in her head.

However, foolish as it all was, it had taught her a lesson. It had called a halt on that idea of hers about the all-importance of money. It was because people put money on such a pedestal that thieves and forgers existed, that fraud flourished. One girl couldn't do much, of course. She could, however, look to herself.

And yet the question remained: How could one live without money? And how could one live well, do good, and give, without plenty of it? Its lack made life sordid and small; it checked all generous impulses at birth; it kept one from meeting the pleasantest people, from traveling, from gaining experience.

"Ah, well," thought Theodora, "some money is certainly a necessity. I suppose the trouble comes when we think more of it than of anything else."

CHAPTER

⚜ X ⚜

t was April when Mrs. Stuyvesant and Theodora returned to New York. Alan Beeckman came to see them at once—without Helen. Then he invited himself to dinner—again without Helen. Next, he asked them to go with him to see some war pictures and insisted on giving them tea afterwards. And then, some days later, Mrs. Stuyvesant sent for her companion earlier in the morning than was her custom.

As soon as Theodora entered the room, she knew that something was brewing. Her employer was nervous; she looked anywhere rather than at the girl she had summoned.

"Sit down, Miss Winthrop. I have something to say to you—something that I greatly regret to say. I have been having several serious talks with Dr. Homans lately, and he absolutely insists on my taking a trained nurse to Fair Acres, and later to Newport."

She paused and Theodora waited. This didn't seem very vital. It didn't concern her. "Yes, Mrs. Stuyvesant," she said, as the silence became awkward.

"The fact is, Miss Winthrop, much as I regret it, I find that for the future I must combine the two positions in one. My companion will have to be a trained nurse."

For just a moment the girl failed to grasp her meaning. Then it surged over her like a wave of blackness that she was being dismissed. She felt like a drowning person. There came a ringing sensation in her ears and her hands turned deadly cold. It was on the point of her tongue to ask how she had failed—for she knew instantly that she was being given a false reason. Why would Mrs. Stuyvesant have to economize by combining a nurse and a companion? She wouldn't, of course. But much as the girl wanted to ask the question, her pride prevented.

Though her voice sounded far away to her own ears, she answered quietly. "I see," she said. "That will be quite all right of course, Mrs. Stuyvesant. I shall look for another position at once. I have been very happy here, and I can't thank you enough for all your kindness."

The older woman still avoided her eyes. "I fear I am never kind, Miss Winthrop," she said, "except to myself. You have filled your position acceptably, and you have made me very comfortable. I am sorry to be obliged to sever our relationship."

Theodora was frankly puzzled. "Thank you very much," she murmured.

"I shall give you the highest references, of course," continued her employer. "That is, if you are thinking of taking another situation."

"Oh yes, I must."

"Must you?"

"I think so, Mrs. Stuyvesant."

"But you will go home first?"

"Oh, no!" cried Theodora sharply. "I don't want to do that."

"You don't want to go home?"

"Not yet."

"Why not? It would seem to me the natural thing for you to do."

"Mrs. Stuyvesant," said the girl suddenly, "if it isn't asking too much, try to put yourself in my place. In the face of my whole world, I insisted on going to work—the first woman of my blood to do it. Do you suppose I want to crawl back now, and tell them that I've been dismissed? I certainly do *not*."

There was an odd compression to Mrs. Stuyvesant's lips; her hands were restless. As for Theodora, she was fast gaining her composure. She was still in the dentist's chair, still in pain, but the tooth was out.

"What do you plan to do, Miss Winthrop?"

"I haven't had much time yet to plan. But I'd like to get another position, and then write home that I'd lost one and found another."

"You must let me help you."

"No, thank you, Mrs. Stuyvesant."

"What?"

"I said no thank you." (This, of course, was the height of foolishness, but it was also unalterably Theodora. Poor dear Theodora!)

"Don't be absurd, Miss Winthrop. This is nothing but temper."

Theodora smiled and shook her head. "As it happens, Mrs. Stuyvesant," she said, "I don't feel in the least tempery this time. But I have my limitations."

"Then if you are determined not to go home, you must stay here till you are placed."

"Had you planned otherwise?" asked the girl quickly.

"Merely when I thought you would go home. You have no friends in New York—"

"No. But there must be boarding-places."

"This is nonsense," exploded the older woman. "Nothing but nonsense! You might get into some terrible place. When I received you under my roof, I became responsible to your mother for your safety. I neither can, nor will, permit you to cancel that responsibility. You are very young and very hot-headed, but I trust you are not too foolish to accept advice from a woman who certainly knows the world. I insist upon your remaining here till you find a position that suits you. Consider the time entirely your own. Sleep and eat here, and use your leisure to place yourself. I will give you the addresses of some agencies. There's today's *Times*—it has always a long list of situations. Look them over; you may find something that strikes your fancy. While you are in the house, run in here each afternoon and tell me what luck you have had. One thing more, Miss Winthrop; I shall positively insist on paying you two months in advance."

"Indeed no," cried the girl instantly. "Nothing could make me take it. I *earn* money, Mrs. Stuyvesant, but I don't accept it as a gift."

"Will you be quiet and listen to me?" cried her employer tartly. "You will do as I say. It is nothing but the two months notice which I owe you. Girls are not turned onto the street without proper notice—at least, not from *my* house. There is my check. Oblige me by taking it without any further discussion."

The girl did not touch it. "I have plenty of ready money," she said quietly. "Since you are kind enough to ask me, I will stay here while I am looking around. It is a very great kindness on your part, and it is positively the only sort that I can accept. May I go now, Mrs. Stuyvesant?"

As she left the room carrying the newspaper with her, the old woman looked at her and fumed inwardly. "The independent little monkey," she thought furiously; "daring to defy me under my own roof? The ridiculous, independent, proud thing! Now,

I suppose I may look forward to a long procession of fools. How I shall miss her, with her brains and her absurd pride! The independent minx!"

Theodora walked down the corridor in a daze. She wanted to cry. It was the hardest kind of work to keep back the tears. Like most persons who are born with pluck, she was given plenty of opportunity to exercise it.

She sat down in her room and read the advertisements in the *Times*. They were so numerous that her spirits revived. No one need lack work, surely.

But all the time she was reading, and all the time she was dressing for the street, and all the time she was going from one address to another, her thoughts were on one subject—why had she been dismissed? Had this happened last autumn at Fair Acres, she could have understood it; she had even expected it then. But this was a bolt from the blue. Unless it had to do with Ned's affair, there seemed to be no reason for it—and surely it would be rather unfair to visit a thing of that sort on her head. It was all a mystery.

For three days she fared unsuccessfully. It frightened her a little to find how differently things may sound, and look. Such wretched holes did she enter, such pitiful stipends was she offered, such tasks and combinations of tasks was she asked to assume, that her heart sank lower and lower. If one didn't know stenography, nor typing, nor filing, nor a switchboard, if one were not already a "skilled hand," as a milliner, or saleswoman, or accountant, if one had no special gift, such as drawing or music, then one must apparently be resigned to doing house-work, or entering a factory or laundry.

Then, on her fourth day of discouragement she came home to find Mrs. Delafield Beeckman sitting with Mrs. Stuyvesant, and to hear that the dashing Blanche probably held the solution to her riddle. "Miss Winthrop," she said, "my aunt has been telling me of your change of plans. I'm wondering if I can't help you. You remember that Mrs. Felton whom you heard speak for suffrage?"

"Oh, yes." Theodora couldn't repress a little smile. "Very well indeed."

"Well, on the strength of that acquaintance she has written me that she is extremely anxious to give more time to the cause, and to speak in public more frequently. But in order to do so, she must find a mother's helper for her two children. She particularly wants one who can speak French fluently, and my aunt tells me that your French is excellent."

Theodora wanted to say, "Yes, the poodles seem satisfied with it," but naturally she refrained. Mrs. Beeckman continued: "Mrs. Felton asks if among my acquaintances there is not someone who is parting with a treasure whom she could secure. Perhaps you might care to try it? At least, it will give you a summer in the country."

The upshot of the matter was that on the morrow Theodora journeyed thirty miles out into the country, and came back employed.

"What are your duties?" asked Mrs. Stuyvesant when the girl came in to report.

Theodora smiled. "A little of everything," she answered. "I am to talk French with two children who don't know a word of it, help them with their lessons, keep their clothes in order, teach them music, give them an idea of dancing, and assist with the cooking and general housework—for there is no servant. As far as I can see, I'm to be everything but laundress. They do hire a laundress."

"But," cried Mrs. Stuyvesant, "this is simply scandalous."

Theodora laughed lightly. "I'm extremely glad to get it," she answered simply.

"What will she pay you?"

"Thirty-five dollars a month."

"I won't permit it," fumed the old lady.

"Mrs. Stuyvesant, please listen to me. I'll admit that I shouldn't care to work long at that price, even though I got my living thrown in. I know that the education that makes me eligible to this position should make me worth much more money—but unfortunately, it doesn't. A combination of cook, housemaid, nurse, seamstress, governess, teacher of dancing and music, and mental companion, seems to be worth just about eight dollars a week plus board—a little over a dollar a day! Less than half what a cleaning woman gets! No *man* would ever dream of giving so much for so little."

"I should think not, indeed! Nor should you."

"No; but I've learned a great deal in these last few days. I find that women seem to be habitually underpaid. Their best chance is a man's poorest—what man would think he had reached the heights, as stenographer or typist? I'm beginning to think there may be something in Mrs. Beeckman's equal suffrage, after all. If a woman had a vote, she would be more valuable. As things are, evidently the only kind of work at which she can hope to get anything like proper wages is specialized work—and unfortunately I've never specialized. . . .I think I'm about ten years older than I was four days ago. And I've come to one certain conclusion, at least."

"And what is that?"

"That I cannot hope to save anything toward old age by working in private homes. I was very fortunate in this first venture, because I got so much besides money. Here with you, I traveled for the first time, I lived charmingly, I met delightful people, I learned much. I shall always be thankful for the experience."

The old lady moved uneasily; but the girl went on, almost as if she were speaking to herself. "I find that thirty-five dollars a month, plus living, is about an average wage. With the slightest possible expenditure for clothes, and allowing a minimum for doctors, dentists, and so on, it would take me seven years to save two thousand dollars. The income on two thousand is one hundred. In other words, it would take me seventy years to save the principal of an income of a thousand dollars, on which to live comfortably in my old age. You see, I should have begun the day I was born—or even a little sooner."

That's why girls grow up to be such disgusting man-chasers; that's why men are coaxed and flattered and cajoled and enticed.

It was a shocking statement—not the sort to tickle and please. "And have you conceived any remedy for this state of things?" demanded Mrs. Stuyvesant irritably. "Of course, there's only one sane one, and that is marriage."

"Yes, and that's just the trouble. It shouldn't be. That's why girls grow up to be such disgusting man-chasers; that's why men are coaxed and flattered and cajoled and enticed. It's nothing but the girl's love of herself, her desire to place herself above the necessity for working. Personally, I'd rather die than marry a man just to be supported by him—even if I had the chance."

As Theodora left the room her employer's eyes followed her. There was an odd look in them. Anyone who didn't know to the contrary might almost have taken it for admiration, mixed with regret. How well the girl walked! How proudly she carried her head! Evidently her ancestors had had the right to look up.

Theodora was to take a three-thirty train the next afternoon. She came in immediately after luncheon to say good bye.

"You'll let me hear of your safe arrival, of course," said Mrs. Stuyvesant.

"Yes, indeed. Thank you once more for everything, Mrs. Stuyvesant—and good bye."

Theodora came and offered her hand. To her surprise she felt herself being drawn gently downward. "Kiss me good bye, child," said her employer unexpectedly, turning a withered cheek to receive the caress. "Good luck to you. I shall miss you."

As Theodora climbed into the waiting motor, there was a lump in her throat and her eyes were blurred with tears.

"I wouldn't have believed it possible," said Mrs. Stuyvesant to herself. "I suppose I'm a fool. But what am I going to do without her? At least, I can keep an eye on her through Bishop Wysong. What a hideous ogress she must think me! Dear me, dear me! But it was simply the only thing to do!"

CHAPTER

☙XI☙

heodora's hand-satchel was heavy, so she took a hack from the Hillcrest station to her new home. No more luxurious private motors for poor dear Theodora!

When the hack drove up to her door, Mrs. Felton was stretched in a hammock on the wide shady verandah. She rose languidly and came forward in kindly greeting. Her anemic appearance contrasted with Theodora's splendid ruggedness.

"Would you like to go to your room and rest?" asked Mrs. Felton.

"Oh, no, I'm not in the least tired, thank you. I've only run out from town, you know."

"Yes; but the very air of New York depresses me. I always come home a wreck."

Theodora hesitated. "I see you're resting," she finally said, "so I won't disturb you. If you'll tell me where my room is, I'll just run up."

"I'd be glad to have you sit and chat with me if you feel like it. I wasn't sleeping, but I made it a rule never to sit up when I can lie down. You know that hygienically the horizontal position is the only proper one. The organs are at rest, instead of hanging in space. It is the difference between a grand piano and an upright."

Theodora listened astonished. Not yet knowing that theories were the meat and drink of this household, she was naturally taken by surprise. "But in that case," she laughed, "I should think the Lord wouldn't have made us upright. We should have been horizontal instead of vertical."

Mrs. Felton smiled slightly. She was a serious person and her smiles came rarely. "I fancy the Lord had very little to do with it," she answered. (According to her convictions, He had very little to do with anything. Certainly He played small part in the life of the Felton family.) "Of course, we had that position originally, but with increased intelligence and activities, we were forced to pull ourselves erect in order to do more. You knew that, I suppose?"

Theodora shook her head. She could hardly keep her face straight. "I'm afraid I didn't," she confessed.

Mrs. Felton looked disappointed. She had been looking forward to a daily companion in theoretic discussion. However, she loved to instruct.

"I'll tell you what would be nice," continued Theodora. "I could run up to my room and get rid of this bag, wash my face, get into a fresh blouse, and then come down and talk to you till you have something else for me to do."

"Very well," agreed Mrs. Felton, who had resumed her horizontal position. "There won't be much to do. I hope you had a good luncheon?"

"Excellent, thank you."

"They always overload their stomachs in the establishments of the rich. They live for nothing but the material side of life. Look at their bloated figures and pouchy fronts as they grow older—"

"Mrs. Stuyvesant is very slender," interjected Theodora.

"She is? She's an exception then, or else she's ill. However, I'm glad you had a good luncheon; we needn't bother over an evening meal. We'll just have a bite out of doors. Mr. Felton is in town and won't be home till after midnight, so you and the children and I can eat a picnic supper. I don't believe in wasting this lovely weather in housework."

"No, indeed. And where is my room, Mrs. Felton?"

"Second floor back, on your left. You'll easily find it. It's just past the bathroom. I'll wait for you here."

"Well!" thought Theodora to herself, as she made her way upstairs. "This promises to be educational, to put it mildly." Following directions, she came to the room assigned to her use and walked in. The room was large and airy, with only a bed, a chiffonnier, and one straight chair. There wasn't a table, nor anything on which to put a book, a portfolio, nor a glass of water. There wasn't a vestige of paper on the wall, nor a single curtain nor shade at any of the four big windows. There wasn't a rug on the floor. There were exactly three articles in that room, and Theodora herself made the fourth.

The bathroom was almost equally bare, but she found a fresh towel hanging on a hook and made use of it. After tidying herself, she went downstairs again, leaving her bag still packed and sitting on the floor.

"Did you find your way?" asked the lady of the hammock as Theodora rejoined her. "Oh dear me, don't take that straight chair. Bring that rocker over, then you can tilt back and prop your feet on the rail. No one can see you."

"This is perfectly comfortable, thank you. Yes, I found my way. And what a lovely big room you've given me."

"Well, at least it isn't all cluttered up. I hate dust-catchers. I never have any hangings, nor ornaments, nor pieces of carved furniture. It sickens me to think of the hours women spend rubbing off dust that begins to accumulate again the moment they stop."

"It never occurred to me that way," mused Theodora. "If you didn't wipe it off you'd soon be snowed under, wouldn't you?—or dusted under, to be more explicit."

Theordora instinctively assumed a relationship with this new employer which was totally different from that which she had held with her former one. She never for a moment considered herself the superior of Mrs. Felton, but she realized that in this new home, she was *expected* to argue every subject that was broached. Should she fail to do so, she would be a disappointment; she would be branded as mindless and conventional.

"I once heard of a Frenchman," she now continued, "who should have your sympathy. He counted up how many hours and days and weeks he'd have to spend dressing and undressing, in the course of an ordinary lifetime—and it discouraged him so much that he committed suicide."

"I don't blame him in the least. Our clothes should grow on us, as they did in the early ages. That's where animals have the better of us." (Theodora thought with inward mirth of all the designers and mannequins she had seen in New York.)

By exercising all her will power, Theodora managed to hold her tongue. She realized that even while this new employer of hers might court ordinary argument, there must be a limit to that, as to all things.

It grew to be twilight, then dusk, then dark. Theodora wondered whether they were to sit there, unfed, all night. What a strange atmosphere! All talk and theory, no action nor effort! And seemingly, no fear of nor love for God! However, Mrs. Felton finally roused herself. "I must go and find the children," she announced with a tired sigh—quite as though she had been working hard. "Then we'll have a bite and go to bed. Your trunk probably won't come until morning. They're terribly inefficient down at the baggage office; there should be a woman in charge. Have you night things with you?"

"Oh yes, thank you. I'm quite all right."

The lady of the house trailed languidly off on her hunt for her offspring. "Eugenia, Walter, where are you?" she called. "It's supper time. I want you to come home."

It was some minutes before she reappeared, heralded by whining and arguing in childish tones. Evidently the young Feltons considered a quarter of nine "the start of the evening," and far too early an hour to have their liberty curtailed.

Theodora wondered how old they might be. In the dark she could get only a vague impression of a tall lanky girl and a smaller boy, neither of whom seemed overburdened with social graces.

Mrs. Felton turned to Theodora. "Do you like raw eggs?" she asked.

For a moment Theodora was too startled to reply that she had never tasted them, but the question unloosed the momentarily bridled juvenile tongues.

"I won't eat raw eggs, nasty old things." . . . "You're always making us have those rotten old eggs." . . . "Can't we have something decent to eat?" . . . "I want something good—*Mother*, can't we have something good?"

"Oh children, be quiet." The tirade evidently bored the mother much more than it shocked her. "I can't hear Miss Winthrop speak. We're great hands here for raw eggs and milk, Miss Winthrop. With those and bananas and shredded wheat, we usually make out a supper when Mr. Felton is away."

"I don't think I care for any eggs," she smiled, "and I'm sorry to say I never drink milk—"

"Never drink milk?" (Theodora might almost as well have confessed to murder.)

"No. But a shredded wheat biscuit and a banana are quite all that I shall want."

They went into the house and turned on one crudely glaring electric light. Theodora, looking about her, found that she was in the kitchen. She had never seen one like it. It was about as big as a closet, and it had one window. There were wall-cupboards, a gas range, a sink, one table, and one high wooden stool. Nothing else.

The entire meal occupied about ten minutes. A raw egg must be swallowed with haste . . .

"My idea of a kitchen," said Mrs. Felton, "is a place where you can stand in the middle, reach all you want, and get out as quickly as possible. I don't believe in intelligent women spending their lives in kitchens."

She went in search of the edibles and Theodora turned her attention to the children. The girl was the older. She looked to be about ten, but tall for her age. She was spectacled, shrewish, stockingless, and sandalled, with dirty clothes, face, and hands. Her brother looked to be some two years younger; he was rather handsome, but very shifty-eyed.

The food arrived and was carried in to the dining-room, where it was dumped on the table in an unappetizing heap, and then eaten as quickly as possible. The entire meal occupied about ten minutes. A raw egg must be swallowed with haste; one shredded wheat biscuit and one banana will not permit themselves to be the excuse for much dallying.

"Now," said Mrs. Felton, "we'll just stack these dishes till morning, and go to bed."

"I won't go to bed," whined Eugenia. "I'm going out to catch fireflies with Eliza Methune. I promised her I would. We saw two fireflies and we're going to put them under a tumbler."

"You're going to bed without another word," remarked her mother.

"I won't. You shut your mouth."

"Eugenia! What do you suppose Miss Winthrop will think of you?"

Eugenia murmured something to the effect that Theodora's opinion was a matter of indifference to her; but she was forced to yield. The house was shut and locked, the one light was extinguished, and in the pitch darkness the four felt their way upstairs.

"I'll tap on your door when we're through in the bathroom," said her hostess. "And I'll do the same in the morning. Can you waken by yourself, or do you want to be called?"

"What time do you get up?"

"Oh, between seven and half-past. The children have to go to school at half-past eight."

"Oh, they go to school?"

"Yes, to the public school—a wretched place, but all that we can afford as yet. I'd planned to take them out; but I found I'd be violating the law unless I put them in some other school. Talk about free countries! The term doesn't end till sometime in June, so music and dancing will be all that you'll have to teach the children till then. I thought through the summer I'd have them coached so they could both skip a grade. Well, good night. You think you'll waken without being called?"

"Yes, indeed. I'm always awake by seven. Good night." And Theodora was left to her thoughts.

She woke long before seven because two of her windows faced the east, and the sunlight streamed in through the unshaded panes in flaming shafts. In vain did she try to cover her eyes and go to sleep again. The light was too strong. "Tonight I'll tie a stocking, or a towel, over my eyes. There's no use in waking at five every morning."

She rose and went to the window. The outlook was very beautiful, with that wonderful newness and freshness of an early summer morning. Around Theodora stretched small lawns, small streets, and small houses—all new, pretty, and well-kept. Lovely old forest trees had been spared by the wise settlers in this new community, and many gay flower beds raised dewy perfumed blossoms to greet the day. Over all was an atmosphere of peace and sweetness.

Fortunately she had stationery and a fountain pen in her valise, so she made good use of the morning hours. Not a word did she write of the homesickness that assailed her, not one of any disappointment.

When Theodora went down to help prepare breakfast, she supposed she would meet her host. But she found that he had fed himself and hurried to town long ago; and again the girl thought what a strange household she had entered.

Breakfast consisted of thin grey cocoa and oatmeal. Theodora accepted the offer of a fried egg and immediately both children demanded like luxuries.

After the children left for school, Mrs. Felton and Theodora washed the dishes and then went upstairs where the girl made up the bedrooms while her employer did the meager marketing by telephone. Such was her habit; it insured, of course, the maximum of cost and the minimum of quality. But then, it was much less trouble.

"And she talks about being poor," said Theodora to herself. "I wonder what she'd think of her husband if he stayed at home and attended to his end of the business by telephone."

During one of the pauses, she asked Mrs. Felton if there were good shops in the place.

"Yes, pretty good. They're down in the village, and it takes a whole hour out of the morning to attempt to go down and market. I haven't the time to waste on that sort of thing." (She hadn't the time, either, to waste on dusting, or housework, or cooking, or taking care of her children. Theodora wondered to what ends her valuable time was spent.)

At that moment a voice called from downstairs. A neighbor had run in to ask if she might dump all her family cares on Mrs. Felton's shoulders, while she herself hurried off to town to do some shopping. The family cares consisted of a long marketing list (to be attended to by telephone, of course), a young baby on the bottle, and a small daughter, to come in at lunchtime. "I've given her her lunch in a box," explained the hurried mother, "if you'll just let her bring it here to eat."

To Theodora's surprise, Mrs. Felton assumed this unlovely burden quite as a matter of course—though the baby was teething and yelled most of the time. After the girl had lived a little longer in Hillcrest, she came to find that such favors were payable in kind. You kept a neighbor's children, and she kept yours. In that way, you were both enabled to get an occasional holiday. It was the "community spirit" and in this instance it didn't work badly.

Dinner, while fairly substantial, was unappetizing. Although the children must have been hungry, they balked at the food. Once more Mrs. Felton exhibited a surprising firmness and patience. Theodora learned more about the chemistry of foods in the course of that one short meal than she had ever before known in her life. Spinach must be eaten whether one liked it or not, because of the iron it contained. It was cheaper than meat and nearly as nutritious. Olive oil and peanut butter were essential foods and might not be sidestepped.

Theodora began to realize that her own healthy appetite would have to be satisfied by purchases in the village. She hoped there were good fruit shops there. The fact that she was barred from the staple articles of Felton diet—milk and raw eggs—and that her palate was unfortunately fastidious about badly prepared food, made her dietic future rather a problem.

The dinner dishes were washed and put away, the baby fortunately decided to sleep until her grateful mother came to carry her home, and so the mental treat of the day was in order. Theodora was told to bring a basket of mending and establish herself comfortably by the hammock.

"I'm writing a paper, and we can talk it over while I work," said Mrs. Felton.

"That will be lovely. What is your subject?"

"Eugenics."

Then Theodora's instruction began anew. She heard for the first time of the Mendelian theory, and of many other things as well. "You see," cried Mrs. Felton, warming to her subject, "now that these things are understood, we have it in our power to raise an absolutely perfect race—simply by cutting out the undesirables and mating the desirables according to fixed laws."

"But won't that also cut out love and preference?"

"Certainly, but they are merely fleeting. Love—what you mean by love—never outlasts a few months."

"A good many persons must have married for those few months."

"Yes, in ignorance. And repented at leisure."

"But I should think everyone would want to marry from preference personally, and then arrange proper eugenic marriages for the rest of mankind. And I should also think that what you call 'undesirables' might often object to being cut out of the program."

Mrs. Felton smiled in pity. "Human beings must learn to sacrifice themselves for the good of the race," she answered.

The conversation passed to the subject of birth control, Theodora now hearing of that remarkable science for the first time. She was frankly startled. "Good gracious," she thought, "I'm glad mother isn't here. What in the world would she think? She'd be horrified. In fact, I think I'm rather horrified myself."

The children came home from school and lingered on the edge of the conversation. Theodora glanced at them nervously from time to time. "Oh," said their mother comfortably, "they know all about such things. I don't believe in fostering morbid curiosity by making mysteries of natural processes. I explain everything to my children. They study sex-hygiene first in plants and flowers, then in animals. We have many pretty games about it."

Theodora was simply speechless. Fortunately a first music lesson was due. It was a relief when they all rose and went in to the piano—Mrs. Felton with the others. She thought she might pick up something by habitually listening to the instruction that Theodora gave her children. She was the most conscientiously serious woman that Theodora had ever met.

"We could have music and dancing on alternate days," she suggested. "And then you might oversee the practicing in between. How would that strike you?"

"I should think it would be an excellent plan. But about the dancing lessons—could you play a simple tune or two while I train the children to dance to it?"

"Mercy no. I can't play a note."

"Then are they to dance without music?"

"Could they?"

"I shouldn't think they could learn rhythm very well, should you?"

"Then, Miss Winthrop, you'll have to sing. I could never carry a tune or I'd do it for you."

Theodora suddenly gulped. She hastily took out her handkerchief and covered her face. The thought of dragging around those clumsy children, instructing them as to steps, counting the beats, and singing, all at the same time, was too much.

When supper time came, the children again responded impudently to their mother's call. Other children in the community did the same. All around, in the still night, Theodora could hear calling parents being invited by their offspring to shut their mouths, and "I won't" seemed to be the local childish classic. Mrs. Felton explained this. "We parents around here," she said, "do not believe in killing a child's spirit. We deplore the old time sternness of parents; we think it creates slyness on the part of the child. A child has as much right to his opinions as if he were an adult. The important thing is not to kill individuality."

Theodora couldn't help thinking that disagreeableness and impudence were far from being individuality, and that respect and self-control were a pretty good foundation on which to build character; but naturally, she didn't say so.

She never even saw Mr. Felton until Saturday afternoon. He was an accountant in New York, and he had many little side jobs which occupied him before and after office hours. So he went early and came late, feeding himself morning and night, and meeting his family once a week only. On Saturday afternoons, all business being closed, he came home early and spent a day and a half on his own domain.

All in all, Theodora had a number of surprises in this new home, but none of them exceeded the one she received on the first Sunday. Coming downstairs in a pretty summer muslin, ready to go to church, she found everyone in the oldest clothes they possessed. The men—both Mr. Felton and the neighbors who appeared on their premises—were in dirty overalls, and all day long they employed themselves in gardening, painting, mowing grass, mending pipes, and so forth. To and fro from house to house they went, borrowing tools and what not. It was a new conception of the day of rest and worship. At least, it was new to Theodora.

The girl went alone to an almost empty church where her appearance was hailed somewhat in the light of a Godsend. That afternoon, she wrote to her mother.

Dearest Mother,

Do you know why your eyelids aren't thicker? Do you know that you were intended to go on all fours, only your ambition got the better of you, and made you stand up on end and stick your fingers into all sorts of pies that weren't meant for you? Why did you neglect my education so shamefully? I never even *heard* of eugenics and sex-hygiene. On the other hand, I was disgracefully prejudiced in favor of religion.

To come down to sense, I'm well and sufficiently happy, and I'm seeing a side of humanity that I never dreamed existed. My world is turned topsy-turvy. One thing I've learned is that the beauty and perfume of life are very valuable things, and that they don't depend on money. If you and I had a little home like this, we'd be perfectly happy and we'd make it a cozy and lovely nest. Just a little willingness to take pains, a little concern over material things, and Mrs. Felton could have a home that was really a home. But she cares for nothing but theories, and she hates trouble as I've been taught to hate the Evil One. However, she isn't very strong. She's always envying me my health. If she had it, she'd probably use it to grab the vote; it must be simply wasted on me.

I've met a few of the neighbors and they all seem to be the same sort. I suppose it's a case of "birds of a feather." I'm always introduced as "our new luxury, Miss Winthrop." Nothing matters here but education. I wish you could see me giving a dancing lesson. I'm teacher, orchestra, and partner, all in one. It's an absolutely joyful sight.

There's one thing that constantly strikes me as odd: there's no consciousness of blood nor of forbears in this family. In Waverly, as you know, it is the whole thing. Here, it is lacking. So, too, is the blood itself, I suppose. But equally so, too, is all pretentiousness about it—which is certainly a mercy.

Suppertime, and I must fly. More love than I can write.

Your own,

Theodora

CHAPTER

ᔥXIIᔥ

uring the heated and one-sided discussions which her employer was fond of having, Theodora realized that there were two distinct elements in Hillcrest society—the serious and the frivolous.

The frivolous women played cards, and they were an abomination. Even though their children might be well cared for, their homes well run, and their husbands well satisfied, these facts carried no weight against the charge that they wasted their time in foolishness, thus copying "society women."

The serious women were devoted to clubs—suffrage clubs, temperance clubs, civic clubs, literature clubs, and clubs for every conceivable serious pursuit. Books seemed never to be read except in clubs. Study was conducted in clubs. Everything was clubs!

From Theodora's standpoint, she'd rather sit alone with a good book, any time.

Mrs. Felton and her friends seemed to view her as a "great laugher."

And when she came to realize the seriousness with which these women took life, she saw how light she must seem to them. Nevertheless, she knew that she could do many things which they could not. Not one of them could speak any living

159

tongue save her own; they knew some Latin, and even a smattering of Greek, but French was a sealed book to them. Not one of them could dance, nor play the piano, nor sing; yet they all wanted their children to do these things. They all hated cooking and sewing and child-rearing, but there wasn't a childless woman among them.

Theodora pondered much over all these things as the summer days and weeks sped by. She used to sit in the quiet evenings, looking up at the stars and praying. Often she found herself asking God to show her what was true about life. She was puzzled by the different standards in different places— even among people of equal intelligence. Everyone was so sure of being right, yet it was obvious that they couldn't all be. Was there such a thing as a fixed standard of right and wrong, Theodora wondered, or was it all a matter of environment, opinion, and heredity?

At the end of June when the Border call came to the men of the United States, Theodora witnessed the selfishness of ultra-theorists. No one in Hillcrest dreamed of doing anything but criticize. The war was a trap, a mess, a mistake, an unnecessary incubus.

"But," cried Theodora, "even if it were all those things and more, someone would still have to put it through."

Ned Charrington rushed at once to join up. His heartbroken mother never raised a finger in protest. Mrs. Winthrop wrote that the boy had been fine, and Aunt Augusta magnificent. But after his departure she had turned to an image of stone. She scarcely ate, and she prowled around the house all night long, often sitting in Ned's room, fingering his possessions.

This, then, was the woman whom Theodora had dubbed hard and cold! This was the boy whom she had feared was a weakling! He had first broken himself of a habit which has mastered many a man, and had then given all that he had to give, at his country's first call. Theodora felt humbled and ashamed.

Fortunately for her peace of mind, Theodora found her older pupil, Eugenia, distractingly clever. The child was unattractive, nervous, irritable, and cold; but she was avid for knowledge. Her brother Walter was his mother's darling; he was handsome and lazy, and soon proved to be the sneak he looked. Theodora never went into the village without meeting him (he was not permitted there and invariably lied about it), and he was always buying food. He gathered up small sums of money all around the house, Mrs. Felton being as careless of that as of all material things. Theodora's own purse was rifled of various small amounts until she took to locking it up.

Theodora realized that the beautiful thing which had seemed to blossom in her heart last winter, was now withered and dead. Whatever it had been, it had disappeared—leaving in its place a dull sort of void. There didn't seem to be much in life now, except an endless procession of identical days. There was no secret joy in her heart, no unaccountable spring in her step, no mysterious feel of hidden future happiness.

And then, early in October, something happened which made Theodora look longingly back to this time of despised quiet and safety. She received a telegram from Aunt Augusta, and it read:

"Come immediately. Your mother very ill."

Theodora would always carry with her the memory of devoted kindness on the part of Mrs. Felton—a memory that wiped out more critical ones from the girl's sad mind. Mrs. Felton showed to her best advantage in times of trouble.

The train that took Theodora homeward seemed to creep at a snail's pace. The girl sat tense and almost motionless, every nerve in her body strained to the breaking point. A year had passed since she had seen her mother. The case must be desperate, or Aunt Augusta would never have sent that message. How could she ever have stayed away so long? Yet if she hadn't, how could she have hoped to improve the family fortunes? But after all, money was nothing; the fact remained that a whole year of possible companionship had been wasted in separation. It could never be made up. Over and over in a fevered and fruitless round did Theodora's thoughts travel.

She arrived unheralded at the station of Waverly. How changed it looked—how small and shabby! The streets, too, seemed dark and narrow, and the house, once reached, shared this impression.

Theodora walked in without ringing. Her aunt was descending the stairs. She looked thin and ill, and she moved wearily. "Theodora!" she exclaimed. "How glad I am to see you! You certainly lost no time in getting here—"

"No, I came immediately. Am I in time? How is mother?"

"She is in great pain, but holding her own."

"Thank God," breathed the girl in low trembling tones. "What is it, Aunt Augusta?"

"Some intestinal trouble. An operation is necessary, but she absolutely refused to have it till she had seen you."

"Will it be a very serious one?"

"Very. But not necessarily a fatal one. The doctors say that her general health is good enough to give her an excellent chance of recovery. Without the operation, she has no chance at all."

"You've had more than one doctor?"

"Yes, we've had a specialist from the city."

"Good. When can I go to Mother?"

"At once, I think. She has hardly been able to wait to see you. Of course you must be very quiet, and you mustn't stay long."

But once inside that room, Theodora never left it, except to follow the doctor into the corridor after his visits, there to get his verdicts and directions. Like a mute she sat by the bed or knelt on the floor, caressing the delicate hand that lay on the counterpane; at nights she threw herself, fully dressed, on the couch. So passed the three days between her return and the removal of her mother to the hospital.

Theodora's impassioned prayers were answered, and the operation was a success. Then there began a strange new routine for Theodora. As soon as the physicians and nurses found what an excellent sickroom companion she was, and how her presence comforted the patient, the girl was given permission to spend every day with her mother. The hospital was some two miles from Waverly, not far from the colony of recently built newly rich palaces. Theodora walked out every morning after breakfast, and returned at dusk. All day long she sat in the sickroom, reading aloud, chatting, or merely lending the comfort of her silent presence.

On her walks to and fro, she did much thinking. Second only to her great thankfulness came the haunting thought of money. What would they have done had she not saved some? What a blessing it had been to be able to assume the expenses and to reassure her mother on the subject! Mrs. Winthrop was never even to guess the size of the bills.

But suppose, thought Theodora, just suppose that one more sickness should fall to their lot! She could not possibly return to Mrs. Felton's. Where, then, would the money be found? Like poor Ned, she became obsessed by the subject. To say the truth, her problem was no easy one. She *must* hereafter spend her life by her mother's side. She *must* materially augment their small income. And there was no possible way to earn money in Waverly.

Nurses made good wages, but they couldn't live at home and their course of preparation took three full years. Her riddle remained still unanswered when Mrs. Winthrop returned home.

Theodora immediately installed herself as nurse, never leaving the house except for a brisk walk each afternoon. One day—a heavenly autumn day—she had walked toward the hospital and beyond it. Coming to a lonely stretch of road, she decided to go no further and turned to face toward home. But she hadn't gone a dozen steps when her foot twisted under her and she came down in a sudden heap—red-hot pains shooting from ankle to knee. She knew at once what had happened: She had sprained her ankle.

She was out of sight and earshot. The effort to walk almost made her faint, and she certainly couldn't crawl three and a half miles. In addition to all else, the sun was slipping away with appalling rapidity. What was she to do? She crawled a bit and limped a bit, and then sank down in despair.

Suddenly, on the hard road, she heard the distant beat of a horse's hoofs. The sound came rapidly nearer, till presently a smart little trap drawn by a high-stepping mare appeared around a curve in the road. Theodora raised herself and began to call. In the gathering darkness she might not be seen. "Will you help me?" she cried. "I've sprained an ankle and I can't walk."

The mare was reined sharply up, and a voice answered.

"Did someone call?"

"Yes," said Theodora, "I did. I've hurt myself, and I'm three miles from home."

"By Jove, that's tough. How lucky that I happened along!" A man sprang to the ground and approached the crouching girl.

"I'm awfully sorry to trouble you," she began.

"Trouble? It's no trouble, I assure you. I'm only too glad I found you. This is a nasty bit of lonely road. It's a long chance if anyone else comes by in hours. Can you stand? Good! Lean on me. We'll get to the trap all right. The confounded thing is so high it's going to be a bad climb for you. Would you let me lift you? That's right. Take your time now—don't hurry. Now, where am I to take you?"

Theodora told him where she lived. "I'm afraid it will be awfully out of your way," she added.

"Scarcely a step. The mare needs a chance to stretch her legs anyhow. Our place is right along here, though I don't come down to it once in a year of blue moons. Waverly's a bit of a dead hole, don't you think?"

"I certainly do."

"I don't know what ever induced my old man to build here. Just a fad, I fancy, and a bit of amusement. Is your foot fairly comfortable now, Miss—"

"Winthrop. My name is Winthrop."

"And mine is Gerald Wyatt."

Theodora recognized it instantly as one that she knew by hearsay. Mr. Wyatt, senior, had been the pioneer builder in the millionaire colony, and his home was said to be more glaring, more lavishly atrocious, than any other there. And here sat she, Theodora Winthrop, hobnobbing with the Wyatt heir and driving by his side through the gloaming. It was ludicrous—ludicrous, but exceptionally lucky and convenient!

At her own home, Mr. Wyatt lifted the girl from the cart and supported her to the threshold, lingering till her ring was answered.

"Won't you come in?" she asked.

"No, I think not. Thank you, Miss Winthrop, but I'll just run on if you're sure you're all right?"

"I'm quite all right and I can't thank you enough, Mr. Wyatt.

But for you, I don't know what I'd ever have done. My family will be so grateful to you. But I hate to think to what inconvenience I have put you!"

The pink of her tea-gown matched the pink of her velvety cheeks, her eyes were deep and starry.

Protesting that it had been nothing but a pleasure and that with her permission he would inquire on the morrow about the hurt ankle, the man said good night and drove off in the darkness.

He was back at eleven the next morning. Theodora, sitting in the library reading to her mother, saw the cart pull up at the door, and ordered the servant to ask Mr. Wyatt to come in. He appeared shortly, his hands full of fruit and flowers.

"Good morning," he cried cheerily. "How's the foot? All bandaged up? That's good. You saw a doctor, of course?"

"Yes, he tells me it's rather a bad sprain. My mother wants to thank you for your great kindness. Mother, may I present Mr. Wyatt—my rescuer of last evening?"

After the introduction, Mr. Wyatt delivered his gifts. "My mother thought you might enjoy these grapes and things," he said. "And she also sent you these posies. She's rather keen on flowers herself, and she thought you might be."

He was a pleasant-faced fellow, with a pair of blue eyes much too tired-looking for his years—which couldn't have exceeded twenty-six or seven. His clothes were exceptionally correct and noticeable; in fact, he would have made an excellent advertisement for a tailor's establishment. His manners were charming. Mrs. Winthrop was surprised. She had expected a cross between a Caliban and a fop.

Theodora was looking especially lovely that morning. The pink of her tea-gown matched the pink of her velvety cheeks, her eyes were deep and starry (they had grown more beautiful of late, reflecting the happiness of her mother's recovery), and her wonderful hair was rolled into the softest and simplest of knots. She breathed wholesomeness.

Now, as for young Mr. Wyatt, the shabbiness of the room in which he sat worried him not at all, but he was distinctly impressed by its old belongings—its portraits of ancestors, and whatnot—and by its two occupants. Mrs. Winthrop, faded and unfashionable though she was, had an air and a manner for which his own expensively adorned mother would gladly have paid millions. As for the girl, she was simply a peach. He saw her plainly now for the first time. Last night he had liked the outlines of her figure, her suppleness when he lifted her, and her lovely voice. This morning he thought her entrancing.

His appreciation of wholesomeness was recent. It was the result of an over-hectic experience through which he had just passed, and from which he had been rescued by the skin of his teeth. As far as the paths of love were concerned, life held few new sensations for this young man. He had been suitor, fiancé, co-respondent—in short, everything but husband. Just at present he was mollified, he was disgusted, and he was keeping his head low. But even though in temporary hiding, he had no desire to dispense entirely with charming female society. He looked upon Theodora as a Godsend.

He spent the balance of the morning and returned the next day. Soon, he was there most of the time. He had nothing else to do, and neither had Theodora. She grew to look forward to

Suitable Gifts for a Lady

The gifts of courtship should be impersonal—flowers, candy, one's photograph, books, and trifles associated with other activities shared in common.

Any articles of wearing apparel are distinctly improper as gifts, as are articles of intimate personal use; the gift of a pair of silk stockings a vulgarism beyond redemption. Ostentation in the courtship gift is in very poor form, and a gift of expensive jewelry in particularly bad taste.

Certain objects, however, are suitable, such as a picture in a silver frame, a silver desk set or silver-mounted desk calendar, a silver paper knife, or even a gold-case pencil or pen without failing in social tact.

—The Book of Good Manners, 1923

his comings, and to miss him sadly on those rare days when he ran up to town on an errand and she thus failed to see him. He showered her with the sort of things that girls may accept—books, flowers, candy, fruit, magazines, and new music (he was crazy about music, and Theodora played to him by the hour). He never made a mistake in taste, and he was always perfectly charming.

Whenever the weather was good (it was November by now, and uncertain), he took Mrs. Winthrop and Theodora out motoring. These trips did the elder woman so much good that the doctor said he wished she could have a few months south. Theodora wished it too, with an intensity that was an ache. Her old money worries returned in fits, and she prayed every night and morning for a solution to her troubles.

What Aunt Augusta thought of the new visitor the girl never asked, and Aunt Augusta never told. Theodora had a shrewd idea that her mother was a sort of go-between, that she occupied herself with telling her sister how surprisingly nice this young man really was. At all events, the subject was never mentioned in Theodora's hearing, though it was as conspicuous by its absence as it could possibly have been by its presence.

Meta was rarely at home except to attend to her duties. The moment they were finished, she was off to see Elise—whose house she was now running. Elise, herself, was spending her time in tea-gowns, cursing the fate that had overtaken her. Sometime in December she was to become a most unwilling mother. Meta took charge of her housekeeping and listened to her railings—Meta, who in Elise's shoes would have been in a seventh heaven of delight! And the man who had chosen between them was a serious, home-loving, child-loving soul.

The degrees by which friendship slips into courtship are too fine to dissect, too familiar to need description. Long before

Christmas, Theodora was conscious that she was being courted—whether seriously or not, she could not determine. With a woman's intuition, she realized that Gerald Wyatt's skill came from long practice. Long practice, and still a bachelor! "He's probably just amusing himself with a flirtation," thought the wise Theodora, "but it's certainly interesting."

As to the young man himself, he was debating the matter in perfectly cold blood. One did not, of course, entangle oneself permanently with every charming girl one met; one kept oneself free for the next—for if Gerald Wyatt had learned anything in the course of a very busy life, it was that the world is full of lovely women. On the other hand, a chap must marry sometime—particularly one who is the only heir to a name and a fortune. Marriage wasn't necessarily the end of gallantry to all charmers save one.

This philosophy formed the cool part of Gerald's cogitations. The warm part was supplied by Theodora herself. She was certainly lovely. He had seen plenty of women he wanted as much, but never one that he wanted as much for his wife.

There came the day when he asked her to marry him. He put his question with few tremors, and was distinctly nettled at her hesitation. Finally he extracted the cause. She wasn't sure that she cared enough for him. She didn't believe she was the kind of woman who could love a man madly.

"I'm afraid I don't love you," said Theodora almost sadly. "I like you awfully, I'm devoted to you as a friend, and I'd miss you terribly if you went away from me. But that isn't enough to marry on, is it?"

"But you will love me. Trust me for that. Look here, Theodora, it's a mighty hard thing to explain to a girl like you; but I know what I'm talking about. There are women who never love till after they're loved. They love in response. They have to be wakened, if you get what I mean. You're that kind. Most clever women are. I reason it out this way: brains hold passion in check and give a woman something else to think about—till something stronger breaks that check. With a decent girl, the only person who can do it is an accepted lover. It's confoundedly hard to explain when I have to be so careful what I say, but your very inexperience makes you doubt your power of loving—just as it makes you specially desirable to me. Do you see?"

"I don't know," answered the girl in rather a daze. "It sounds a little frightening to me."

"Not in the least. That's just your innocence. The main thing is that I know that I can make you love me. I'm perfectly willing to take the risk, unless, that is, you are in love with someone else. You're not, are you?"

Theodora hesitated perceptibly before answering. Then, "No," she said. "No, certainly not."

"Then it's all right."

"But suppose that this wonderful love that you think you can call to life doesn't come?"

"You'll still be free to break your engagement. An engagement isn't a marriage. But I have no fears on that head. You won't want to. I know your type. All you need is to have your eyes opened. It's my luck that I happen to be the one to do it."

It wasn't at all what Theodora had imagined a proposal of marriage would be, although the man was certainly in earnest. Then Theodora recalled those old puzzles of hers—how it was that Elise, with no more experience than her cousin and but little more beauty could always make men aware of her, could always understand them and get what she wanted from them. Perhaps this was the answer; perhaps Elise knew all these things innately.

But she couldn't make her momentous decision quickly. She must have time to think it all out. In addition, there was one other important matter to discuss.

"There's another thing," she said. "I couldn't leave my mother. There are just the two of us, you know."

Gerald took this lightly. "That's all right," he said easily. "She can be with us as much as you like—live with us permanently if you choose. The governor will undoubtedly give us a couple of places—town and country, you know—and she can always have her own rooms—"

"You're certainly an angel," cried Theodora gratefully. The praise was like wine to her lover. He became quite self-consciously generous.

"We'd probably travel quite a bit," he said. "Perhaps she'd like a jaunt with us, now and again? I'm very fond of your mother, you know."

Theodora suddenly put out her hand, shyly but warmly. The man seized it and carried it to his lips. And that, she certainly did not dislike.

"Will you do something wonderful for me?" she asked. "Will you give me a day to think this over? And will you go now, without touching me at all?"

He was wise enough to humor her.

She thought it out, shut and locked in her own room. And she came to the conclusion that if Gerald was right, if her love would indeed awaken to his call, then she was a very lucky girl. Where else could she hope to find an answer to her problems—even to her prayers? What other man would be so wonderful about her mother? To think that she would be able to give that mother every luxury in the world, and that they need never again be separated! It was almost too good to be true!

Then, too, the thing was merely a trial. She wasn't going to get married yet—just engaged. If everything didn't go right and according to Gerald's promise, she would still be as free as air.

The next day Gerald Wyatt received the answer that he expected. And the week before Christmas, three important things happened in the Charrington-Winthrop household: Ned came home from the Border looking simply magnificent; Elise gave birth to a little son; and Theodora's engagement was announced.

"I must tell you," wrote Aunt Augusta to the Misses Duncan, "of poor dear Theodora's latest remarkable whim. She has engaged herself to the son of the man who built the first of those awful houses—Mr. Wyatt. My dear friends, I do hope you won't be too shocked."

That, however, was Aunt Augusta's sole diatribe. To Theodora herself she never made one criticism. Ned was jubilant; he liked Gerald, and he talked openly about "Brownie's luck," which he vowed she richly deserved. Mrs. Winthrop was too delighted to hide her pleasure; she knew her future son-in-law quite well by now, and she certainly saw nothing in him to criticize. While the fact remained that no one could really deserve Theodora, Gerald was a dear fellow and seemed to come as near it as anyone could. Elise, of course, said many biting things; but then, that was to be expected. It didn't even ruffle the general feeling of happiness.

PART FOURTH

A Questionable
Engagement

CHAPTER

☙XIII☙

lise Sewall lay on a couch, fretting peevishly over the unfairness of the world.

Here she was, young and fond of life, saddled with a baby and forced to listen to her husband's constant rhapsodies on the subject. Meta was just as absurd. To hear those two, one would suppose that no other child had ever been born. It was all very well for a man and an old maid to make such fools of themselves—what did they know of the pain and inconvenience of motherhood?

Her brother Ned was another thorn. Ned had always had the soft end of all the bargains. All the money in the house had had to be scraped and saved for his college course; he visited at rich houses; he got away from disgusting one-horse Waverly. In answer to the Border call, he had gone off to what proved to be a perfect cinch—no fighting, no danger, and a summer of travel! Yet on his return, he was hailed as a hero.

And now, to cap it all, he was invited to spend the Christmas holidays at a beautiful New York home, and his engagement to the only daughter of the house was to be announced. Theodora knew the girl—Marjorie Gary—and said she was lovely. So there was Ned, finely fixed for life!

But more irritating of all, adding insult to injury—was Theodora's own engagement. Nothing but the purest luck! A sprained ankle on a lonely road, and a millionaire fiancé as the result! Theodora, the girl who had forsaken her poor mother in order to go out into the world and hunt up a good time, while her cousin Elise stayed virtuously at home and got the mean end of the bargain! Elise's husband had no fortune and no future, except a country doctor's practice; Theodora's husband would be a fashionable idler all his days, would give his wife everything, would take her everywhere!

But that was always the way. Elise hadn't met her cousin's fiancé yet because of her state of health, but she had seen the sapphire-and-diamond engagement ring, and the superb pendant that had been Theodora's Christmas gift—jewels fit for a queen. The sly Theodora had always pretended not to care greatly for such things, while she, Elise, with her usual honesty which never seemed to bring her any reward, had frankly confessed to a love for them.

It wouldn't be pleasant, thought Elise, to have Theodora down here at Waverly in the summers, living in a palace and lording it over her poverty-stricken relatives. Of course, they'd all kneel down and worship her when once they saw her possessions—all, that is, except Elise. Theodora was to go off in a day or two to make a little visit at the Wyatt's town house, and to be presented at a huge dinner. Elise had never been to a real dinner party in her life. One didn't count those old-maid affairs at the Misses Duncan's.

While Elise was thus amusing herself with envy, malice, and all uncharitableness, Theodora was busy making a frock for the announcement dinner. She had gone to town and bought some yards of heavy pale pink satin, as delicate in tint as the inside of a seashell. With no embellishment save a real lace fichu furnished by Mrs. Winthrop, and a velvety artificial rose, the dress turned Theodora into a rose herself.

She was a little nervous over the approaching meeting with Gerald's family. "Mother," he had told her, "is something of a fusser, but okay when you really know her. The governor has to be handled with gloves, but he'll fall for you all right. Just pet him up a bit and humor him, and you'll own him. My sister Marguerite has the brains of the family, but she'll bite your head off if she doesn't happen to like you. She drives the old lady crazy. She's always letting out the truth about things—just to be devilish, you know."

"Is she pretty—your sister?" asked Theodora. To tell the truth, she was not tremendously reassured by the picture her lover painted of his home circle.

"No, not in the least. She's the sporty type. Loves horses, rides like a centaur—you know the kind. She's thin and dark, and she doesn't make up at all—not even powder on her nose. The old lady powders and rouges and wears a pound of false hair. She's always 'reducing'—afraid to eat this, or that, or the other thing. Beauty doctors are her meat and drink; she must spend thousands a year on them. She's determined to have Marguerite marry a title, but she's so darned independent I don't know how it will all turn out. She couldn't *love*, I'm sure of that. She's as hard as nails, and has been all her life. She was the most disagreeable child that ever was born."

Theodora's heart was failing her for fear. Here were types that she didn't even know. She would be as strange to them as they to her. Probably they wouldn't like her at all. She wished devoutly that the visit was over.

The day that she was to start, Gerald came to luncheon and drove her in to town in the limousine. Orchids were in the hanging vase, a sable-lined coat was on Gerald's back, and the chauffeur was muffled in furs; and Theodora, the heroine of the occasion, wore a cheap ready-made suit, and carried in her small trunk two simple homemade frocks.

They stopped eventually in front of a huge new house; it was of grey stone, turretted like a medieval castle. The butler who admitted them wore white kid gloves; he handed them over immediately to a footman in prune livery with scarlet facings. This impressive person preceded them to an enormous drawing room where Theodora found her future mother-in-law awaiting her.

> Mrs. Wyatt was a portly woman. She could no more have lifted her own handkerchief from the floor than she could have flown.

Mrs. Wyatt was a portly woman. She could no more have lifted her own handkerchief from the floor than she could have flown. Her hands were white and pudgy, and they blazed with huge gems. Her flabby cheeks bloomed with a girlish color that never varied, and her grey head was a miracle of the hairdresser's art. Her black-and-silver tea gown left the neck and bust bare, and sheathed the rest of the body like a close-fitting glove. As to her real face, one never got that far—the accessories were too blatant.

"Well, my dear," she greeted, holding out one of her hands, "we're very happy to welcome you, I'm sure." Theodora printed a light and careful kiss on the tinted cheek, and Mrs. Wyatt continued: "My son has told us that we had a great pleasure in store, and I can see that he was right." Then to the waiting servant, "Tell your master that the young lady is here."

Theodora couldn't help noting how she'd been referred to. But what difference did it make whether Mrs. Wyatt said "Miss

Winthrop," or "the young lady"? Such things were mere conventions.

Mr. Wyatt soon appeared, and was presented to the young lady. His portliness, unlike his wife's, was far from restrained. His fat stubby hands were covered with a thick growth of reddish hair. Gerald inherited his blondness from his father. Mr. Wyatt, however, lacked his son's gift of light conversation. "Well, well," he said, and pinched Theodora's cheek. "Well, well! Here we are, are we? So you're going to take that son of mine in charge, young lady? I wish you luck with him. He needs a heavy hand—a heavy hand."

"Now, Poppa," warned his spouse (she always addressed him either as "Poppa" or as "R.S."—his name being Richard Smith Wyatt). "Our son went to Harvard," continued the fond mother, turning to Theodora, "and the stylish young men at Harvard are never very quiet I guess. Poppa's getting old. He forgets he was young once."

"I was never too young to work," he announced. "I went to work when I was twelve, Miss, and I ain't ashamed of it."

"I think it was splendid," agreed Theodora. Then rather shyly, "And you're going to call me Theodora, aren't you?"

Two men-servants had been busying themselves over a tea table in the rear of the room; one of them now approached Theodora with a tray. Just as she served herself, a young woman in riding clothes entered and was introduced as Miss Marguerite Wyatt. Acknowledging the presence of her future sister-in-law with the barest of nods, the daughter of the house walked to the table and elected to try a cup of tea, as she had a "rotten headache." After one bare mouthful of the tea, she turned to her mother in disgust.

"That's the vilest dope I ever tasted," she remarked. "Where, in the name of all that's holy, did you pick it up?"

"It ought to be all right," contended Mrs. Wyatt. "It costs seven dollars a pound, and it's exactly what Mrs. Hamilton Woods always uses."

At this, Marguerite honored Theodora with her first direct remark. "We don't know Mrs. Hamilton Woods," she said, "but we know all about her tea."

"Oh, cut it out, Midge," said her brother. "Theodora's going to hear enough wrangles in this house without starting in before she's been here a half hour."

Theodora was glad when the time came for her to go to her room and rest for the approaching festivity. She felt depressed, and as the guest of honor she would naturally be expected to sparkle.

No sooner was she safely shut in the luxurious suite appointed to her use than Mrs. Wyatt turned to her son. "She's lovely, Gerald," she said. "I wasn't expecting such a beauty. But that was certainly an awful suit she had on. It couldn't have cost a cent over thirty dollars. I do hope she's got something better for tonight. The Arments are coming and it's the first time I've ever been able to get them. Mrs. Arment's such a dresser, and she always notices clothes so much—"

"And she looks like a cook, out on a holiday," interrupted Gerald hotly. "And so will all of the rest of your guests when they get near Theodora. Can't you see what she is?"

"Well, of course, Gerald."

"What more do you want, then? When Theodora is my wife, she'll dress with the best of them. In the meantime she has what all the money in the world can't buy. She makes Midge look like a barmaid."

"Now, Gerald, your sister has a style of her own. You know Count Petrezelli always said so. I don't think it's nice to talk that way about your own family."

"Who began it, I'd like to know? I never come into this house for as much as an hour, without running into a row. I'll be glad enough to get a home of my own."

Tears brimmed into his mother's eyes. She really adored this good-looking son of hers; but her life was so harassed with ambition, and the rungs of the social ladder proved disappointingly slippery, that she was always tired, generally fearful, and often unhappy. Like most of the unhappiness in the world, Mrs. Wyatts came from kicking against life's thorns—fighting age, fighting fat, fighting facts, fighting snubs.

"Theodora is very handsome, certainly," she now said, and Gerald softened instantly. He really had a very charming disposition—which is by no means the same as saying that he had a charming character. His sister reversed this order; her character was far better than her disposition.

"Theodora could dress in calico," exclaimed Gerald, "and still go anywhere, believe me!"

Mr. Wyatt, senior, having just returned to the room, now put in a word.

"Yes," he said. "And she'll bear fine children. I'll bet she won't sidestep her duties in that line, either."

All of which comforted Mrs. Wyatt no little!

As the dinner guests gathered, it was obvious that Theodora was in a class apart. Mrs. Wyatt wore a gown that had come from Paquin, and cost six hundred dollars. In fact, before the evening ended Theodora knew the maker and the price of nearly every costume in the room. The information was always dropped as a negligible aside. Marguerite wore a sheath-like flame-colored gown with a big green parrot perched on one shoulder. Her sleek dark hair lay so close as to look as though it had been painted on her skull, and huge gold hoops swung from the lobes of her invisible ears.

Theodora was forced to admit that Marguerite understood her own style. Conventionally garbed, she would have been merely a homely and unnoticeable woman; in these clothes, she looked like a tailor's correct model.

Theodora was introduced, not only as the coming daughter of the house, but as the intimate of the Neilson-Duncan set. Over and over were her references given, as the guests gathered.

The dinner and the service were elaborate and expensive. Mr. Wyatt, rising to propose a toast to the coming generation of Wyatts, was silenced by his spouse. In spite of the cut of her gowns—a concession to the demands of the fashion—Mrs. Wyatt was an essentially modest woman. She was kept on the constant alert to intercept the jokes of her husband and the frank remarks of her daughter—neither of whom could have been accused of over-modesty.

All the women wore startling *décolletages*; they were too new to the world of fashion to dare to assert their own opinions in the face of the names of the great Parisian fashion designers—and their husbands were too well trained to object.

The dinner went off brilliantly, as did the remainder of Theodora's three-days visit. She had never before had so much gaiety squeezed into so little time. Before she left, there arose the question of her accompanying the Wyatts to Palm Beach in February. "We're going in a private car," said Mrs. Wyatt. "You really must come, my dear. We won't take no for an answer."

"Dear Mrs. Wyatt," cried the girl, "it is simply sweet of you to want me! I'd love to go, of course; but I really couldn't leave my mother for so long a time. Since her sickness, she depends particularly upon me."

"She shall come too. One more in the car won't crowd us."

"Oh, that's lovely of you; but she really couldn't." Not only did Theodora realize that her mother's limited wardrobe would never warrant the trip, she knew how unhappy Mrs. Winthrop would be under the circumstances. Indeed, with each passing hour, she grew increasing worried about the blend of the two households. "It is all very well," thought the wise Theodora, "to say that one marries an individual, and not a family. As a matter of fact, it can't be done. One must marry family standards, and family traits, and family blood." Indeed, as Theodora turned the matter over in her mind, marriage appeared to have as many sides as a well-cut diamond, and as many pitfalls as a lawsuit.

But when the girl returned home with her invitation, her mother insisted on acceptance. "It is only right," she said, "and I am quite well again. A month will soon fly away. It will be your first chance at real pleasure, for last year you were working, and had none of the dances and gaieties that are the natural right of young things like you."

Theodora could hardly explain that last winter would probably outrank this one; so she wrote to Mrs. Wyatt accepting the invitation, and thereby plunged herself into another immediate discussion. Her future mother-in-law insisted on presenting her with an elaborate outfit for the trip. In this, however, she was instantly overruled—to her great disappointment. Theodora set to work immediately to fashion the simple costumes she would take—linen skirts and blouses for the morning, two more frocks for the evening, some self-trimmed hats, and a wrap manufactured out of an old paisley shawl.

One day in late January, she and her fiancé were sitting in the library of the old Waverly house talking over the coming trip. Gerald had just said that he must be going when a little car drove up to the door, and Elise got out.

"By Jove," said the man, "who is that beauty coming in here?"

Theodora crossed to his side. "That is my cousin Elise," she answered. "Mrs. Sewall, you know."

"Not the one who's just had a baby?"

"Yes. The baby's over a month old now."

"Why, she looks like a schoolgirl."

"She's two years older than I," responded Theodora, and at that moment Elise entered and Gerald was presented.

He stayed as long as she did, which was after dark. Then he insisted on driving her home in his closed car, leaving hers for her husband to fetch later. But when Theodora next saw Gerald, he never as much as mentioned Elise; so she supposed that he had had the good sense to be disappointed on closer acquaintance.

Some few days later, she was expecting him again; but as she sat waiting, a boy came running up from the station with a telegram. (The Waverly house did not afford a telephone, to the great disgust of Theodora's fiancé. Like many another, he didn't mind the stigma of poverty, but he heartily detested its inconveniences.)

The telegram was from him. To his disappointment he found himself prevented by business from leaving town that afternoon, but he would certainly see Theodora on the morrow. So, remembering that Meta had some wine jelly to be carried over to Elise's, Theodora offered her services for the errand.

She took a long walk first, and was stopped by a poor woman who had a sick baby. Seeing Theodora pass her door, Mrs. McCarty sent a scurrying child after her. "If ye do be passin' by Dr. Sewall's, Miss Theodora dear," said the anxious mother, "would ye be askin' him to stop in before night? I'd sleep easier like, if he seen the baby."

Theodora promised. At the Sewalls' house, she followed her custom and walked in without ringing. Immediately, she heard her cousin Elise's voice in the library. Theodora, unwilling listener though she was, distinctly heard those mocking tones of

Elise's, saying: "Poor dear Theodora! She *is* so terribly down-right, isn't she?"

"Dr. Sewall must be at home," thought Theodora, and gave a little call to announce herself. Following her own voice, she walked into the library. There sat Elise on a deep sofa near the fire, and there—rising with a haste which failed to hide the fact that he had been sitting excessively near her—stood Gerald Wyatt.

⚜XIV⚜

hey got out of it really very neatly.

"Bless my soul, here she is now," cried Gerald, after a pause which, although a trifle too long for natural-ness, was still marvellously short considering the amount of thinking he had to do. "I was just coming over, dear. I jostled my old business around and beat it after my telegram. That's the beauty of having no telephone in the house; you see, I couldn't let you know." For once in his life, Gerald Wyatt blessed this absence of telephone. He was growing almost jovial as he found how well his story hung together.

"Yes," Elise's voice took up the dialogue, "and on the way Mr. Wyatt did an act of mercy. I was trying my first walk and I found I had attempted too much. So, seeing a car coming, I waved for it to stop—with never an idea who was in it. To my great delight, I found it was my future cousin—and if I couldn't ask a favor of my own relation, who could I ask it of?"

"So I just stopped in for a moment," Gerald resumed, "and I was making my adieu when I heard your voice."

"Mr. Wyatt had just said," (this from Elise), "'Won't she be surprised to find me here!' And I had answered, 'She'll never understand it. Poor dear Theodora! She *is* so terribly down-right, isn't she?' when you appeared in the doorway."

She had actually the aplomb to repeat, not only her own words, but her own accent and intonation. There she sat in slippers and house-frock, with no hat nor wraps (nor was there sign of any such in the room), and looked at Theodora with the eyes of a baby.

"Is Dr. Sewall home?" asked Theodora rather heavily. "As I passed poor Mrs. McCarty's door she begged me to send him over if I could. Her baby's sick again."

"No, he isn't home," replied Elise with exaggerated regret—delighted that the conversation was taking a new turn. "He's away for the entire day. Isn't that a shame? It hardly ever happens, as you know. But this is the day of his monthly visit to the Upland Hospital; he won't be back till late tonight. Mrs. McCarty should have remembered that. He always goes the last Friday in the month."

"I don't suppose she could choose the time for her baby to fall ill," said Theodora dryly. "Here's some jelly Meta sent over. I must be getting back."

"Wait till I call the car," cried Gerald.

"Don't bother," answered the girl without looking at him. "I'd rather walk."

"Then we'll walk, of course."

"You needn't come," Theodora told him. "I have an errand to do."

But he followed her out, with merely a backward nod to Elise. For some distance they walked—Theodora maintaining a stony silence, her companion chatting lightly on all sorts of subjects. Finally, realizing that he couldn't carry off the situation as easily as he had hoped, Gerald changed his tactics. Stopping dead in his tracks, he faced the girl—blocking her further passage.

"Look here," he said, "I want to know exactly what is the matter with you. Answer me, please." For Theodora showed signs of still evading the issue.

"I think you know," she finally replied.

"I most sincerely hope that I don't. It would grieve me greatly to find that you were a very different girl from the one I took you to be—that you were so jealous, so suspicious, as to fly into a tantrum merely because I happened to spend ten minutes with your own cousin, whom I have met at your own house, and to whom I had just rendered a trifling service. And she, a married woman, at that!"

"Gerald," said the girl unhappily, "you can't expect me to believe that tale—"

"What tale? I most certainly *do* expect you to believe what I tell you. What is there so incredible in it? Didn't Mrs. Sewall say exactly the same thing?"

"That wouldn't convince me."

"Let that go, then. You know your cousin better than I do. But when it comes to refusing to take my word for a thing, I call it mighty rough. A nice outlook that makes for the future!"

"There doesn't have to be any future."

"What do you mean?"

"I mean there doesn't have to be any joint future for us—"

"Theodora," cried the man sharply, "are you crazy? No girl in her senses would be so stubborn over a mere trifle."

"Gerald, it isn't a trifle. Look at my side of the case. You broke an engagement with me—"

"Which I was rushing to resume, thanks to my eagerness to see you. Can't a man ever change his mind, or his plans?"

"But—oh, Gerald, there are so many things."

"Let me hear them, please. That, at least, is my right. You can't condemn a fellow unheard."

The girl's pride made it very difficult for her to state her charges. "Well," she said at length, "how could Elise have been walking in those clothes—slippers, and tea-gown, and so on?"

"So that's the trouble is it? She ran up to change the moment we got in."

"But you said you'd only just arrived."

"Which was perfectly true. I don't think it was two minutes before she was back again. Probably she had worn that frock under her coat. She ran up, begging me to wait for her just a moment, and I could hardly refuse. When she came back I found that she wanted to give me tea—as a sort of hospitable reward, I suppose. I had just declined it when we heard your voice. Are you sufficiently convinced now?"

Theodora did not answer.

"Are you?" demanded the man.

She shook her head.

"Then for heaven's sake, let's have the balance of your remarkable charges."

"I think it is strange," she said, and her voice trembled a little, "that this should have happened on the one day in the month when Dr. Sewall is away."

"What in the name of all that's holy has that got to do with it? Except that Mrs. Sewall would probably never have attempted that walk if he had been home—as I wish to heaven he had been."

"And your position when I came in—"

"My position?"

"Yes—where you were sitting."

"I was sitting where any man would have been sitting—on the far end of the divan."

"Oh, well," said the girl wearily, "let's stop talking about it."

But Gerald wouldn't. And the longer he talked the more absurd he made Theodora's stand appear. She consented eventually to give him the benefit of the doubt—thereby making her first great mistake. While appearances may sometimes prove deceptive, generally speaking, the first time that an honest woman feels convinced that her beau is lying to her, she would be wise to end the relationship—if it is not already too late. To be over-generous is merely to defer catastrophe.

This first mishap with Gerald worried Theodora not a little; but having promised to try to believe him, she did her best to put the matter from her mind. Everything mitigated in favor of her fiancé, who was himself more charming and tactful than she had ever before known him. Had Theodora stopped at home alone and cogitated over the matter, she would probably have broken her engagement. Caught in the mesh of the modern whirligig, she was largely aided to forgetfulness and forgiveness.

❧❧❧ ❧❧❧ ❧❧❧

The Wyatt party reached Palm Beach in the middle of their second night of travel, but they elected to remain on their car until morning. Mrs. Wyatt spoke confidentially to Theodora on the subject. As she sensibly put the matter, why get off a private car in the middle of the night with no one to see? In the morning there was a likelihood of the hotel verandahs full of guests, and the debarkation could be made with some degree of grand display.

Ever since finding that she was to return to Florida, Theodora had thought a great deal about the man who had so enhanced the pleasure of her first visit there. Would Alan come back this winter? Had he gone to the Border last summer with the troops? Was he married yet? He might be at Palm Beach on his wedding trip. In that case, she'd probably see little or nothing of him.

Mrs. Wyatt must have been bitterly disappointed about the arrival. There were very few guests on the verandah, no one bowed, and no one showed any signs of being impressed. The newcomers went straight to their rooms and ordered breakfast trays sent up. After refreshing themselves, they planned to rest till noon, then appear in all their glory at the morning concert.

Theodora, however, found she couldn't wait. After a bite and a bath and a change into summer apparel, she hurried downstairs and out of doors to greet again the wonderland that she loved. Before she had gone a dozen steps along the palm-shaded avenue, she heard herself hailed.

"Mais—Mademoiselle!—Mademoiselle vient donc d'arriver?" And then two little black noses were sniffing around her ankles, four snowy white paws were clawing wildly at her gown, and a pair of intelligent poodles were threatening to go into apoplexy over this fortunate encounter with an old friend. Louise stood smiling a welcome and trying to restrain the warmth of the canine overtures.

"How they know you, Mademoiselle! Down then, Blanchette; down Poilu! Have you no manners?"

Greetings and inquiries followed. Theodora found that Mrs. Stuyvesant had arrived a week previously and that she was "much the same as formerly." Then Louise asked discreetly whether Miss Winthrop was "with another lady."

"No," smiled Theodora. "I'm here with my fiancé's family, Louise."

This elicited a torrent of congratulations and questions. Louise managed to get an excellent view of Theodora's superb engagement ring, and her conclusions were not hard to draw.

An hour later she came on the porch seeking Theodora, whom she found awaiting the arrival of her party. Mrs. Stuyvesant begged that Mademoiselle would come to her apartment; she was impatient to greet Mademoiselle at once.

"Well, my very dear Miss Winthrop," cried the old lady— quite as though she and Theodora had parted the previous week, and without the shadow of a misunderstanding—"what a great pleasure to see you again! And what is this wonderful and delightful tale that Louise has been telling me? You have decided to take my advice, and do the only sensible thing? And pray, why didn't you write me the good news? I feel very much hurt."

"I didn't know you'd be interested," answered Theodora. Stooping, she printed a light kiss on the cheek offered to receive it. There was certainly a look of pleasure in Mrs. Stuyvesant's keen old eyes, and she retained the girl's hand much longer than a mere greeting demanded.

"Then, my dear," she answered with all her old vigor, "if you didn't know that I'd be interested in news of that sort, and concerning you, you are much less intelligent than I supposed. Tell me all about it."

Theodora obeyed.

"Is your fiancé here with you?" was Mrs. Stuyvesant's next question. "He is? Then you must be sure to present him to me—and his family as well."

Theodora answered that she would be delighted. "They—" she began, and then stopped. "I shall love to," she repeated rather lamely. "My future sister-in-law is really very amusing. I think you'll enjoy her."

Mrs. Stuyvesant was an astute old worldling. Silence was often as enlightening to her as speech. "Where did you meet the young man?" she asked. "And by the way, what is his name?"

The girl explained the circumstances of the meeting. "But how romantic," cried the older woman. "You say that Mr. Wyatt's family have lived some time in Waverly, but that you had never met them?"

"No, we never had. They live there only in the summer, and the old residents of Waverly lead a very quiet life. They rarely call on newcomers. Then, too, these new people live in a style that Waverly could not afford. It makes two separate worlds— a quiet one and a gay one."

"I see. I'm sure your future parents-in-law are devoted to you?"

"They are kindness itself. Yes, I think they are fond of me."

"To be sure they are!" And Mrs. Stuyvesant had the history of the romance in a nutshell. She knew that the Wyatts were probably among the new wealth, that Theodora's circle had regarded them as outside the pale, and that they were delighted with the match as much on account of Theodora's birth as of her personal charm.

Theodora asked after Mrs. Delafield Beeckman and heard that she was well, and she learned that Miss Burrill was as busy as ever.

"Is Miss Burrill coming down this year?" she asked.

"No," replied Mrs. Stuyvesant. "Not this year." And somehow, the subject seemed to be marked as definitely closed. Theodora was longing to inquire for Alan Beeckman—both her other questions having been intended as leaders to that end—but she found herself unable to do it. She would be self-conscious, and the fact would never escape Mrs. Stuyvesant's notice.

Before luncheon, the various members of the Wyatt family were introduced to Mrs. Stuyvesant. She chatted pleasantly enough with them for a few moments—to Mrs. Wyatt's very great delight—but she studiously restricted her later intercourse

with them to smiling bows. With Theodora, however, she was
notably friendly, seeking her, sending for her, and inviting her
constantly for tea, Bridge, and chair-rides.

At first, the girl was tempted to attribute the change in her
attitude to snobbery, and to resent it as such; but she became
speedily convinced of the unfairness of such an explanation.
The older woman was too plainly pleased to have the girl near
her again, too genuinely anxious for her society. Theodora
finally ceased worrying over the matter, and accepted the situation simply and sweetly.

From Marjorie Gary Theodora eventually extracted the
information that Alan Beeckman had been with the troops on
the Border, and that he had returned. Marjorie didn't know
whether he planned to come down or not. She hardly thought
so, for Helen Burrill was abroad.

"Abroad?" echoed Theodora.

"Yes. She has gone to England to work among the blinded
soldiers. Isn't it perfectly splendid? But it's just like Helen. She
is so good!"

"But what about her engagement?" Theodora was suddenly
terribly interested in the handle of her parasol.

"Her engagement? Oh, to Alan, you mean. Are they really
engaged? It has never been announced."

"Mr. Van Rensselaer Beeckman told me they were."

"Yes, I suppose they are. I know that they're always together,
and have been for years. As to that, I suppose Alan hopes to be
over there himself very soon. All the men do. You know they
say we will positively be in the war by spring. But, oh,
Theodora, it frightens me to death when Ned says he is going.
I couldn't keep him, I suppose, even if I wanted to. But he positively shall not go without me. We'll be married, and I'll go too.

And I suppose you have the same worry? Mr. Wyatt is probably making the same plans?"

Theodora felt suddenly ashamed. Nothing would have induced her to admit that she had never heard Gerald voluntarily mention the war. Gerald Wyatt was excessively proud of his fiancée, but he was also excessively fond of himself, and of what he considered a good time. And for his sort of good time, Palm Beach offered almost unlimited opportunity. He would have vowed hotly that he gave Theodora all the attention that any engaged girl had any right to expect or demand. Yet she missed something. She didn't receive from him anything that struck her as being devotion.

As a matter of fact, having caught his car, he saw no further necessity of running for it. Moreover, one didn't travel the length of the United States in order to sit exclusively beside the girl that one could see at home. Neither did one pose as a monk in a place which, as far as opportunities for amusement were concerned, was second only to Paris.

Marguerite, on the other hand, warmed toward Theodora as the days went by. She fell into the habit of wandering into Theodora's room for odd quarter-hours of chat. Wrapped in the weirdest of dressing-gowns, Marguerite might have posed as model to some futurist artist. Her conversation was apt to be as startling as her appearance. "You know," she would say frankly, "you're a great deal too good for Gerald, and you ought to realize it. The Lord knows, he's no saint. I only hope he'll give you a square deal, but I don't think there's much chance. . . . If you were the sort of girl who would marry for money, I wouldn't give a hurrah what you got handed out to you. But you're not. You really love Gerald, I suppose?"

"I should never marry him if I didn't," evaded Theodora.

"That's what I thought. Is this your first love affair?"

"Yes. I've known very few men."

"Exactly. Now see here—don't think I'm a brute, but do you by any chance imagine that you are Gerald's first flame?"

"I never thought about it. No, I suppose I'm not."

"You bet you're not. And you don't mind?"

"How could I mind what happened before he ever saw me—unless it were something very terrible."

"And if it were?"

"Then I think I should be told."

"But you'd hate the person that told you?"

"Not necessarily."

"Well, suppose again that it was not anything very 'terrible' according to the standards by which the world judges a man's life—merely a long line of the sort of thing a fast fellow goes through?"

"Why, I don't know. What do you mean, Marguerite?"

> "Most women are content to be a man's last flame, even if they can't be his first. How would you feel if you weren't even that?"

"Most women are content to be a man's last flame, even if they can't be his first. How would you feel if you weren't even that?"

"I don't understand you."

"I mean how would you feel about your husband having affairs with other women, right under your nose?"

"I wouldn't stand it of course. If I knew it was true, I'd leave him."

"Yet that is what most women find they have to put up with."

"I don't believe it," flamed Theodora hotly. "Excuse me, Marguerite. I know that you think that sort of thing is universally true, but I most certainly do not. Some men are bad, I know, and some women have to suffer for it, but not most. What would women marry for, if only to be cast aside and insulted?"

"Bosh! You can't teach me anything about life, Theodora. I'm thirty—I'm older than Gerald, you know. I've seen most of my schoolmates marry. Without exception, they tell me the same tale of faithless husbands—or someone else tells it for them. In my set, the women accept the fact that their husbands will amuse themselves with other women, after a time. Some of the women claim equal privileges, some merely put up with a thing they know they can't help, and others pull out. They have their choice of those three courses."

Theodora didn't and wouldn't believe it. "That must be only in a certain set," she contended.

"Possibly. It's the set you're about to marry into, however. Let me tell you, Theodora, if things of that sort are going to worry you, you'd better shake the whole thing before it is too late. If you think you can stand marriage as it is—or as it surely will be with a man like Gerald—then you're all right. But for heaven's sake, don't shut your eyes to the truth."

"Marguerite," said Theodora with sudden vehemence, "I know you think all this is true, but I'd rather die than believe it. I'm sure such things are a woman's fault more often than not. If she's willing to condone them, she'll surely have them to condone. But if she'd never stand them for a second, if she makes her husband realize this, and if he really loves her, I should certainly think he'd behave himself. And if he didn't love her, why did he choose her? If a woman can stick to one man, why can't a man stick to one woman?"

The moment she had said this she was comforted. It sounded so sane, it must be true.

Marguerite rose to go, and then paused. "Did anyone ever tell you of my other brother?" she asked. "My mother's oldest child?"

Theodora shook her head.

"He died of paresis in an asylum. It was the result of dissipation. Well, good bye. If I stay any longer we'll both be late."

Marguerite Wyatt went to her room convinced that she had done a kindly act in a clever way, yet uncertain as to the result. For few persons would she have taken the trouble that she had just taken for Theodora. Marguerite held no doubts as to her estimate of her brother. But had she helped matters any? That was a question that troubled her.

That same evening the entire Wyatt party were sitting together listening to the after-dinner concert. A bellboy came from the desk carrying the mail which had just been sorted, and handed the family pile to Gerald, who happened to be sitting on the end of the line. Fumbling in his pocket for a coin, Gerald dropped the top letter to the floor. He stooped to regain it, and Theodora held out her hand.

"That is mine I know," she said. "It is one of Elise's rare letters. No one could fail to recognize her violet stationery and her dashing hand."

Gerald glanced at the letter, then put it in his pocket. "You're a very poor guesser," he said blandly. "That letter is mine, and it's from a woman you never saw. She is the wife of one of my college chums. They've struck hard luck and I've been making some investments for them. Let's pull out of this and get over to the Club. It's slower here than molasses in winter."

At the Club there was of course no chance for a confidential talk. Theodora watched her fiancé curiously as he took his place at one of the roulette tables. He played habitually, rather heavily, and in fairly good luck. If he had lied about that letter—and Theodora could not doubt it, for added to the evidence of her eyes was that of her cousin's favorite sachet—then he was the most practiced and consummate liar that she had ever met.

She kept thinking it over. The girl well knew that no matter what she might say, Gerald would smoothly deny. She could prove nothing. But she did decide the moment she got the chance, she would say, "Look here, Gerald, unless there can be frankness and honesty between us, I'm certainly not satisfied to go on with my engagement." She would then be exactly where she was that afternoon when she found him sitting with her cousin. Exactly. And unless she broke her engagement, she'd probably be there many times again in her life.

The next morning, Theodora decided to take her breakfast downstairs alone. She used her time in planning her greeting to Gerald when he should finally appear. After breakfast she wandered onto the porch; and there, something happened that drove the subject of letters from her mind for the time being. Mrs. Stuyvesant was out earlier than usual, and she was sitting in conversation with a man—a young man whose back was turned to the passers-by. At the old lady's bow he looked around, and then sprang to his feet and held out his hand to Theodora. It was Alan Beeckman.

"Come here, my dear," cried Mrs. Stuyvesant. "Sit with us a bit and give my nephew a chance to offer his good wishes. I've been telling him about your engagement. Doesn't he look well after his months on the Border?"

They talked quite awhile before Theodora moved on. Alan noted her direction and presently followed her. This gave them a short *tête-à-tête* before any member of the Wyatt family appeared. Theodora was conscious of a lightness and a happiness which she explained to herself by the fact that this man belonged to a life which she herself had regretted ever leaving.

Nowhere had she met as many interesting people, or heard as much interesting conversation, as under Mrs. Stuyvesant's roof. Was it not natural that she should since have missed such opportunities?

Gerald finally appeared and was introduced. The greetings of the two men were ordinary, yet Theodora was conscious of a certain aggressiveness on Gerald's part, a certain surprise on Alan's, a certain apologetic attitude on her own.

Together the three strolled to the beach, and went in for a swim by the dock. Theodora looked lovely in—and out of—the water and her fiancé was ordinarily very proud of the fact. But today, he seemed anxious to curtail the bath. He found the water chilly, and insisted that Theodora was in danger of taking cold. He was fractious and critical the balance of the morning. Only too well did Theodora know that that was no time to discuss the letter.

Soon, Palm Beach was Alan Beeckman to the girl. She didn't realize the fact herself, as yet. She merely ranked him as the most attractive, and the most congenial, of her friends. But she never opened her eyes in the morning without wondering how soon she should see him, never a chat did they have that didn't seem all too short, never a word did he say that she didn't remember and rehearse. Although she never forgot for a moment that she was the betrothed of another man, although every word of their conversation might have been overheard by all the world, the fact remained that a distinct warm friendship sprang up.

On the other hand, the friction between Gerald and Alan grew. Gerald was terribly quarrelsome these days, anyhow. His mother explained it by saying that he wasn't sleeping well; she'd have come nearer the truth if she'd said that he wasn't sleeping at all—except for naps between dawn and nine in the morning.

Gerald Wyatt thought that Palm Beach nights were too good to waste in sleep.

One morning he and Theodora happened to be alone, a rare thing of late. That in itself puzzled the girl. Under normal conditions, Gerald should certainly have wanted to be alone with her; had he wanted to, he could easily have accomplished it. She was glad of her freedom, but she couldn't understand it.

"Gerald," she said this morning, "Mr. Beeckman predicts that we'll be in the war in another month or two. Will you go?"

"Beeckman's an idiot," answered Gerald irritably.

"But would you go?" persisted the girl.

"Good Lord, Theodora, how you shoot questions at a fellow! No one can cross a bridge until he comes to it. . . . Of course I'd go, if other chaps did."

"But what difference would that make?" demanded the unwise Theodora. "Wouldn't you choose for yourself?"

"I suppose it would be little loss to you," replied the charming Gerald, "to have me blind, and armless, and legless. That's about the point of view of the ordinary hysterical female—provided she herself sits safe!"

At that very moment, Alan Beeckman joined them. Coming from behind them while they talked, Theodora was almost sure he had overheard Gerald's last speech. Thinking to make light of it, she asked laughingly: "Mr. Beeckman, would you call me an ordinary hysterical female?"

Under the circumstances it wasn't a very clever thing to do, but she was surprised at the sudden look of wrath that leaped to Gerald's eyes. Without giving Beeckman a chance to reply, he said levelly: "Mr. Beeckman's opinion of you is not vital to me, Theodora—unless, indeed, he knows you better than I've been privileged to, which I hope is not the case."

The girl looked as though she had been struck. Beeckman, who had just sat down, sprang to his feet. The hot color surged into his face, and his lips almost formed the word "cur." Then, without as much as glancing at Gerald, he looked straight into Theodora's eyes and said: "Are you bathing this morning, Miss Winthrop? Yes? Then I'll see you at the beach." And he raised his hat and walked off.

Somehow, the look that she caught on his face as he turned away became one of Theodora's most precious memories. Naturally, neither she nor Beeckman ever referred to the incident, although they came soon to have more and more time together. Gerald's temporary vigilance and aggressive proprietorship speedily relaxed; there were other fish to fry. A certain little vaudeville actress appeared upon the scene and immediately became the pursued of all masculine pursuers.

Theodora was not a little astounded at the frankness with which she was discussed. One heard the name of the man who had given her her pearls, of the one who was paying her present bills, of the other with whom she had been stopping in Paris when the war broke out, and so on, indefinitely. She was as pretty as a nymph, and apparently as soulless. Whenever and wherever she appeared, she was the immediate center of attention.

Very early in the game, she began to bestow some of her choicest smiles on Gerald Wyatt. He couldn't, of course, notice her when Theodora was near; but there came to be more and more times when Theodora was not near—or rather, when he was not near Theodora. The girl to whom he was engaged would naturally be the last to hear gossip about him—thanks to the perverted blindfolding system so decried by Marguerite. She was the one who finally cut the knot of silence.

"Theodora," she said, "if I were you, I'd get Gerald out of this place in double-quick time. It's simply scandalous for him to be

Proper Relations
for Engaged Couples

When a couple is engaged to be married, neither man nor woman should assume a masterful or jealous attitude toward the other. They are neither of them to be shut up away from the rest of the world, but must mingle with society. The fact that they have confessed their love to each other ought to be deemed a sufficient guarantee of faithfulness; for the rest let there be trust and confidence.

Nevertheless, a young man has no right to put a slight upon his future bride by appearing in public with other ladies while she remains neglected at home. He is in future her legitimate escort. He should attend no other lady when she needs his services; she should accept no other escort when he is at liberty to attend her.

—Etiquette for Ladies and Gentleman, 1877

acting as he is, right under your nose. It might be all very well for a man without ties; but for one in Gerald's position, it's insulting and disgusting."

"What are you talking about, Marguerite?" asked Theodora rather wearily.

"I'm talking about Gerald and that little cat of an actress—and so is everyone else in the place but you. He's rushing her till it's the scandal of the season. I'll bet you're the only person here who doesn't know of the affair."

"And what do you think I should do?"

"Make a row and get the family to start home at once. I'll back you. I'd do it myself, only it's none of my business, if you don't care. But 'don't know' and 'don't care' are two very different things. We're going in a week anyhow; just make them hustle it up a bit."

"I couldn't make a fuss, Marguerite. I don't believe I could make you understand how much I hate to discuss my private affairs with anyone; I'd rather just speak to Gerald and tell him what I've heard, if you really think it's necessary. But I can assure you I'd be very sorry to believe half the things I hear here."

"Bosh, Theodora! Don't be a fool. Take my word for it, you'd better believe this. And you'll be wise to speak to Gerald—or to someone. It's high time somebody did some talking."

Theodora accordingly spoke to Gerald, but she merely succeeded in driving him into a fury. He denied everything, and demanded to know "what cat had been talking." Theodora's greatest surprise in the whole affair was not Gerald's attitude—but her own. She seemed to be getting callous, so little did the report really affect her.

"I've had too much of this sort of life," she said to herself. "I'm getting hardened, like the rest of them. It will be good to get out of it all, and into a quieter, cleaner atmosphere. When I'm home again, I'm going to thresh out a lot of things, all by myself."

But in spite of his temper, the warning had a salutary effect on Gerald. He was still as anxious as ever to have Theodora for his wife. And when he saw himself in danger of losing her, he was wise enough to pull up. He became quite charming and devoted again—thus redoubling the problems of Theodora.

CHAPTER

☙XV☙

he trip home was an anticlimax. But one great piece of
good fortune (from Theodora's point of view) awaited
their return. A telegram called Gerald to Chicago,
where he was to be best man at the wedding of a college chum.
The wedding was being hurried on account of the gathering
war-clouds which everyone knew must soon break; America
could no longer avoid entrance into the World War. The wedding, however, was not to be weighted by sorrow; and Gerald's
presence was indispensable. It would be hard to say if the summons was a greater relief to Gerald, or his fiancée.

And so at last, Theodora had the chance to thresh out all her
problems unhampered, and she used it to advantage. Her
thinking time was night; she was sure then not to be interrupted. Through the days, one half of her was the girl who
chatted with the family, answered questions about her trip, read
aloud to her mother, helped with the familiar household tasks.
The other half was thinking subconsciously, "When Gerald
comes back, I'll have to tell him, and them. I wish I'd done it
before he went." Thus, through the days she admitted the facts;
but at night she admitted the reasons.

There was but one thing that she could tell Gerald: that the
love which he had promised had failed to come, and that

without it she could not marry. It would be vain to plead her constantly increasing distrust, to paint the picture she was coming to have of what married life with him would be, to discuss the incompatibility of standards in the two families. There remained but one valid objection which he could not dispute. And though he might rage, he could not force.

. . . a romantic woman would have thrilled to the thought, "At last, true love has found me!"

It would have been enough that Theodora did not love the man she had promised to marry, but it was as nothing compared with the flood of certainty that at last surged through her heart that she did love another man—and a man, at that, who had never even mentioned love nor marriage to her, and who was himself engaged to another woman. Theodora knew now what had been the nature of that vague and lovely thing that had entered her heart a year ago—it had been the first tender shoot of the exquisite plant called Love. Its fragrance had permeated her days, making the past inconsequential, the present rose-hued, and the future golden-bright.

And then, before she had as much as grasped the meaning of this new feel of life, along had come the tempest— uprooting her little plant and leaving it to wither.

It had been the haunting memory that there existed such things as love and its wonderful perfume, that had made Theodora first fear to engage herself to Gerald. All through her affair with him, her heart had beat so sanely, her pulses had lain so quiet, her poise had been so normal. There had been none of that foolish certainty that *something* was about to glorify life, and that nothing really mattered, except that one was alive and young and not too unattractive. There had never existed that wonderful feeling that right around the next corner one would suddenly catch up with perpetual bliss.

An experienced woman would instantly have recognized the symptoms that had made Theodora wonder; a cynical woman would have said to herself, "Here's another swoon. Now I shall be restless and unhappily happy till it's over"; a romantic woman would have thrilled to the thought, "At last, true love has found me!" Poor dear Theodora, being neither experienced, nor cynical, nor especially romantic, had no clue to her mystery.

But now, at last, she faced the truth. She made her bitter self-confession. She *loved* a man who *liked* her. And that is tragedy. She knew that Alan was her friend, she knew that he was fond of her; but that was less than enough. The fact remained that he was the betrothed of another woman. It seemed strange that the engagement should never have been announced, and that the marriage should have been so long delayed—and that Helen Burrill should have gone to England alone. In any case, Theodora's own position remained unchanged—she had given her love unasked and unsought. Poor dear Theodora, with her pride and her sensitiveness, and her inability to extract comfort from self-deception or tears!

To her joy, Gerald's stay was greatly lengthened. He visited one friend after another, and long before he returned, America was at war. Private quarrels lost importance in the face of all that came to pass.

Dear old Ned enlisted at once; he wouldn't even wait for Plattsburg and a possible commission. He wanted to get "over there" as quickly as possible. He could have stayed at Yale and trained in the artillery; he could have enlisted in that vague branch of the service known as the naval reserves (immediately so overcrowded with applications), and so have deferred his going indefinitely; he could have chosen the air service and the probability of an instructorship; and he had his girl as an excuse. But his one idea was to get into the trenches and avenge his country's honor.

Mrs. Charrington was simply splendid. Ned was the apple of her eye, but she had no thought of holding him back. She tolerated no tears—at any rate, no public ones—and asked for no sympathy. Theodora, watching admiringly, realized that the same sternness which used to make Aunt Augusta so unapproachable, was now showing its reverse side of magnificent strength. Had she been softer, she would have been more lovable; but she couldn't have been finer.

Gerald came home, and Theodora braced herself to her task. She broke the engagement on their first meeting, and it was even worse than she had expected. She had not made sufficient allowance for Gerald's vanity. He was furious. Theodora heard herself called a "jealous cat," a "common jilt," and a "fool." But she was firm, and the man finally left in a fit of temper, leaving the girl to break the news to her family.

Mrs. Winthrop said, "You know best, of course, my dear. I wouldn't have you marry a man you didn't love." But she plainly showed her disappointment. Having come to regard her daughter's future as splendidly assured, she was now thrown back to the old standpoint of worried uncertainty. Aunt Augusta merely said, "I'm very glad to hear it. That is the best news I've had in some time." Whatever other fault might be charged to Aunt Augusta, she was certainly consistent. Meta said, "Oh, Theodora! Really?"—which was about as much as one could expect of Meta.

But in the eyes of Elise when she came to hear the news, there shone a hard sort of triumph. "What happened?" she asked, holding one of her rings up to the light and watching the sparks of light its gems threw out.

"Nothing at all," answered Theodora coldly.

"How remarkable! I suppose you simply said, 'Well, good bye; I'm through'; and he said, 'All right; just as you please.'" (Elise was plainly feeling her way; mocking at everything, yet trying to elicit news.) "Did you give back his gifts?" she continued.

"Certainly. Do you think I should have kept them?"

"That, of course, is a matter of taste. And now I suppose that he's heartbroken and that he will fly away from Waverly again?" (So that was what she had been driving at! There *had* been something between them. The violet letter *was* from her, and Gerald had lied. Theodora had been sure of it, but here was proof. Oh, how glad she was, how glad, to be finally extricated from the falsehood and deceit!)

As Theodora's romance died, Ned's flowered into perfect life. He had been ordered to a camp, and his division would probably be one of the first to be sent overseas. In order to be near him while he stayed, and to follow him when he went (orders to the contrary not yet having been issued), Marjorie insisted on marrying him at once, and there became immediately apparent one of the first great effects of even an embryo war— its power to wipe out the false and conventional and to replace them with the elemental and the genuine. Marjorie Gary and Ned Charrington cried, "Do not separate us unnecessarily." And their elders responded fittingly, "Our children are right. We must give them their chance at life, even as we have had ours."

So Marjorie and Ned were married in a tiny church near his camp. The wedding was simple with only the nearest relatives present. Mrs. Charrington went over, and Elise (being the only other member of the family who could afford the trip) accompanied her. Oh, how Theodora longed to go—for many reasons! But it was out of the question.

Ned had already received his degree from college, and he was granted a three-days leave for his wedding trip. A bungalow near the camp was found for the little bride. When Ned went overseas, she was to follow immediately, and to do canteen work. And *this*, thought Theodora, was the spoiled and pampered Marjorie Gary!

During the absence of Elise at the wedding, Meta brought her little nephew home, the better to take care of him. Theodora was astounded at the temporary transformation in this meek and homely cousin of hers. With the baby entirely her own for the time being, Meta was a happy woman. Her voice cooed caressingly during bath hours and bottle times. She bustled smilingly about her household tasks, and the task of wheeling him through the shady village streets was sufficient to glorify her entire day.

"Do you know," said Theodora to her mother, "all that Meta needs in life is the shadow of happiness. If she could have that baby to keep, she'd never want another thing. I wish she could afford to adopt one!"

"Oh, my *dear*!" cried Mrs. Winthrop, "that would be a terrible risk! And it wouldn't be the same thing at all."

"No," admitted Theodora. "This baby is our own blood. And Meta was fond of his father before Elise got her clutches on him."

"My *child*!" exclaimed the shocked parent.

"Oh, Mother dear, for goodness sake don't be so timid. I only said what you thought. People discuss things nowadays, instead of swallowing them and choking on them. Just wait till I get you out into the world, and see what shocks you'll get!"

"I prefer the old way," insisted Mrs. Winthrop with gentle dignity.

"Well, I don't," responded the fearless Theodora.

"Poor child," thought the parent. "She has had much to bear. I must be patient with her."

"Poor mother," thought the daughter. "She's never had a chance. I must be patient with her."

Yet with all their consciousness of forbearance, each of these two burned to regulate the other's life—a sad mistake, no doubt, yet one which every human being insists on making at some time or another.

Aunt Augusta came home perfectly in love with her new daughter-in-law. Elise, on the contrary, didn't think her either pretty or attractive. From both of them Theodora tried to elicit the particular information that she wanted. But all that she could ascertain was that there had been but one Mr. Beeckman at the wedding, and he was addressed as "Van." He, by the way, was the only guest for whom Elise had a word of praise. With him, she seemed to have hit it off wonderfully.

As the days went on, and Theodora wrote to Ned and Marjorie, she asked them about Alan and his whereabouts. But the very detachment with which she self-consciously put her question, ended by defeating her purpose. Neither of them remembered to answer it. Just once, Marjorie referred to it. "Yes," she wrote, "dear old Alan is in the service, too." And that was all that Theodora ever heard. She couldn't very well write and say, "Won't you please make a point of telling him that my engagement is broken?" And even if she could, what good would it do? Her engagement wouldn't affect his.

Meta was absorbed in the baby. Ned was gone. Elise grew more detestable daily. Aunt Augusta had that trying kind of sadness that hotly resents comforting. Except for her mother's presence, there was nothing to make Waverly life bearable to Theodora. And her mother could not be moved unless money could be made.

Three or four days later, Marguerite's card was brought up. Theodora received it with trepidation, but as it turned out, Marguerite's visit was one of congratulation purely.

"You're well out of it, Theodora," she said. And in proof of her statement, she proceeded to make a series of the most startling revelations.

"Oh, Marguerite," cried Theodora, "don't tell me any more. These things can't matter to me now."

"I just want to show you that you've made no mistake. You'd have had a horrible life, believe me. Men, Theodora, have no hearts. Most women have none, either. But if you ever do happen to run into a heart, it will be sure to be a woman's. Men are bunches of selfishness and self-indulgence and passion and desire. That's all."

"Don't say such things," begged Theodora. "You think your father has a heart, don't you?"

"Indeed I don't; and neither would you if you knew the things he's done to make his pile. He'd knife his best friend in the back. He's done it."

"But his family?"

"Affections, perhaps; and pride and habit. That's about all. But if you want to see him show real feeling, just watch any one trying to get the better of him in a deal! Gerald and I inherit our coldness from him. Mother's weak and silly, but she really has a heart. By the way, Gerald is just adding one more to his list of charms. He's a slacker. His one thought at present is how to keep out of danger without making himself look cheap—a sort of 'what-can-I-do-to-be-saved' attitude! As I say, you're well out of it all. And what are you going to do now?"

"I wish I knew," replied Theodora.

"You're a brick," cried Marguerite unexpectedly. "To need money as much as you must, and to turn Gerald down! I bet I can help you find a job. You know, all this war work is going to give women chances at wonderful wages. One of my friends wrote me the other day that her former cook was getting forty dollars a week in one of the new factories, and that without brains or education. But you mustn't go into a factory. There are better things than that for an intelligent woman like you. The women's Motor Service will all be voluntary. So will most of the Red Cross work. You don't know stenography, of course?"

"Unfortunately not. I could learn it, but it takes so long."

"I'll tell you what wouldn't take long—a switchboard. I know a girl who is going to study that. The government will need telephone service, and they say if you are fluent in French you'll be able to get as much as thirty or thirty-five a week—"

"*Thirty-five!*"

"Yes. Would you take that?"

"Would I take it? It would be heaven. My mother and I could live on it, and have something to give away!"

Marguerite's shrewd eyes softened. "Well," she said brusquely (she prided herself on her lack of emotion), "if you could, you certainly deserve it. This girl's position was to be in New York—"

"Oh," interrupted Theodora breathlessly, "I'd *love* to get one there. I'd far rather be there than here."

"I think you're right. The field's bigger, and you ought to get in ahead of the rush. I'll write to my friend about you tonight. She's to take a three-week course at the switchboard for ten dollars, and then to step into this thirty-five-dollar job. If she didn't know French, she'd have to take ten dollars less. I bet you could get your training here in the city—you could go in each day—and then perhaps this friend of mine can find you a position in New York. She'll probably have some ideas about boarding-places, too. She's a Hartford girl, and her people have lost all their money."

"Marguerite," cried Theodora, "I can't thank you enough. It all sounds too lovely for words. How kind you are!"

"Nonsense, that's nothing! Look here, Theodora, I'm going to pay you the compliment of treating you like a sensible being. If you happen to be a little short, I wish you'd let me lend you something—just till you're on your feet, you know."

The tears were very near Theodora's eyes. "I have all I need," she said. "But thank you just the same. You are kindness itself. And you tell me that your mother has the only heart in the family?"

Marguerite colored as though she had been caught in some blunder.

"Nonsense," she said gruffly, "that's nothing. Any idiot would do as much for a pal!"

ne November morning Theodora sat in a New York office at her switchboard. The hands of the clock pointed to half-past nine. The door opened and a pretty painted girl, who didn't look more than nineteen, entered apprehensively. Her eyes flew to the clock and then to the manager's desk. A look of relief lightened them. The manager's chair was empty.

"Hasn't the boss been in yet?" she demanded. A dozen girls looked up from the nails they were manicuring so elaborately. "No," they answered. "He's late. Gee, M'ree, you're some lucky baby! Out last night?"

Marie (whose other name was Maginnis) nodded.

"That new fella?"

"Yep. Some spender, believe *me*! Say, girls, he wants to give me a ring. I don't know as I'll take it, though."

"No, you don't! A swell chance he's got! What kind of a ring?"

"Blue-white diamond. I was talking about that being the only kind I liked, and he said a pretty hand like mine ought to have one."

"What'd you wear?"

"My new black velvet."

"Seal coat?"

"Hm-hm."

"It ain't real, is it?"

"Real? Sure it's real."

"Well, Rosamund says you can't get a real seal under three hundred."

"You can't," put in Rosamund. "I was into Ganter's pricing them, and the man told me. Of course I don't know anything about the common places—only Fifth Avenue."

"You got your cheek with you, ain't you?" cried Marie, though without anger.

"Mine's real and it cost a hundred and eighty. And it didn't come from any cheap place either. I guess I know as much about refinement as you do, Rosamund Strauss! Say, girls, my fella's going to call me up about lunch. Whichever one of you get the message, keep it a secret and slip it to me quietly, will you?"

Marie had hardly taken her seat, adjusted her headband, and plugged herself in, when the door opened again and the manager entered breezily. Nail files and buffers were hastily bundled away, and every girl became absorbed in her work.

"Good morning, ladies." The manager's voice was as crisp and breezy as his manner.

"Good morning, Mr. Harmon."

"Everyone on time this morning?"

"Yes, sir."

"How about you, Miss Maginnis?"

Marie looked at him with limpid eyes. "I was here," she said simply.

"Glad to hear it. Ladies, I am receiving complaints as to private use of these wires. Now, I'm prepared to back this office against the world; but remember, if I catch any of you at that, it's good night nurse! You understand? Have any of you made private use of these wires?"

Denial was immediate, unanimous, and indignant.

"Very well. See that you don't."

Mr. Harmon walked over to Theodora. "Well, Miss Winthrop," he said. "How about that extra Liberty bond?"

The color flew to Theodora's face. She had repeatedly told him that she was carrying all she could afford. "I'm sorry," she answered, "but I couldn't possibly."

"Oh, come now, Miss Winthrop! We're all doing more than we can. It will be paid by installments from your salary."

"But I've already taken two that way, Mr. Harmon. I can't spare another cent from my salary if I'm to pay my bills."

"Bills? Good Lord, I wish I knew who was going to pay mine! But everyone's in the same boat. The other evening I heard a speech from young Hannaford down at the club." (Young Hannaford was one of New York's sensational millionaires.) "By Jove, he was actually wearing shoes that had been tapped—he showed them to us; and he was smoking Meccas—the cheapest things on the market."

Theodora's lip curled. She was no longer ashamed in the face of such a shameful argument. However, three months in an office had taught her much. "Mr. Harmon," she said, "I know how wonderful the rich have been. Nothing could detract from their credit. But for them, I don't know where the country would be. Just the same, and in spite of their generosity, they are still able to live in luxury. *All* my shoes are tapped—it's so much a matter of course that it would never occur to me to mention it. The question is how I can go on wearing shoes at all. And I couldn't afford a club, and I couldn't afford to smoke. And though I'm very sorry, I cannot take another bond."

He walked away, leaving her with the sensation of being in disgrace. She felt apologetic, yet indignant. Since she first entered that office she had never been late a minute, never sick a day; she had never asked for a holiday, though she had learned all the tricks by which one might be obtained. She had never once asked another girl to take over any of her duties, though she had often assumed those of others. And yet, because she would not buy a thing she could not afford, she was under a cloud.

It was a pity the issue had arisen. Theodora had just come into her own in the office life. At first, the manager and most of the employees had looked askance at her. She was not the conventional office type. She wasn't pert and she wasn't self-assertive—at least not here; she stuck to her work even when the "boss" wasn't around; she asked no privileges; although perfectly pleasant with everyone, she was above gossip; she was educated and intelligent. Altogether, there had been a strong prejudice against her, for the reason that she was actually, in practice, what an ideal office employee is supposed to be in principle.

Then, by dint of courtesy and fairness, by minding her own business and never putting on any airs, she had made her own place. It was rather an isolated sort of place. The girls attempted no "dates" with her. They never gossiped with her. The boss never came and sat by her as he did some of the others; but he appreciated her and he respected her. All had gone well until the question of Liberty bonds had arisen, and then the girl who took the most bonds became the one to be favored and praised.

Probably it wasn't Mr. Harmon's fault. He seemed worried. The girls said that a certain amount had to be subscribed in the office, and that it was his business to see that it was done. They told each other that as soon as the campaign was over, he would be himself again. No nice man enjoys hectoring women.

❧❧❧   ❧❧❧   ❧❧❧

Theodora had been in the office three months now, living in a hall bedroom in order to save all she could toward her mother coming to New York to join her. Today after work she would go straight to the station to meet her. One of the girls here had a tiny flat that she wanted to sublet; her husband had gone off to the war and she was going home to her parents in order to economize. So Theodora took her flat. It was up three flights and there was no lift, but it had a cunning kitchenette and room enough for two people to live entirely comfortably.

At a quarter past five that afternoon, Theodora was hurrying happily to her rendezvous when a hold-up at a Fifth Avenue crossing brought her face to face with a waiting motor in which sat Mrs. Stuyvesant. Two minutes later, Theodora was spinning down the avenue by the side of her former employer, exchanging with her items of news.

"Just think," said the girl, "my mother hasn't seen New York for nearly twenty years, and she has scarcely slept outside the Waverly bedroom for fifteen."

"And you've taken a position in order to support her?"

"Her and myself. She has a small income."

"And your engagement is broken?"

"Yes," said the girl quietly. "And Marguerite Wyatt was the kindest friend you ever knew. It was through her that I got my present position."

There was an odd look in Mrs. Stuyvesant's eyes. "I wish you'd come back to me," she said impulsively. "I've never had a companion who did anything but rattle around in your place."

The girl glanced at her curiously. The old query rose again in her mind—why had she been dismissed? "That's very kind of you," she replied; "but—my mother, you see."

"I shall come and call on your mother," announced Mrs. Stuyvesant, and took the address. "I am very much alone these days, Miss Winthrop. Everyone is busy—and it is right that they should be. But there is no more of the old-time visiting and entertaining. Mrs. Delafield Beeckman is abroad doing canteen work. So, of course, is Marjorie, and her parents simply spend their lives in Red Cross work. Helen Burrill is in England. I can't tell you how alone I am."

"Has Mr. Alan Beeckman gone yet?" asked Theodora. Her voice shook as she put the question, and her heart beat to suffocation. At least she would know something definite!

"Yes," replied the old lady. "He went in October. He is Captain Beeckman now."

Only too well did Theodora realize that further inquiries would look over-eager; only too well did she realize that her companion was waiting to see whether she would make them. She said no more.

Mrs. Stuyvesant dropped Theodora at the station, and before many minutes mother and daughter were clasped in each other's arms. It was a very dazed Mrs. Winthrop who followed her daughter to the cab—it was a nervous and astounded one who rode through the crowded streets of the great metropolis. But when the little apartment was finally reached, it was a very happy pair that explored it together.

"I'm sorry about the stairs," apologized Theodora, "and I'm sorry I have to be away so much. But you'll soon get used to finding your way around, and there are so many lovely things to do! There are provision shops right in this block, and a little restaurant that we will often patronize. Then we'll have our

> *If they try to reason with Elise, she goes into hysterics and cries that all her family hate her, and that she wishes she was dead.*

evenings and our Saturday afternoons and Sundays together. It seems too wonderful to be true."

The long evening chat was a treat worth waiting for. "And so dear Ned went overseas in September," said Theodora. "The darling! And wasn't Marjorie lucky to get across too? They say that soon no wives will be allowed to go." There was a wistful tone in her voice. She tried hard to guard against jealousy and that deadliest of poisons—self-pity.

"Yes," replied Mrs. Winthrop. "Marjorie is in Paris, and your Aunt Augusta thinks from Ned's letters that he is somewhere in Champagne."

"So I gathered. I suppose Aunt Augusta is as wonderful as ever, and that Meta is still living for everyone but herself. How's the lovely Elise?"

Mrs. Winthrop moved uncomfortably and lowered her gaze. "What is it, mother?" demanded the girl. "What is she up to now?"

"She is behaving very badly," hesitated the parent. "If she continues, she will break your aunt's heart, as well as Dr. Sewall's."

Theodora had a sudden flash of illumination. "Gerald Wyatt?" she asked point-blank.

Mrs. Winthrop gasped. "Why, Theodora," she cried. "Who told you?"

"No one. But I'll tell *you* a few things about that pair." And she proceeded with a recital that scandalized her mother.

"Well," said the older woman, "he is at Elise's constantly. Dr. Sewall can do nothing to stop it, and your aunt can do nothing.

If they try to reason with Elise, she goes into hysterics and cries that all her family hate her, and that she wishes she was dead. She has taken to running to the city twice a week for music lessons, and several times Mrs. Neilson has seen her lunching with that man. It really doesn't seem as if it could be our family, with such dreadful things happening in it," finished Mrs. Winthrop plaintively.

"Well, Mother, Elise is just exactly what she's always been," observed Theodora with complete nonchalance. "I don't know why we should expect her to change all of a sudden. Now, I'm going to put you to bed. You've had a wearing day."

"Very well. My dear, I'm very thankful you broke off your relationship with that man."

"So am I, dear. I'm sure none of us will ever regret that," agreed Theodora cheerfully. "That was certainly one time when Aunt Augusta proved a better prophetess than any of the rest of us, didn't she?"

Mrs. Stuyvesant made the promised call, and she carried Mrs. Winthrop home with her for luncheon. The visit must have been a success, for it was the forerunner of many similar ones. Soon it became the accepted thing for Mrs. Winthrop to lunch at least twice a week with the old lady.

"Do you know, Theodora," she said to her daughter, "She's really very lonely; and she detests her present companion. She tells me that she has never ceased to miss you. She is evidently devoted to you."

"At one time she took a very odd way of showing her devotion, then. Yet I'm bound to admit that she has seemed genuinely fond of me ever since. Does she ever mention her nephew, Captain Beeckman?"

"Never till today. Miss Lorrimer, her rector's daughter, writes all her letters to him. I happen to know, because Mrs.

Stuyvesant had mislaid the envelope to the last one, and I had to address another for her." Theodora picked up a magazine and became absorbed in the picture on its cover. "What was his address?" she asked. "Do you happen to remember it?"

"Yes. The 165th Infantry, 42nd Division."

So there was Theodora with her long desired information, and the only good it would do her would be to enable her to follow the movements of the division as reported in the papers. She couldn't very well write to an engaged man and say, "I thought you would be glad to know that my own engagement is broken." Nevertheless, the knowledge was a comfort.

One January afternoon she returned from the office feeling more tired than usual. As soon as Theodora opened the door of her little flat that day, she knew there was something amiss. Mrs. Winthrop looked as though she had been crying and her manner was perturbed. After some futile conversation, the trouble came out. "Read that," cried the mother, thrusting an envelope with the Waverly postmark into her daughter's hand.

"Your poor aunt! I fear she will never get over this blow!"

Theodora read the letter to the accompaniment of her mother's sniffs and murmurs. The news it carried was rather in the nature of an earthquake considering the people it concerned.

Elise was going to Reno for a divorce. "That man" (Aunt Augusta could not bring herself to write Gerald Wyatt's name) was evidently putting up the money for the trip; in all probability he would join Elise out there. She was leaving her baby to Dr. Sewall, apparently without a regret. And she had been sufficiently unprincipled to seize that handle open to the wives of all physicians—fictitious jealousy of her husband's women patients and his undue interest in them. "And *that*," wrote poor Aunt Augusta, "is the thing I can least forgive her. No better man than Andrew Sewall ever lived, and his wife must know it well. But she spares no one. Meta will take the boy. She will bring him up better than his mother ever could. But for Andrew, I see no comfort anywhere. My heart is broken by my thankless child. Poor dear Theodora—I hope this miserable business will not cause her any unhappiness. She is well out of her entanglement with that man!"

Theodora laid down the letter with a long breath. "Poor Aunt Augusta," she said.

"She'll never get over it," moaned Mrs. Winthrop.

"Well, Mother, Elise is a miserably selfish woman, but we've always known that. She's deserting her child, and she's doing her best to break her mother's heart—and her husband's. But apart from that—I mean, as far as disgrace is concerned— Aunt Augusta needn't worry. In Gerald Wyatt's set and in all the sets that Elise will ever care to enter, this sort of thing is too usual even to cause comment. It's an everyday occurrence."

"I can't see how Elise ever learned to be so wicked," sighed Mrs. Winthrop. "She had just the same training as you and Meta."

"Oh, no, she didn't, mother. Elise has been spoiled and humored all her life. Maybe Elise couldn't help herself after all—though it's my private opinion that she could. At any rate, I'm going to write to poor Aunt Augusta this minute."

This she proceeded to do. "Above all, dear Aunt Augusta," she wrote in conclusion, "don't worry about me. I never loved Gerald Wyatt. Elise apparently does. She'll make him happier than I ever could, and she'll probably be happy herself. The baby will have a wonderful mother in Meta, and Dr. Sewall will surely get over his unhappiness after a while."

Theodora honestly believed that her cousin would be happy when she had attained the money and luxury for which she had always longed. But of course she was mistaken. As long as there lived a human being courageous enough to give Elise Charrington the cold shoulder, as long as there existed a clique in which she was not welcomed as a queen, as long as there were women with more money, or beauty, or gems, or clothes, or youth than she, just that long would she have cause for wretchedness. And it would be strange should Gerald, who his whole life long had loved women only to leave them, suddenly discover that there was but one woman in the world, after all. And it would be doubly strange if the sum of one selfish human being plus another selfish human being should equal perpetual bliss!

PART FIFTH

Love's
Sweet Surprise

☙XVII❧

heodora sat at Mrs. Stuyvesant's dinner table and looked around the softly lighted, softly perfumed circle.

At the head of the table Mrs. Stuyvesant presided with all her sparkle and charm, happy to find herself once more a hostess. On her right sat Bishop Wysong, a visitor in New York and tonight's guest of honor. Next to him, on his other side, was a transformed Mrs. Winthrop. Theodora looked at her mother in happy amazement. Less than three months absence from Waverly had made a different woman of her. As she turned from Bishop Wysong to Mr. Lorrimer who sat on her right (and who was Mrs. Stuyvesant's permanent pastor and her own temporary one), she was actually animated, actually almost gay.

Next to Mr. Lorrimer sat Theodora. Theodora, one-time dependent in the Stuyvesant household, now its frequent and welcome guest; Theodora, a little pale, a little thin, decidedly more silent and less assertive, distinctly softened and restrained, but no whit less wholesome and charming and honest; a far gentler Theodora, yet a Theodora with occasional lapses into her old intensity—as she presently proceeded to prove.

They were talking, of course, about the war. Who in the civilized world was not, at that particular period? Mr. Lorrimer's curate, young Mr. Fosdick, sat between his hostess and Theodora and completed the party. He was a great admirer of the girl, and they had just been discussing volunteers versus drafted men. There happened to be a general conversational pause as Theodora replied to a remark of her companion.

"I think I can stand anything," she was saying "better than the men who enlist only when they find that they are about to be caught in the draft anyhow. That makes me hot. They haven't the physical courage to go if they don't have to, nor the moral courage to admit that they were forced. I could admire an out-and-out-slacker more."

She glanced up and caught the bishop's eye. It held a certain look that she recognized. Immediately her face flamed scarlet, and she addressed herself directly to him. "I suppose it's none of my business," she said. "It's their shame, not mine."

The bishop threw back his head and laughed—he couldn't help it. But there was a very tender note in his voice, as he replied: "You're learning, dear child. You're learning fast."

"But," persisted Theodora, "we can't help noticing things, can we?"

"Certainly not. We can only help feeling that their punishment and denouncement lie with us."

"Nevertheless, sir," Mr. Fosdick rushed to Theodora's support, "I fancy that most of us feel privileged to criticize unworthiness."

"Undoubtedly we *feel* so," smiled the bishop. "I think no one will deny that."

"I heard the present crisis very aptly named the other day," said Mr. Lorrimer. "Someone spoke of it as the 'Sieve of Flame'; the sieve that separates the wheat from the chaff."

"They may call the war anything they choose," cried Mrs. Stuyvesant, "as long as they don't call it a blessing in disguise. I confess, that is more than I can stand."

She turned to Bishop Wysong. "You make no such claim for it, I hope?" she demanded.

"Most certainly not. It is a holocaust. It is no more a blessing than would be some horrible plague, or devastating fire, or sudden outbreak of crime. It is a terrible evil, and like all evils, it must be met and fought."

"The sad part," said Mr. Lorrimer, "is the way it has made the world poorer. I don't mean in money, of course; but in happiness, in heroes, in good men and women, in geniuses, in trust, in normal progress. The wastage has been appalling. For that, if for nothing else, its perpetrators must be indicted."

"The only way," said the bishop, and he spoke like a man inspired, "the only way that this war can be turned into a blessing, is by seeing that its lessons are never forgotten."

"What?" cried Theodora eagerly.

"In this season of mourning," continued the old man, "we have learned much. We have learned to be tender and pitiful, to bear heroically, to give our lives to others, to forget unnecessary social distinctions, to pray more than we ever prayed before. We have learned to shudder at greed. We have learned that materialism can find no answer to any of the great questions. We have learned to believe in miracles. And therefore I say that only if safety brings forgetfulness and return to carelessness, will the war have been wasted. It lies in our human hands. The watchword of the world should henceforth be, 'Lest we forget.'"

There was solemnity in the silence which followed his words. Mrs. Stuyvesant was the first to speak.

"How are you going to make people remember?" she demanded. "I know it's the singsong of the moment to talk of the spiritual reconstruction of human nature by the war, but I have absolutely no faith in it. Serious people, decent people, were serious and decent before the war, they're serious and decent during the war, and they'll be serious and decent after the war. But the burden of sorrow and of reconstruction will all be on their shoulders. Greedy people are willing to grow rich even by forgetting Germany's crimes. How are you going to keep such people 'remembering' once the danger is past?"

> Theodora's beautiful eyes were gazing intently into space. They were seeing the vision painted by this man of God.

"The little leaven that leaveneth the whole lump," murmured Mr. Lorrimer.

"Exactly," nodded the bishop. "Make it the fashion to be decent. Above all, show the boys who come back that religion and decency are the style. Help them to cheerfulness and happiness, but at the same time prove to them that while they've been thinking of serious things, so too have we. Do your own part. You, dear Mrs. Stuyvesant, and women like you, are vested with a wonderful power. But even so, you haven't by any means the corner on influence. No one has. Welcome or unwelcome, it is the possession of every human soul, and its circles widen and widen till they reach undreamed-of boundaries."

Theodora's beautiful eyes were gazing intently into space. They were seeing the vision painted by this man of God. Never in all her life was she to forget that which he had just made her see. His influence, in this instance at least, had not gone for naught. "Lest we forget. We mustn't let the war be wasted."

"But you don't think, do you," she cried eagerly, "that anyone really *could* forget?"

The bishop shook his head sadly. "People can do anything," he answered. "Anything in either direction. I alternate between hope and fear. My faith bids me hope. My perception makes me fear."

༄༄༄ ༄༄༄ ༄༄༄

When Theodora and her mother returned home that evening, the late mail had been dropped into their letter-box. There was one letter that the girl carried to the light, scanning it anxiously. "Here's an overseas letter," she said, "in a writing I don't know. I do hope there's nothing the matter with Ned." Tearing open the envelope she hastily turned the sheet to read the signature. "Oh," she gasped, and her cheeks began to flame.

"What is it?" demanded the mother anxiously. "Not bad news?"

"No . . . no, it's all right. It's just—just a friendly letter from a man I used to know—Mrs. Stuyvesant's nephew, in fact, Captain Beeckman. He ran into Marjorie in Paris and they got to talking about me. She gave him my address."

Before Theodora slept, she knew that letter by heart. She could see it projected on the darkness before her wide-open happy eyes. It was nothing unusual, but it didn't sound like the letter of an engaged man. If this man were in love with Helen, why should he be writing to Theodora? To be sure, it was a mere friendly sheet. Captain Beeckman wrote of his pleasure in hearing of her "even indirectly," and of his surprise at the news of her broken engagement—"and since it was your pleasure to break it, perhaps you won't mind if I say that it was my very great pleasure to hear of it." He wondered if she could spare an occasional half-hour to send him a line. "Letters from home are the finest thing a chap gets, out here. He has plenty of time to

235

look forward to them, and to learn them by heart after they come." Then he signed himself, "Yours, Alan." Nothing but those two words—yet to Theodora they were the most important ones in the letter.

How changed was the world the next morning! How pleasant were the people in the office! How beautiful were the morning sunshine and the afternoon storm! How foolish and negligible was food! And above all, how blessed was the luncheon hour when, instead of eating, Theodora wrote. Wrote, and tore, and re-wrote, and finally posted. Her letter didn't please her, but she knew she'd never be able to write one that did; how could one manage to say just enough, when one didn't know what that "enough" might be?

One question Theodora determined to settle definitely and permanently. "It must be a comfort," she wrote, "to have Miss Burrill on the same side of the water, even if she is not in France." Then she drew her pen lightly through the words "Miss Burrill," and substituted "your fiancée." "There," she said grimly to herself, "now I'll know."

She began to count, first weeks, then days, then hours and minutes. Yet when Alan's answer finally came (which it did at the first possible opportunity), she almost feared to open it. She wished she had not said that about Helen Burrill. Perhaps he wouldn't like it.

His letter lay awaiting her return from the office, and the first thing that she noticed was its thickness. It must be long!

The man began by expressing his very great pleasure in hearing from her.

"What you say about Helen Burrill," he wrote, "may, I hope, be the answer to many things that have puzzled me—even sometimes hurt me a little. Was it because you believed me to be engaged to her that you never wrote me of your own broken engagement? Never sent me a single line before I sailed, or since I landed? Had I had any such line, rest assured I'd never have left without seeing you, nor given you any rest from my letters once I was here.

"I have never been engaged to Helen, nor to anyone. Who ever told you that I was? Not Aunt Honora, I am sure, though I confess that it has long been the dearest wish of her heart to see us married—a wish, however, which was shared by neither of us. I'll explain it to you.

"My aunt had an only son whom she adored. He was rather the type of my cousin Van, attractive but selfish. Eight years ago, when he was a man of thirty-five, he engaged himself to Helen, who was then only twenty. His mother was in a seventh heaven of delight. The wedding day was set and the cards were actually out, when my cousin shot himself and was found dead in his apartment. It nearly killed Aunt Honora, and it turned Helen into a recluse. She and I had been boy and girl friends—there is less than a year's difference between us—and I was consumed with pity for her. We came to be together constantly; in fact, for a long time I was the only person she would consent to see. But it was always the relationship of a brother and a sister. Not only was she a little the older actually, but her tragedy made her seem very much so. I was her 'little brother,' the person to whom she turned for sympathy, and also for help in the splendid charities with which she soon began to busy herself. And watching the development of a mind and character such as hers, I came to find the ordinary society bud insipid and silly.

"Then Aunt Honora, whose pet and favorite I had always been, set her heart on a marriage between Helen and me. It became the dream of her life, and she did everything in her power to bring it about; but of course to no end. There was never the ghost of that sort of thing in our fondness. Helen had

had her romance, and mine had never even come—until I saw you. And now my secret is out.

"My dear, in this life over here, a chap gets down to facts. He forgets how to be graceful, and becomes primitive and elemental. That must be my excuse for what follows.

All through the days after we declared war, all through the long weeks that I spent in camp waiting for orders to sail, you were my one thought.

"I loved you, I think, from the first moment that I ever saw you. Do you remember those evenings at Fair Acres, and how I kept coming back to you? I think now that Aunt Honora guessed my secret and sent you off. Then I went almost immediately to the Border, and when I came back you belonged to another man. As far as I knew, you were entirely in love with him. Still, I couldn't forget you. All through the days after we declared war, all through the long weeks that I spent in camp waiting for orders to sail, you were my one thought. I kept thinking that if I could only see you once—married or single—I could go the more easily. And since I got over here, the longing has been worse. Your face is always before my eyes, your voice calls to me from every wind that blows. Sleeping or waking, I can never forget you. Perhaps at home I might have managed it in time—but I don't think so. Out here, the memory of you is intensified till you are life itself.

"And now, perhaps I needn't try to forget. If I come back, perhaps I'll have a chance to make you care for me. I used to think last winter that you liked me a little. My dear, my dear, if I come home again, is there any hope for me?

"This may sound bald to you. You may think I should have wooed you by more graceful degrees. If you were out here you'd understand. You'd know that there isn't time. There isn't time for anything but plain truth.

"If you can ever love me, I pray that I may live to come back. They say the big push is on soon. But no matter what happens, I'm glad I told you that I love you. Of that, you must have never a doubt.

"Yours,
Alan."

⁕⁕⁕ ⁕⁕⁕ ⁕⁕⁕

There may be happier moments in the life of a woman than the one when she first knows that the man whom she loves loves her, but human experience scarcely warrants the belief. Theodora could have asked nothing more in the way of bliss. And it was Marjorie Charrington, Ned's little bride Marjorie whose happy love story she had been almost envying, who had been the unconscious means of bringing about this miracle.

It was early in March when Alan's letter reached Theodora. She answered it immediately, as frankly, as freely, as yearningly, as he himself had written. She poured out her heart in an abandonment of love and happiness; but the great question soon became whether the letter would ever reach him. Word was sent almost immediately that the American soldiers were in the trenches, and that the big drive was on. The days grew steadily blacker to those waiting at home. Men's hearts failed them for fear, and women's almost stopped beating.

Everyone tried to extract comfort from the talk of "strategic retreats," and "unbroken fronts" and an approaching unified command. The fact remained that the Allies were being steadily driven back over their hardly recovered ground which had taken months to win. For the first time, Hope died in many a breast. Men and women who had not prayed for years, or perhaps never at all, prayed now. Those who had prayed all their lives, now found their sole comfort in prayer. There were few who cared to scoff at such things in these days.

It was impossible not to read the papers—one read five and six editions in a day; yet it was so depressing that it took all one's courage to accomplish it. There came a day when Theodora was called to the manager's desk and told that she was wanted on the private wire. It was her mother speaking from Mrs. Stuyvesant's. She had never before called up during business hours, and her voice sounded strained and unnatural. "My dear," she said, "could you possibly get the afternoon off? Mrs. Stuyvesant is not well, and she wants to see you at once. No, it is not one of her heart attacks—at least, not yet; but the doctor rather fears one, particularly if she does not soon see you. Come at once, dear, if you possibly can."

☙XVIII❧

rs. Winthrop was waiting downstairs to intercept Theodora and explain the situation to her.

"Mrs. Stuyvesant has had bad news from France," she said. "Her nephew has been dangerously wounded in action."

Theodora collapsed onto a chair. Her breath seemed to stop, but she managed to ask: "Captain Alan Beeckman?"

"Yes. Why, Theodora! Why, my dear child! What is the matter?" For Theodora had begun to weep silently. Not since she was a little child had her mother seen her shed tears.

"Mother," she said piteously, "I've been going to tell you about it. I love him."

"My dear," she cried pitifully, "I'm so sorry. Tell me about it."

She couldn't help feeling relieved to find that the girl's love had not been given unsought. Poor dear Theodora was always so full of surprises that her mother was prepared for any-thing—anything that is, that might be the outcome of a warm, honest heart and a terribly independent mind. Mrs. Winthrop petted and comforted and attempted to cheer, and for the first time in years she felt as if she had her little girl back again.

"Now," said Mrs. Winthrop after a time, "do you think you could go up to Mrs. Stuyvesant? She wants you so much."

"Is she alone?"

"Yes. I just left her to come down and look for you. Marjorie's mother has been here for quite a while, but she's gone now. Louise is in the next room, of course, but Mrs. Stuyvesant seems to want no one but you."

"How do my eyes look?

"They are quite all right. Will you go up?"

Theodora needn't have worried about her eyes. It was not a moment when such things were conspicuous. She was shocked to see the ravaged face which Mrs. Stuyvesant turned to greet her entrance.

"My dear," she said, and opened her arms wide. Kneeling by her side, clasped in her embrace, Theodora read the dread message: "Regret to report Captain Alan Beeckman, 165th Infantry, 42nd Division, severely wounded in action."

"Dear, dear Mrs. Stuyvesant, it mayn't be as bad as you think," cried the girl, though her own heart was full of the blackest fears. American casualties had but begun to come in; for years, one had read of the martyrdom and permanent crippling of the Allied soldiers, and that word "severely" carried its own message.

"Oh, but it is—it is. Somehow, I feel it. And look at the report—"

"Yes, but many of the men get well again, even after they are badly hurt."

"But Alan would rather be dead than maimed. I'm sure of it. He was so vigorous, so straight and beautiful! From the time he was a little boy. . . . But oh, the worst of it all is that I made him unhappy; I *tried* to make him unhappy. I, who pretended to love him! I saddened his going, and I kept telling myself that I knew best."

242

"Never mind." Theodora's sole impulse was to comfort. "He knows how much you love him."

The older woman's hands were lying in her lap so tightly clasped that the knuckles showed white even against their chalky surface. All at once she bit her lips as though in sudden resolve, and threw her head up proudly. Turning, she faced the kneeling girl. "Theodora," she said (it was the first time she had ever so spoken), "Alan loved you."

"And I love him," answered the girl simply. "I've been wanting to tell you about it."

"So I robbed you both!"

"No, no you didn't. Let me tell you—you've made it so easy for me to do it; just remember that and forget everything else." And with the same lack of self-consciousness with which she did everything, the girl told her love story.

"Thank God," murmured the old lady. Then she asked sharply, "And did he have time to get your letter before—before *this?*"

"I don't know," answered the girl softy. "I'm hoping so. He wanted me to know; I want him to know."

"But even so, I've cheated you. If you and Alan loved each other, you might have been married before he went out."

The girl shook her head quickly, and turned her face aside. This was more than she could bear. Then very quietly she answered, "No. You see, I was still engaged when he enlisted."

"Was it because of him that you broke your engagement?"

"Largely. That, and other things. But I didn't know then that Alan cared for me." A lovely color flooded her face as she pronounced his name.

"Theodora, listen to me. Don't try to stop me, for it will do no good. I want to explain this thing to you. I had other plans for Alan—very cherished plans."

"Yes, he told me."

"He told you about Helen?"

"Yes, Mrs. Stuyvesant. In my first letter—the first I had ever written him—I spoke of his fiancée. You see, Mr. Van Rensselaer Beeckman had told me that they were engaged."

"No, they never were. But it was a thing that I desired with all my heart. Did Alan tell you about my son?"

Theodora nodded.

"You see, I couldn't yield the hope that I might some day have the daughter that my own dear boy had planned to give me—for Alan is like a son to me, and his wife will be like a daughter."

"I can understand it perfectly," said Theodora gravely. "What I think is wonderful, is that you should be ready now to take me in the place of Helen."

"My child, don't say that. All that I ask is that you and my boy may be spared to each other, and that you will both forgive me."

"There is nothing to forgive," Theodora assured her sweetly. And they fell to talking of Alan.

Mrs. Stuyvesant and Theodora were now to learn the full meaning of the word suspense. They lived through days that seemed centuries long. They learned the weariness of companionship, and the sadness of solitude; the dread look and smell of newspapers, and the heavy hours of waiting for them; the jump which a heart may give at the sound of a postman's whistle; the vain effort to eat; the awful realization of powerlessness to affect the final issue. It seemed a wonder that human hearts and human nerves could stand such a strain, while human bodies continued their accustomed round.

Nearly two weeks passed before they received any definite word concerning Alan Beeckman, and it proved them to be among the blessed. He would recover, and he would not be permanently maimed. He had gone splendidly through two operations, and his weeks in hospital might well be the means of saving his life, since, while he lay hovering between this world and eternity, the terrible drive went steadily on, and with it went many of his former comrades.

The dreadest part of the good news about him was that he would eventually be able to return to the Front. Then it would all have to be lived again.

It was long before Alan himself even dictated a letter, and longer still before he wrote one. In those weeks of waiting Theodora grew to know anew Mrs. Stuyvesant. She grew so much more appealing and human that Theodora was worried. Once in awhile the old spark would flare to life, only to give place to almost immediate softness.

Her self-will showed itself in one direction more than in any other; she was determined that Theodora should give up working, and that she and her mother should come to live in the big lonely house where they now spent so much of their time. "If it hadn't been for me," she often reminded the girl, "you would have been my niece by now. The least you can do is to let me adopt you."

But to this plan Theodora would not harken, and her mother upheld her. "I hate to have you obliged to work," said Mrs. Winthrop; "but of course, we could not make any such permanent arrangements as that."

Theodora never forgot the day which brought Alan's first pencilled note. He had received her original long letter just before going into battle. "I can never make you understand what it was to me," he wrote. "To get it in those surroundings was like standing in hell and seeing heaven waiting a few steps ahead. I know it was the word your letter brought that carried me through. The first thing I did after the operation was to make them give me that letter, and it has never left me since. Because of it, I fought for my life like a tiger."

And so it came to pass that Theodora joined the pathetic army of Waiting Women.

Romances born in war days are sad and abnormal. Proper love affairs should be a series of meetings and thrills, of short partings which only make possible further meetings, of jealousies and reconciliations; they should concern beautiful maidens in beautiful dress, and enamoured beaus hovering ever near. Such love affairs are delights. But the maidens whose heart flowers bloom in those sad days when their country is at war, can hope for no such romances. For them, there are no recurrent meetings—there is one great parting, and then an aching void.

Therefore the romance of a warring man and a waiting maid can never sparkle and scintillate and dazzle. One sole soft ray lights the path of the maid who waits for the lover who fights afar—and that is the gleam from the star of Hope, which only comes through prayer. And it was only by dint of never closing her eyes to this soft beam, that Theodora's heart was guarded by God against the blackness of despair.

※ ※ ※

By the first of May, Theodora's lease expired, Mrs. Winthrop was beginning to feel the confinements of city life, and Mrs. Stuyvesant was anxious to get to Fair Acres—where she planned to spend the entire summer, foregoing Newport entirely. Theodora and her mother consented to spend the summer with her. Mrs. Winthrop had by this time become almost indispensable to the old lady; she read to her, wrote for her, drove with her, and was a delightful companion for her days of loneliness.

Theodora came and went, and she nearly always found her mother and Mrs. Stuyvesant waiting for her in the motor when she stepped off the afternoon train. To them she brought the news of the busy city, and from them she received much affection.

In June Mrs. Stuyvesant received a letter from Helen Burrill announcing her engagement to a blinded British officer of the Coldstream Guards. The old lady handed it to Theodora to read. "I'm not much of a success in the role of Destiny," she observed. "My dear, dear Helen! What sacrifice of her young life this seems!"

"But how wonderful for the man," said Theodora. "And she seems blissfully happy."

"Yes, she evidently is."

July brought the news that Ned was reported among the missing. He was Sergeant Charrington now. The word "missing" had come to be dreaded almost more than the word "killed." Aunt Augusta, in her agony of suspense, broke through her frozen calm and wrote heartbroken letters to her sister. Through Red Cross channels, Mr. and Mrs. Gary managed to get passports to France, and they sailed at once. But poor Aunt Augusta had no such solace. Like Theodora, she joined the army of Waiting Women.

☙XIX❧

he first Victory Day found Theodora sitting at her desk, listening to New York's bedlam and wondering if the war could indeed be over. The thought was almost inconceivable. Without that black monster of war, what would the world be like—what would daily life be like? People would be quieter and kinder—not gloomy, but thoughtful. Life would be simpler. Naturally, standards must be higher. Four awful years must surely have seared some scars in selfish hearts!

New York had gone mad over the report of an armistice. Papers were being issued every hour, their huge black headlines announcing the news in the most theatrical of terms:

"Germany Crawls"

"The Kaiser, Beaten to His Knees, Acknowledges That America Proved His Finish"

"Crown Prince a Suicide and Hindenburg in Prison"

"Crown Prince Weeps as He Dons Overalls"

One could read anything and believe what one chose. Whistles, sirens, horns, engines, bands, and human voices combined to make a hideous ensemble that almost killed the power of thought. Invitations to the Kaiser's funeral were being distributed on the streets; screaming mobs accorded him a mock burial; telephone books were shredded into confetti and show-ered from high office windows. The rites of joy were as crude as they were noisy.

It had all come about so suddenly that Theodora feared to believe. Might it not be some trap? Could Germany indeed have been beaten in a campaign of less than four months? Could she really have fallen to pieces so suddenly? She who had so often lied, so often duped the decent world, might well be at her old tricks again.

If the war were indeed ended, how marvellously blessed was she, Theodora! To have had two loved ones in the struggle and to get them both back unmaimed would be almost a miracle. Alan had written two weeks ago; he was still safe then. Ned, too, was back in the fight. After having been wounded in the Second Marne, he had managed to crawl into a shell hole. There they found him three days later, apparently dead. But after six or eight weeks in hospital, he had rejoined his unit and gone back to the front. How wonderful it would be if they should both return unharmed! Life then would hardly be long enough to show one's gratitude.

✿ ✿ ✿

It might have been supposed that the false Victory Day would have discounted the real one, but such did not prove to be the case. On the real day, Theodora awoke between four and five o'clock in the morning to the sound of the city whistles answered by those of all the suburbs and nearby towns. (She was back in New York by now, and she and her mother were stopping with Mrs. Stuyvesant while seeking an apartment.)

Creeping out of bed, the girl knelt on the cold floor in an abandonment of gratitude. For so long now, prayer had been but an agony of supplication. The answer had come; the curse was lifted. What was there to do but make it the pinnacle of thankfulness?

Finding further sleep an impossibility, Theodora dressed and went out. She wanted to get into a church. Surely she could find one open—she cared not what its denomination might be.

> Where were their souls? How many of them had been into a church that day? How many had even remembered to pray?

She had walked but a little distance when she heard the sound of singing, and then she came upon the singer. In a narrow open space that had been cleared for her, a woman stood, surrounded by a reverent crowd. The men's heads were bared and the women's were bowed. In a high clear soprano the singer chanted the Doxology; over and over again she repeated it, till its four simple lines of praise and worship became a recurrent anthem. Eventually the crowd joined their voices to hers; more and more of them sang; it was a beautiful ceremony of the utmost simplicity.

"Oh," thought Theodora, "It's going to be all right. They're remembering to pray. I'm so glad—so glad!"

The first church that she found open was a Romish one, and she went in to early Mass. The service fitted wonderfully into her mood of reverence and awe. To Theodora's delight, the church was thronged.

She returned home before going to the office, and she found her mother and Mrs. Stuyvesant in the same state of fervent exaltation that she herself was experiencing. "Oh," cried Mrs. Stuyvesant, "I hope everyone will remember to thank God for this mercy. I hope they won't forget!"

"They won't," Theodora assured her, and told what she had seen and heard.

But as the day progressed, she began to have qualms. A day of solemn thanksgiving is one thing, a motley carnival is quite another. Where were the hearts of the people in those ever-increasing hectic crowds? Where were their souls? How many of them had been into a church that day? How many had even remembered to pray? Should prayer be kept as the expression of fear, while drunkenness and debauchery stood for relief?

In the afternoon Theodora made her way home through streets that were growing nearly impassable. At the house she found Dr. Powers, who had run down from Grosvenor to see the celebration. Mrs. Stuyvesant suddenly decided that they must all dine at one of the quietest of the big hotels, in order to watch the crowds. Her physician could not dissuade her.

"What difference will it make to my health whether I eat my dinner there or here?" she insisted. "You will be there to take care of me. And this is probably the greatest day the world will ever see. Theodora, telephone and ask whether you can get a table. Use my name. Then invite Mr. Lorrimer and his daughter to join us. I'd ask Van, but of course he'll be flying off to some gayer party. A quiet affair like ours would bore him."

Theodora succeeded in getting the table and the guests. "How gay we shall be, with our two gentlemen!" cried Mrs. Stuyvesant. "One man to a pair of women isn't a bad proportion for an impromptu war-time dinner."

They were glad enough for their escorts when they reached the hotel. It was jammed. Halls, lobbies, dressing-rooms, were almost impassable. Mrs. Winthrop was dazed—she had never seen anything approaching it. Dr. Powers and Theodora were concerned for Mrs. Stuyvesant. "We must keep a sharp watch over her," said the physician, in a low voice. "She shouldn't be here at all."

It wasn't long before they decided that they should none of them be there at all. Each member of the party kept this conviction secret, however. They all smiled, and tried to chat above the din, and to pretend that there was nothing incongruous between their feelings and their surroundings. Less than twenty-four hours after the first authentic word of the Armistice, and many hours—many weeks and months—before actual peace and victory, the city was drunk, debauched, disgusting.

It grew harder and harder for the members of Mrs. Stuyvesant's party to hide their distaste for the scene around them. The hostess suddenly proposed going home. "Let's get out of this din," was the way she put it. "We can have some coffee and nuts and port around my library fire, and I think we shall be much better off. I don't know how it strikes the rest of you, but I don't feel decent here."

It was with genuine relief that her party accepted her proposal. As well as they could, they made their way through screaming, jostling, maniacal crowds. Inside the car, they sat silent and depressed—a sinister sensation of dread bearing down upon them. Was this what relief would mean to the world? Was this the way that it would be expressed?

Theodora was the first one to speak. "The awful thing," she said, "is that nearly all those crazy people tonight must have someone they love 'over there.' How do they know their own boys are safe, and not lying cold and dead—" She bit her lip to still its trembling.

"Exactly," cried Miss Lorrimer eagerly. "That's what I kept thinking. The victory was won by the boys out there. *They* fought for it, and *we're* celebrating it. And even though we know that many of them are filling nameless graves, many facing long lives in which they are never to see again, never to walk again, never to be carefree and happy again, we can forget them all and act like drunken savages. It's simply awful!"

Once at home and clustered around the fire in Mrs. Stuyvesant's library, they resumed their discussion. "To me," said Dr. Powers, so slowly and so quietly as to give a peculiar force to his words, "to me, the world has long seemed like a very sick man—a man who has lived far from purely. He thinks he's going to die. He's frightened. He's repentant. If by any miracle this life can be saved, he's willing to promise anything in the way of future reform. And he really believes he's sincere. He'll live simply, he'll work cleanly, he'll give up all his bad habits, and go to church, and say his prayers.

"And then," continued Dr. Powers, "just tell such a man that he's going to get well! What becomes of his good resolutions and his new righteousness? They're gone. The first things he demands are a cigar and a drink; the first thing he chuckles over is the new deal he's going to put through, and he decides on the lawyer who can best keep him out of jail. Well, that's what you're going to see this reprieved old world doing before you'll believe it possible."

"Oh, *no*," cried Theodora sharply. "Not forget!"

Dr. Powers looked at her with sympathy and sadness in his shrewd eyes. "Yes, my dear," he said, "forget. Forget everything—fright, repentance, good resolutions, wholesome work, the simple life, everything. The world has always forgotten easily, and it always will."

"But not all of us," cried the girl.

"No, not all of us—and in just that fact lies possible salvation. It all depends upon how many of us remember, and how strong we are, and how hard we're willing to work without growing discouraged. We must never forget that though people do not remember, God always remembers. He alone can help us. But we're going to be saddened every day of our lives. . . . Well, I must be saying good night."

"So must I," said Mr. Lorrimer, rising. Everyone was dispirited, yet this talk had been a tonic. It left the feeling that hope was not entirely lost and that help was still possible.

When the guests had departed, Theodora made her early office hours an excuse for going to bed. "You see," she remarked to her mother and Mrs. Stuyvesant, "I must be off in the morning before either of you two sleepyheads is up."

❧❧❧   ❧❧❧   ❧❧❧

But as it happened, Theodora wasn't "off in the morning," as she had expected to be.

Before seven o'clock, one of the maids tapped at her door. There was a telegram for Mrs. Stuyvesant. Should she be called, or would Miss Winthrop attend to it?

"I'll take it, Mary," said Theodora. She opened the message and ran her eyes hastily over it, then with a low cry of horror and with hand pressed to heart, she hurriedly reread the words, in a vain effort to discount their meaning. After that she simply stood frozen, her eyes staring into space and her lips repeating mechanically, "Oh, God, don't let it be true. Please don't let it be true!"

"What is it, Miss Winthrop?" demanded the frightened maid. She had lived in the house since long before the time Theodora had first entered it, and in common with the rest of the servants was devoted to the girl. "Can't I do anything for you, Miss Winthrop?" the poor soul repeated in distress. But Theodora seemed stone-deaf to her voice.

"There now, sit down till you feel better." Mary drew a chair forward and almost pressed the inert figure into it. Theodora's eyes were still wide and faraway, but her lips had ceased to move. "Sit there, now," repeated the kind-hearted servant, "till I run and fetch Mrs. Winthrop."

When the two came, they found Theodora in a transport of grief. She had flung her arms wide on a nearby table and bowed her head on them. Lying so, she had given herself up to her sorrow. Her entire frame was convulsed with almost noiseless sobs.

"Oh, my darling, my darling, what is it?" cried the poor mother. "Tell Mother, my baby, what is it?"

"Alan," almost whispered the girl, and the parent's heart stood still in fear. Noticing the telegram on the floor, she picked it up with one hand while with the other she never ceased caressing the poor bent head. To her eyes leaped the dreadful words, "Killed in action, Captain Alan Beeckman." With a low cry of pity, the mother threw both arms tightly around her poor hurt child in an agony of futile sympathy. To think that she could do nothing to soften this blow—nothing to comfort!

"Don't mention this downstairs yet, Mary," she warned. "We must decide how to tell Mrs. Stuyvesant." And that was the first speech that seemed to penetrate Theodora's consciousness.

"How can we tell her?" she asked. "Oh, Mother—" and again she fell to sobbing.

Eventually, Mary was dispatched to the telephone to send two messages—one to Dr. Homans asking him to come at once, and the other to Theodora's office saying that she would not be there that day.

After the maid had gone, Theodora began to talk in broken snatches. Sad as were her words, they were a relief from that frozen silence, that noiseless sobbing.

"Just think, Mother," she said, "last night was only last night! It seems ten years ago. And this was true then."

After a bit she spoke again. "I'm thankful this didn't happen last summer when my darling was wounded. At least, he had time to know of my love and to tell me of his. But, oh, Mother, Mother, that makes it all the harder to give him up. What am I to *do*? To think of that little bit of faraway happiness being all that I shall ever have! I must live on those few letters for the rest of my life."

"I know, my child, I know! And you so richly deserve happiness. All your life you've been my good, good daughter—so plucky and sweet and brave! My great loss came to me, dear, when I was scarcely older than you, and I was left with a little fatherless baby."

"Ah, that was where you were fortunate! You had your baby, and you had the name of the man you loved. There was at least the memory of a few happy years. I have nothing. Nothing. Not a handclasp, not a single caress, not a farewell. Just a few letters that I shall read and reread all the rest of my life. Oh, mother, I'm thankful to have even them—little as they are."

Presently Mary came to say that Dr. Homans was downstairs and wanted to see Miss Winthrop.

It was a very grave conference that they held. The doctor, knowing nothing of Theodora's personal loss and attributing her tear-ravaged face to sympathy for the family sorrow, asked her to break the news to Mrs. Stuyvesant.

"Someone must do it," he said, "and I'm sure you would be the best one. You are so tender with her, and she is so devoted to you. Her relatives seem to be scattered or dead. Will you undertake it, Miss Winthrop? I will be near, with the restoratives."

"Oh, Dr. Homans! Suppose the shock should kill her! I'd never get over the feeling that I'd bungled. You know you've always warned me against excitement."

"Yes, but I meant the excitement of temper, rather than of sorrow. Sorrow is quieter, less dangerous—at her age, especially. Nature seems to blunt its edge providentially to the old. At any rate, the issue cannot be avoided. Mrs. Stuyvesant must be told. The only question is whether you are willing to undertake the task."

"Could I do it?" ventured Mrs. Winthrop.

"No, Mother," said the girl with sudden resolve. "I believe Dr. Homans is right. I'm the one to do it." After a little more talk and some advice, she professed herself ready. While hard, it was probably the best thing that could have happened to her under the circumstances. In thinking of Mrs. Stuyvesant, she was forced to stop thinking of herself to a certain extent.

The task proved much simpler than she had dared hope. Her face spoke for her the moment she entered the room.

"What is it?" asked the old lady quickly and sharply.

Theodora went and knelt on the floor by her side, taking a veined and knotted hand in both her young strong ones. "I've had bad news," she answered simply.

"Your cousin?"

Theodora shook her head.

"My boy?" Then before Theodora could answer a word—"I knew it. He is dead. Alan is dead. I knew it."

Her grief was heartbreaking in its stoic calm. She asked no questions—even the thought that another few days would have seen the war over and Alan safe did not seem to add to her grief, as it had to the grief of so many bereaved ones all over the world. The mere fact that Alan was dead was all that seemed to make any difference to his old aunt. She never even knew that her physician was in the house, and after an hour or so of waiting he felt safe in leaving. It was not until the early evening that he was hastily summoned again. The dreaded attack had come.

For hours they worked. At midnight, with the patient dozing under opiates, the doctor pronounced the crisis once more past. "It is surely an incomprehensible plan," he said, shaking his head. "Once more we see an old life spared and a young one taken. It is one of the things that we cannot understand. God must have a reason for it. Such things don't just happen. Of that, I'm very sure."

For the first week, life merely drifted. Everyone tried to hide personal sorrow and to comfort others. Mrs. Stuyvesant and Theodora were, of course, the principal sufferers in the tragedy, and it drew them closer together than ever before. Each of them knew the look of a sleepless night as reflected in the eyes of the other. Each knew that even a night which brought blessed sleep must also bring the reawakening to the sickening sense of loss.

From the first they talked constantly of Alan. He was a member of their fireside circle. Mrs. Stuyvesant brought out two photographs of him—one in civilian clothes and one in uniform—and gave them to Theodora.

With this came a time when she broached to Theodora the thing which was now the dearest wish of her old heart. "My life is nearly over," she said. "It cannot last much longer now. But if there has been a purpose in sparing me, it is surely that you and I might be together. If Alan had lived, you would have been his wife. Even with this thing lying in wait for him, you should have been married to him before he went out. I, alone, prevented it—you surely will not refuse me the right of partial reparation. Pride, my child, is all very well; but mercy is better. Whom have I left but you? As Alan's wife you would have had an ample fortune. I shall leave you exactly what I should have left him. It is my great consolation that I can thus make you comfortable for life. And that I may have the enjoyment of you while my days last, I want you to promise to give up all thoughts of working, and to stay here with me. You, mother, too, naturally. It is my only chance of comfort. Just think how lost I should be without both of you!"

And so it came about. Pride and independence didn't seem the wonderful things to Theodora that once they had seemed. They were all very well in their way, of course; but there were much better things, deeper things, than they. Pride and independence had to do exclusively with material things; things of the heart and spirit must unquestionably outweigh them.

After her long stretch of strenuous office days, a more leisured life seemed at first to be odd and wrong. But Theodora soon found ways of filling it. She was quick to seize the opportunities for service. Canteens, hospitals, work on voluntary committees and on various relief corps soon gave her all that she could do. The days were never long enough. Her black robes unsealed many lips for the telling of sorrows and the asking of comfort and help. "You've lost someone, too," other black-robed women would say, and immediately the bond would be established. Maimed men in hospitals would ask about her loss; they realized broken hearts might be as hard to bear as broken bodies. And Theodora, on her side, watching their pluck and cheerfulness, could never allow herself to sink into self-pity.

"To think," she would say to herself, "to think what they are facing with never a murmur!" She saw every degree of cripple; she saw men who had given their services to their country only to come home and find that the ones they loved best in the world, the ones for whose sakes they had been fighting, had died while they had been gone. Unless a heart is very hardened indeed, there is nothing that so makes its own burdens shrink as watching the burdens of others.

And thus there came about in her a regeneration of which she was not even conscious. It was strange that she should not have recognized the effect of the greatest lesson she had ever learned. Of all her other lessons she had been keenly aware. She knew well what she had learned when she first started out in the world for herself and went to live with Mrs. Stuyvesant. She had learned patience first, and self-control. She had learned to hold her tongue, even when she knew she was right. She had learned a sort of humility that had in no way lessened her self-respect, but rather increased it. And she had learned, above all, that seemingly haughty hearts can also be very kind ones.

At Mrs. Felton's, too, she had learned much—and again consciously. She had learned the valuelessness of theory as opposed to practice; she had learned that the beauty and perfume of life are essential. Also, she had learned that it is better to mind one's own business than to mind that of anyone else.

During her engagement to Gerald Wyatt she had certainly learned at least two useful lessons: first, that money is by no means the answer to happiness; and second, that marriage without love is well-nigh a crime. It isn't enough that one doesn't love anyone other than one man; one must love that man.

It was during her business life that Theodora thought she had learned the most. There, she had learned that a girl's own attitude is her best protection. She had learned that kindliness does not necessarily mean intimacy; that petty cheating does not pay in the long run; that employers generally prove to have rather level heads and decidedly decent hearts; that boasting deceives no one very long; that morality and decency vary as greatly in one class as in another; and that discouragement is rarely as black as it first looks.

From Alan and from his love, Theodora had learned the meaning of happiness—that wonderful lesson that makes life blossom like Aaron's rod of old. And with that, she would have told you that her lessons had ceased.

As a matter of fact, his death had taught her the greatest lesson of all. It had taught her tolerance; it had taught her soft-ness; it was teaching her the triumphant answer to that sublime question: Oh, Grave, where is thy victory?

Theodora had always been plucky and she had always been honest. Honesty was the groundwork of her character, and its reverse side had been a hot intolerance for all injustice and all deceit. Over the sad and the weak and the oppressed she could ache with a protecting pity; but at the oppressor, and at all injustice and deceit, she must be free to rant hotly.

And now, suddenly, she no longer wanted to rant. The cloak of pity and tolerance spread its soft edges even over her pet aversions. It was not that she disliked them any less, but she felt that their punishment was not her affair. She was too busy with love to have time for hate; sinners would undoubtedly be punished, but she was content to leave their punishment to hands more powerful than her own—hands in which no task could fail. Where once she had said, "God is love, but He is also just," she now said, "God is just, but He is also love." And the difference is greater than may at first appear.

Once in awhile, some tale of injustice would waken the old spark, but quick on its heels would come reaction. When assailed with hot hatred for the arch-fiends who, after plunging a universe into mourning and pain, had temporarily escaped punishment and achieved seeming safety, Theodora first raged, and then thought: "What good, after all, will it do them? They can't get away from God!" This was merely proof that she was achieving a longer vision; she was learning resignation, coupled with faith in the promise of old: "Vengeance is mine. I will repay, saith the Lord."

※ ※ ※

When Theodora had been in mourning some six weeks or two months, there came to her one day two letters in the same post, and both in Alan's writing. She stared at them a moment, and then she understood. Alan had written them just before he was killed. They had been posted either just before, or just after, his death, and delayed in delivery. Precious as they were, she felt that the reading of them would be one of the most heart-breaking tasks she had faced. They were almost like a message from beyond the borders of the grave.

CHAPTER

❧XX❧

heodora and her mother sat in excited conversation. The girl's cheeks flamed, her eyes were deep wells of wonder and bliss, and there was that in her face which made Mrs. Winthrop's heart sing with thankfulness.

"It must be true," said the girl, for at least the twentieth time. "You see the dates, Mother. December the fourth and the ninth. He speaks of the armistice coming ten days after he was wounded, and of how he has been entirely without letters in the hospital—you know all my late ones were returned to me. You see, he says he'll have to stay in the Bordeaux hospital 'a long time yet.' Mother, it simply must be true! There's been no fighting since the date of these letters. They couldn't both be dated wrong. And anyhow, he writes of the armistice. There *can't* be any mistake. This wonderful thing is *true*. What have I ever done to deserve it? What have I done?"

All this was more than an hour after the first reading of the letters. Theodora had been puzzled, then incredulous, then wild with hope. She had carried the letters to her mother's room, and together the two women had allowed themselves to be convinced. With conviction had come a gratitude so deep, a joy so overwhelming, as to be almost pain.

"Oh, Mother! How will I ever thank God enough?" Theodora cried. Relief from a possible danger is wonderful enough; but relief from an accepted tragedy is at first too dazzling to be grasped.

"The first person I'm going to talk to," said Theodora, "is Mr. Lorrimer. And the next is Dr. Homans. Mother, do you realize that this will have to be broken to Mrs. Stuyvesant as carefully as that other awful message?"

"I can't understand how the first one ever came to be sent," mused the mother.

"Just a mistake. When you think of the millions of men who are out there, you realize that there must be some false reports. I've heard of such cases, but I never dreamed of connecting them with myself. I should think that the worst thing about such errors would be that everyone who got bad news would keep hoping for a miracle like this."

"But for you to be so long without news—"

"I had to wait till Alan could write himself, you see—more than a month after he was hurt. He didn't know about the other report; he thought we must know all about him. And I suppose that the hospitals must be so crowded and the nurses' hands full. Alan must have been very badly wounded—a month, before he could send me a single line! You see, he says there's a chance that he may always limp, even after the successful operation. Mother?"

"What, my dear child?"

"There's a thing that makes me ashamed. A number of times lately I've caught myself envying people who had lost no one in the war. I'd feel hard and bitter about it—as though they had been specially favored at my expense. Of course, I always tried to stop such thoughts, but I'm ashamed now that I even had them. The idea of envying anyone happiness—of wanting them to feel the way I've been feeling, instead of the way I feel now! No matter what happens to me, I hope I'll never do anything as wicked as that again."

"You couldn't help it, dear. You had a bitter sorrow and you bore it very bravely. We never ceased to admire you. But I cannot excuse the blunder that caused you such unnecessary suffering."

"I don't know," said the girl dreamily. "Perhaps it was good for me. I don't mean, of course, that I'm glad I had it, but I can see that it taught me something. And without it I'd never have known that there was such a thing as the sort of happiness that has come to me now. I feel as if life wouldn't be long enough to pay my debt of gratitude. I can't help remembering all those poor others who are still where I thought I was, and who will never find that their sad news was a mistake."

⁂ ⁂ ⁂

Dr. Homans advised that Mrs. Stuyvesant be told of this new development as though it concerned some stranger, then little by little be led to realize that it was her own nephew who was being given back to her like a man risen from the dead.

"It will be rather a ticklish piece of business," he said. "Especially after that last shock. I fear the reaction more than I did the original effect. You must be very careful. You read the papers to her, don't you?"

"Yes," replied Theodora.

"Then I think I'd go about it this way: take home an early evening edition with you. Pretend you have just read of this strange case. First merely give her a plain statement. Then begin to specialize. Say, 'Why, the man was a New Yorker. He was a captain. He was wounded ten days before the Armistice. He was in the Rainbow Division—the 165th Infantry,' and so on.

It seems childish, but it is safer. Taking it in bit by bit, being led up to it step by step, the shock will be lessened; she'll be gradually prepared. You must keep watching her carefully. You know the danger signals. I'll be within call."

Whether or not the plan was the necessary precaution that the physician considered it, it worked perfectly. When Theodora, in fear and trembling, said "the 165th Infantry," her task was over. Mrs. Stuyvesant suddenly sat alert. Her hands gripped the sides of her chair and her head was thrown proudly up with that old vigor which Theodora had once so greatly admired, and which had all but disappeared of late.

"And his name was Alan Beeckman," she said sharply. "Thank God! Thank God! Don't be frightened, child. I won't die. I'm going to cry, of course; I'm no graven image. I'm going to cry" (she was already doing it), "but I'm going to live to see my boy come back—to give him to you, and you to him. Oh, my boy, my boy! You won't know your managing old aunt in the foolish woman who'll be waiting to take you in her arms. Theodora, what are we going to do with all the days that must pass before we can get him back? How can we fill them? Where's your mother? Go and get her. Don't leave anyone out of this day of rejoicing. Your mother will have a son. You'll have a husband. And I'll have the best pair of children in the world. I'll never let them out of my sight again. Make up your mind to that!"

As a matter of fact, the days both flew and dragged. Flew, when measured against all the happy and useful tasks which they must hold—dragged, when one took time to look forward to one's heart's desire. But the one sure thing about days is that they will pass.

It was not long before Ned's little wife returned with her parents. A happier trio it would be hard to find. In the days before the war, Mr. Gary would probably have been voted a bore by his friends—so full was he of pride and anecdote. "That boy of mine," Mr. Gary would say to each newly met friend and acquaintance, "has made a record of which I don't mind admitting I'm rather proud. Went out as private, because he didn't want to waste time getting a commission. Before he'd seen three months of service he was a corporal. Then a sergeant. He's coming back a lieutenant—a *first* lieutenant, if you please. I can tell you, when a man is lucky enough to have a son like that, there doesn't seem to be much sense in pretending not to be proud of him! At least, that's the way I feel about it!"

After a long time, news came that Alan Beeckman was well enough to be sent home as a "casual"; the next word was that he would probably sail in the near future. Then ensued a wait that seemed interminable, but eventually the eagerly anticipated telegram arrived: He had landed at Hoboken en route for Camp Merritt.

It seemed as if miles of red tape had to be unwound before permission could be obtained to see Alan—for neither his aunt nor his fiancée wanted that first meeting to take place in the always crowded Hostess House just outside the grounds. And in order to get inside and see him more privately, a special permit was necessary. It came one evening—as a matter of fact, less than two days in the wake of the telegram, and those two days had been devoted to the various sanitary processes through which all returned soldiers must pass—and the next morning found Mrs. Stuyvesant's limousine speeding over the frozen roads, carryings its owner, Theodora and her mother, and Dr. Homans.

The day had dawned at last—the wondrous day that marked the termination of waiting and separation, and that opened to at least one of that party the gate to the Garden of

After a while—beginning with broken murmurs—they started to make up for the long months of silence.

Delight. How the sun blazed in a golden glory of promise, how the air pulsed with myriads of mysterious messages, how the heart of the girl fluttered in response to their call!

No one talked much—conversation is always superfluous in times of deep happiness, always impossible in times of deep sorrow. At best, it is but communication between minds; hearts have ever laughed it to scorn.

Arrived at the camp, the chauffeur flashed his pass and carried his party triumphantly to the Red Cross headquarters. It was in that building, that must have seen so many pathetic partings, so many blessed reunions, that Alan was to meet them.

The half-hour that they waited there was longer than most years. Suddenly Theodora, who was sitting near the window sprang to her feet. "There he comes," she said in a queer muffled voice. And there indeed, leaning on his stick but making excellent headway, nevertheless, came Alan. How tall he was—how bonny! Under his service cap his close-cropped yellow hair gleamed crisp and shining. His shoulders had surely broadened, and even his stick and his limp could not rob him of his jaunty swing. There wasn't, of course, another soldier in the camp as handsome as he! Probably there wasn't another in the army!

They were all standing when he entered, and Mrs. Stuyvesant called his name. "Alan," she said—and he turned from the crowd around the desk where he had been about to make his inquiries, and faced them. "My boy," cried his aunt, and held out her arms. But even before he limped into their embrace, his eyes found Theodora's.

He was introduced to Mrs. Winthrop and greeted by Dr. Homans. And then somehow—neither of them knew how it came about—he and Theodora found themselves pushed into a little room alone, and the door shut between them and the world.

❀✿ ✿❀ ✿❀

It was some time before they spoke, but after a while—beginning with broken murmurs—they started to make up for the long months of silence. Dispensing with sequence, breaking in upon each other with this memory and that, they told and listened. Theodora would not yet mention the terrible experience of the false report; it seemed too awful to tell a man that you had long mourned him as dead. But she did speak of the returned soldiers whom she had been visiting in hospital, contrasting her own happy fortune with the tragedies that had come to some women.

"In the face of what others have to bear," she said, "my love seems selfish. For I can't think of a thing now except just you and me."

"That's enough, dearest. What do you suppose I was spared for, if not that we should be happy together?"

"That's true. And it wouldn't make anyone else happier for me to mourn, even if I could."

"Assuredly not. Do you know, dearest, I've about decided that love is the biggest thing in the whole world. Just think a minute! If Germany had had a particle of love for her fellow men we'd all have been spared quite a bit. Love pulled off the Allied victory—love of freedom, of justice, of firesides, and of the women and children clustered around them. I know it was love that kept up our hearts in the trenches, and that gave us strength to see the thing through. Look out that window there. Every man that you see, every man that ever went out to fight, came into the world through human love and human mating. Back of each one of them is a love story. And back of each one of them is God's loving the world so much that—"

270

He stopped suddenly, laughing at his own eloquence. "You see what you have done to me," he said. "You've taught me about love, till I can't think of anything else."

Theodora's eyes were wide with the birth of a new thought. She gazed into her lover's answering eyes, and on beyond them down into his heart. "I see," she breathed. "I see. And we aren't selfish to take our share of this lovely thing. We're *meant* to take it. God wants us to. Because only then can people do their part in a way that is bigger and better and more beautiful."

"Exactly. And it is by love that women like you can wipe out the past for chaps like me."

Theodora was thinking. It was love that had made Ned pull himself up, and that had turned him so fine. It was love that was giving Meta her reward in the little boy she so adored. It was love that had softened Mrs. Stuyvesant so beautifully. "Why, Alan," she said, "you're here because two people loved each other, and I'm here because two people loved each other—why, it isn't only personal, at all. It's as big as the world!"

"Bigger, sweetheart. It's as big as the world—and heaven beside."

"It's wonderful," whispered Theodora.

❈   ❈   ❈

There came a tap at the door. "Have you two finished talking?" called someone. "You've had an hour, and it's time to go home."

"An *hour?*" cried Theodora incredulously. With lips pressed deep in her soft cheek, her lover murmured, "Soon, my darling, we won't be counting hours. They all be ours together." Then with arms entwined, they walked to the door and opened it.

There stood the three waiting ones—Mrs. Stuyvesant, Mrs. Winthrop, and Dr. Homans. All were smiling, but at least two pairs of lips trembled, and two pairs of eyes glistened with unshed tears. And in all three breasts the hearts were soft with the thought of love—of love past, present, and future—and of this girl and this man who stood transfigured with the revelation of its wonder.

THE END

DATE